"Lie down,"
Cort ordered.

If she'd had a means, Jessy would have gladly strangled the offensive man.

"I said lie down. Tomorrow I'll decide what I'm going to do with you."

Jessy considered refusing, but thought the better of it. Besides, she might be able to escape while he slept. Obediently she lay on her side, facing away from him. The next instant, an arm circled her waist.

"What are you doing?" she demanded.

"I'm making sure you stay right where you are for the night."

"Get your filthy hands off me!" Jessy tried to kick her feet and swing her arms but the blanket impeded her efforts. Just as she managed to get a leg free, he swung his leg over hers, pinning her down.

"If we continue this much longer, Mrs. Turner," Cort whispered in her ear, "we'll be spending the night in more enjoyable pursuits. Or maybe that's what you want...."

Dear Reader:

We appreciate the feedback you've been giving us on Harlequin Historicals. It's nice to hear that so many of you share our enthusiasm.

During the long winter months, everyone looks forward to spring; and coming in April and May we'll have a wonderful surprise for you. In an unprecedented publishing venture, acclaimed Western romance writer Dorothy Garlock, writing here as Dorothy Glenn, joins forces with popular Kristin James to produce companion historical romances. *The Gentleman* and *The Hell Raiser* tell the stories of two Montana brothers who were separated as children, raised in entirely different life-styles and reunited as adults—only to clash bitterly and fall in love with each other's woman! Each book stands alone—together they're sensational. To celebrate the occasion, the heroes will be featured on the covers. Look for both books this spring from Harlequin Historicals.

As always, we look forward to your comments and suggestions. After all, these books are for you; so keep those letters coming. Meanwhile, enjoy!

The Editors
Harlequin Historicals
P.O. Box 7372
Grand Central Station
New York, NY 10017

Fire and Ice

DeLoras Scott

Harlequin Books

TORONTO • NEW YORK • LONDON
AMSTERDAM • PARIS • SYDNEY • HAMBURG
STOCKHOLM • ATHENS • TOKYO • MILAN

Harlequin Historical first edition February 1990

ISBN 0-373-28640-6

Books by DeLoras Scott

Harlequin Historical

Bittersweet #12
Fire and Ice #40

DeLORAS SCOTT

believes her writing is derived from a love for historical novels, a strong dash of humor and an excellent support group. A full-time writer, she enjoys the freedom of being able to create characters and have them come alive in plots of her choosing.

The mother of five grown children, she and her husband have lived and traveled throughout the U.S. A native of California, she now resides in the state of her birth.

Prologue

Kansas, 1878

The smoke-filled saloon smelled of whiskey, unwashed bodies and the cheap perfume of painted women. The ceiling was peppered with bullet holes from quick-tempered ranchers, sodbusters and cowboys. There had already been several fights that night, but the five men sitting around the poker table in the back paid scant attention.

"I'm out," declared the big, redheaded man named BJ.

Jonathan glanced across at the only person still in the game besides himself. The stranger had a thin cigar clenched between his teeth, and other than squinting his eyes to keep out the smoke, his sun-darkened face remained expressionless.

"Five hundred," Jonathan said, pushing the last of his money to the center of the table.

The stranger looked at the sizable stack in front of him. "I'll see your five and raise a thousand."

Jonathan felt the sweat begin to trickle down his temples. It always happened when he became excited, and the three jacks he held were sure to make him a winner.

"Will you take an IOU?" he asked.

Dark brown eyes studied Jonathan for a moment. "What do you have to back it?"

"My wife's diamond and ruby necklace. It's worth a lot more than a thousand."

The stranger let out a grunt of disbelief.

"He's telling the truth," said the merchant seated to BJ's left. "I've seen it."

"Very well, but I suggest you don't try to weasel out of a payment. I'm a man who collects his debts."

His low, quiet voice caused Jonathan to fidget in his chair. "That's an insult, sir," he said in a huff. "I'm good for it."

When the note was signed, the two men laid down their hands. The three jacks lost to a full house.

After collecting the pot, the stranger dressed in black shoved his chair back and stood. "That'll do it for me tonight, gentlemen," he announced.

"You can't leave without giving us a chance to win back what we've lost!" BJ declared angrily.

The stranger's hand dropped to the gun at his side.

"I didn't mean it that way," BJ quickly assured him. "Maybe we can continue this tomorrow night?"

"Maybe."

When the man left the table, a cowhand took his place.

BJ laughed nervously. "Quick-tempered, ain't he? I think it's time we changed decks. Don't you, boys?"

The other men nodded their heads in agreement.

BJ smiled at the cowboy. "New cards, new game."

"You'll have to stake me, BJ," Jonathan said, relaxed now that the stranger had left the saloon. "Maybe I can win back some of what I've lost."

The game continued for another hour, with BJ and Jonathan winning most of the hands. The cowboy became suspicious, accusing them of using a marked deck. Hot words were exchanged, and the cowboy settled the argument by drawing his gun and shooting Jonathan. Before he could turn his weapon on Jonathan's pal, BJ drew and fired. The young man fell to the floor, dead.

"How bad is it, Jonathan?" BJ asked leaning over his friend.

Jonathan knew his death was just a matter of time. A coward and no-account throughout his life, he suddenly found courage. "I'll be all right, just get me home. Jessy will know what to do."

Chapter One

Jessica Turner raised the white, lacy handkerchief to her eyes while surreptitiously checking to be sure she was alone in the small funeral parlor. Satisfied, she looked at the closed wooden coffin sitting a short distance away.

"Well, Jonathan," she whispered, "your death stirred up a hornet's nest. Early this morning the merchants you owed money to paid me a visit. They took just about everything in the house, plus the cow, the wagon and that fancy horse of yours. They even ripped up the straw mattress looking for all the gambling money they thought you'd stashed away. BJ always was a bad influence. I told you to get rid of him, but no, you wouldn't listen."

Jessy hiccuped. "Guess I can't complain. You weren't much of a husband, but you took care of me when my folks died." A soft giggle escaped her lips. "I have to admit, Jonathan, it feels awfully good knowing I'm going to be on my own now."

Jessy pushed back a wisp of silver-blond hair that had worked its way loose from the large bun atop her head, then leaned down and removed a small flask from the reticule sitting by her foot. Tears filled her eyes when the potent whiskey reached her throat and snatched her breath away. She sat there coughing before she finally regained her breath. Upon hearing heavy-booted footsteps approaching from behind, she slipped the flask into the reticule and began sobbing loudly.

"The men are ready to take Jonathan to the cemetery, Jessy," Harry the undertaker stated as he patted her shoulder. "I don't like seeing you grieve like this. Jonathan wasn't worth it."

Jessy bowed her head and managed a sniffle. "How can you say such a thing, Harry? Even though Jonathan left me penniless, he was still my husband."

"I reckon so. Good thing the traveling preacher passed through when he did. Jonathan might not've had a proper funeral."

"Yes, it was fortunate, wasn't it?" Jessy hiccuped, but stifled the sound with her handkerchief. "I'm ready," she moaned.

As Jessy stepped outside the small log cabin, the sudden warm breeze made her dizzy. There's no doubt about it, she scolded herself, you've had too much of Jonathan's whiskey!

As she tried to focus, Jessy's gaze came to rest on a tall man standing in front of the saloon across the street. He wore black pants and a black vest, and the silver around the crown of his black hat sparkled in the sun. Though the hat was pulled low and shadowed his face, Jessy had the distinct feeling he was watching her. Then everything began to spin.

When Jessy started coming to, she heard Mrs. Tinker say, "It's disgusting. You can smell the liquor on her breath, and her poor husband hasn't even been placed in the ground yet!"

Jessy slowly opened her eyes and saw Harry's wife, Betsy, leaning over her.

"Are you all right, dear?" the kindly woman asked.

"If she isn't, it's certainly not due to grief!"

Jessy looked up at Myrtle Tinker, the self-proclaimed leader of doing away with all sin and corruption in the small Kansas town of Binge. Jessy wanted to tell the woman to go to hell, but instead lifted her hand to Harry who was trying to help her up. Though still a bit wobbly, Jessy did manage to stand. Glancing across the street, she discovered the man in black was gone.

Feeling considerably more sober, but still allowing Harry to support her, Jessy made an effort to brush the dirt from her black dress. "I'll be fine now," she assured the handful of people who surrounded her.

After Jonathan's burial, Harry and Betsy offered to drive Jessy to her house, but to Jessy's aggravation, she didn't have an opportunity to accept.

"As Jonathan's best friend, I'll take his wife home," BJ declared.

Not wanting to cause an argument, Jessy climbed onto the rented buggy without saying a word. As BJ urged the horse down the hard-packed dirt road leading away from town, she moved as far away as the seat would permit. Her head was pounding. She wasn't sure if it was due to her drinking or the strain she'd been under.

Jessy thought about the man beside her. Billy Joe Johnson had changed little during the thirteen years Jessy had known him. His carrot-red hair was still shaggy, and his face remained pinkish, refusing to darken from hours in the sun. Large freckles stood out on his skin, reminding her of big flecks of dirt. Though not tall, he was solidly built.

When they were children traveling west by wagon train, the Johnsons' wagon was only two wagons up from theirs. BJ was always causing her trouble. Even at fourteen he had a cruel streak, and his father wasn't much better. Jessy could still remember how the wagon train often passed dead stock or buffalo on the trail, and Billy and his friends discovered that if they dived onto the stomach of a large, sun-bloated animal, it would fling them high in the air. They'd tried to get Jessy to do it, but even at ten she wasn't that stupid.

"Naturally I'll spend the night."

"Why?" Jessy asked, astonished at BJ's statement.

"You need me to take care of you, that's why. You'll soon know what it's like to have a real man in your bed. I've told you for years you married the wrong man. Reckon we should see a preacher right away, 'cause you'll be carrying my baby in no time."

Jessy had been scared and vulnerable when her parents died, and had foolishly agreed to marry Jonathan. But she was older and wiser now, and she would die before she'd marry the likes of BJ! "I'm twenty-three, Billy, and I want to live alone for a while," she stated flatly. Seeing a dark scowl cross his face, she quickly added, "Of course that doesn't mean I'm not going to marry you. I'd be a fool to turn down a man that owns so much land."

Billy's bird eyes lit up with pleasure. "You're damn right you'd be a fool!" He broke out in one of his high-pitched laughs, a spittle of tobacco juice escaping the corner of his thin lips. "So, you've finally come to your senses. I've waited a long time to hear you say you'd marry me." He reached over and placed a rough, possessive hand on Jessy's thigh.

Gritting her teeth and unable to bear the sight of him, Jessy looked out over the flat land. A movement on the horizon caught her attention. Even with the late sun in her eyes, she could make out a lone rider atop a sleek, gray horse some distance away. The man's black vest was accentuated by a white shirt.

"BJ, do you know that man?"

"Who?" Billy asked, looking to where Jessy pointed.

"He must be behind that stand of trees," she replied, verbalizing her thoughts.

Billy pulled the horse to an abrupt stop. "I don't see anyone," he said when the dust had settled. "Was he riding fast?"

"Now that I think of it, I'd say about the same pace we were setting." Jessy shaded her eyes to get a better view, but BJ started the horse again.

"It's just your imagination. If someone was riding out there, he'd have cleared those trees by now. You're just jumpy."

Maybe he's right, Jessy thought as she rubbed her temples. Especially after what I've been through today.

When they came to a halt in front of the sod house Jessy called home, BJ started to climb down.

"Just a moment, Billy," Jessy said, effectively stopping him, "I'm still upset about Jonathan."

"Jonathan, hell! You never cared for him." He quickly removed his worn buckskin jacket.

Seeing his beady eyes already turning glassy with lust, Jessy had to bite her tongue to keep from screaming obscenities at him. "Please, Billy," she purposely pleaded, "allow me this night alone. Tomorrow night I'll show you how much I appreciate your consideration."

Indecision was written on his face.

"Please?" She gave him as sweet a smile as she could muster.

"Tomorrow night?"

"Yes. I know you've waited a long time, but you're certainly man enough to wait one more day."

BJ hesitated a moment before answering. "All right, I'll be here at eight."

"Thank you, Billy." Jessy maintained her smile and quickly stepped down. But as soon as the buggy was out of sight she spit on the ground in front of her. "Bastard!" she mumbled.

Lifting her black skirt, Jessy entered the sod house, her eyes scanning the interior of the small, single room. It still came as a shock to find the place so barren.

"I think we need to talk."

Startled by the deep voice, Jessy whirled and saw a tall man leaning against the door frame. Fear ran up her spine. This was the first chance she'd had to see his face, but she recognized the clothes. He wasn't pretty like Jonathan. No, his face was more sculptured and lean . . . handsome, but in a very masculine way. Even the small scar running along his jawbone added to his good looks. But his dark brown eyes frightened her. Some sixth sense told her he was a man who could be dangerous. Jessy straightened her shoulders, refusing to let him know the effect he had on her.

"We have nothing to discuss. I don't know who you are and I certainly do not appreciate you following me."

He gave her a lazy smile, showing even white teeth. "How else was I to know where you live?"

What did the man want? Jessy knew she was at his mercy. The only weapon she owned was a small pistol, and it was inaccessible. She would have to try to bluff her way out of this new mess. Something she seemed to be doing a lot of lately.

"You have no business in my house. I demand you leave immediately!"

"And if I don't?"

Though he hadn't moved an inch, he was the most intimidating man Jessy had ever had the misfortune to meet. His shoulders almost filled the doorway. Why now, Lord? she silently asked.

Jessy held her stance. "You said we had something to discuss. Tell me what it is, then be on your way. If you've come to rob me, you're too late. There's nothing left."

The stranger chuckled as his eyes traveled from her head to her toes, then back again. Jessy shuddered.

"Oh," he drawled, the smile still on his face, "I could think of a couple of things that would prove most enjoyable."

"You wouldn't dare!" she gasped as she stepped back.

"Lady, there's very little I wouldn't dare. You're a very attractive woman, and I've never seen silver hair and lavender eyes before. Most interesting."

Fury suddenly took over, and Jessy's hands balled into fists by her sides. "I'll fight you until one of us is dead!"

He raised a dark eyebrow. "I doubt it."

Jessy watched him take a step forward. He ducked his head to keep from hitting the top of the doorway. She knew exactly where to plant her foot if he came any closer. But he stopped and straightened to his full height. To Jessy, the already small room seemed to shrink. She felt like a mouse needing a place to hide. For the first time, she noticed the gun belt hanging low on his slim hips. The holster held a fancy .45, and was tied to his leg, gunman style.

"I came for only one thing, Jessica Turner," he said, the smile gone, "the necklace."

"What necklace?" she demanded.

"The one your late husband lost to me in a poker game."

"You must be out of your mind!"

"Your husband lost a card game the night he was shot. I have his IOU, and I've come to collect." He pulled the slip of paper from his vest pocket and held it open so she could see the writing.

"Even if I had a necklace, which I don't, I certainly wouldn't hand it over to you." In an effort to put distance between them, she moved to the cold fireplace, her hand only inches from the iron poker.

"It's either the necklace or a thousand dollars. Give it to me and I'll leave."

Jessy laughed bitterly. "Well, you've wasted your time as well as mine. What my husband did has nothing to do with me. I never had a necklace worth that amount." She waved her hand toward the almost barren room. "As you can see, I certainly don't have a thousand dollars. Jonathan's debtors cleaned me out."

The stranger's face grew hard. "Lady, I've talked to quite a few people in town. More than one has seen you wearing that necklace, and none of the men who came here have it. The game is up. Your husband is dead, and the necklace is mine. You, Jonathan and BJ were in cahoots."

"That's ridiculous! I don't even know how to play poker."

"It wasn't necessary. You were the bait. You and that necklace."

It suddenly occurred to Jessy that from all indications, the stranger didn't intend to force himself on her. The knowledge gave her strength.

"This is all a big misunderstanding," she whimpered. Pulling the white, lacy handkerchief from her sleeve, she dabbed her nose. "I admit there was a necklace Jonathan asked me to wear, but it was made of glass. I don't even know what happened to it. And I certainly had no idea my husband used it for gambling purposes." She smiled weakly. "I regret you've lost money, but in all truthfulness, I am innocent. No matter what my husband did, in my eyes, gambling is the devil's work. You see, my father was a preacher. I was raised to believe gaming is a sin."

Jessy started sobbing, but not too loud. "Please leave, I've had a terrible day...I just buried my husband...I need to be alone."

"I'll leave, but you can bet I'll be back tomorrow."

He left as quietly as he had arrived. This time Jessy closed the door and shoved the wooden bar into place. "If I survive this day," she uttered, "it will be a miracle."

Assured that there would be no more intrusions, Jessy collapsed onto a wooden chair and gave thought to Jonathan, now lying cold in the ground. Try as she may, she could feel no sorrow at his loss. She was finally free, and that was all that mattered. Over the five years they had been married, she'd grown to dislike her husband almost as much as she disliked BJ. Although they owned good land, all Jonathan wanted to do was gamble. She hated the way he bragged about cheating, then ran with his tail between his legs if some man challenged him.

Jessy smirked. When it came to women, however, Jonathan tried to prove his manliness by using force. One of many things he'd learned from BJ. But Jessy had known how to outsmart her husband. After their wedding night, she started throwing tantrums, and she swore that if he ever touched her she'd kill him in his sleep. Jonathan believed her, and no matter how many times BJ told him he was a fool, Jonathan never again laid a hand on her.

Suddenly realizing how dark the room had become, Jessy pulled herself off the chair and lit a candle. The time had come for her to get down to business. Removing her black dress and skirts, she climbed into Jonathan's old work clothes, which she had tossed on the bed prior to leaving for the funeral. The faint odor of Jonathan's Lavender Water still clung to the material.

Wooden hairpins landed on top of the dress, and after allowing her thick silver mane to fall around her hips, she deftly weaved it into a single thick braid, securing it with a piece of twine. Ready to leave, she took one last look at the small house she'd called home and blew out the candle.

As Jessy left the sod shelter and headed for the out-house, she had to force herself to walk slowly. If by chance BJ had sent someone to keep an eye on her, she didn't want him to become suspicious. At least one thing was in her favor. There were a few drifting clouds in the sky darkening the night, and the moon wasn't out.

After entering the smelly outhouse and closing the rickety door, Jessy waited a good five minutes before peeking through the half-moon that had been cut out of the door. Seeing no one, she slipped outside and hurried to the big branched tree in the back. Well hidden in the shadows, Jessy crouched and remained motionless, her eyes scanning the darkness for any sign of movement. Nothing. Her spirits began to soar. She was almost free. Jessy left her hiding place.

Jonathan had told her that as soon as the town learned he'd been shot, everyone he owed money to would come to collect. So she had been prepared. She'd stashed food away and staked the old mule far from the house. Then she'd buried Jonathan's carpetbag with all his poker winnings and the necklace in a secret bottom compartment. What little clothes she'd need had been piled on top.

Chapter Two

Long streaks of orange and yellow sunrise were beginning to splash across the sky, but Jessy continued urging the mule onward. Knowing BJ would be tearing up the countryside in search of her, she'd decided her fastest route would be to go to Atchison and catch the train to Kansas City. But there was still a long way to travel, and she needed to get as many miles behind her as possible.

She shifted painfully in the wooden saddle. It would be a miracle if she could ever sit again. But she was free, and intended to stay that way. She'd be in Kansas City soon, with ample money to purchase new clothes and anything else she needed. Jonathan had told her about the city, and she'd see for herself. Then she would purchase a house and rent out rooms to young ladies, thereby securing her own livelihood. It wouldn't afford her the luxury she'd known during her young years in Tennessee, but those days were long past.

It was nearly three in the afternoon when Jessy finally stopped at a clearing by a wide creek. She'd already dozed off several times, and on more than one occasion had nearly fallen from the saddle. Though she hated having to stop, sleep was imperative. She couldn't go another mile.

The small area abounded with green trees and low scrub bushes, creating a perfect hiding place and providing shade from the blistering sun. After watering the mule and hobbling it, Jessy spread her blanket on the ground and stuck her small pistol under the edge. By the time she was ready to lie down, she was already half asleep.

Hearing the mule bray brought Jessy awake with a start, but upon remembering where she was, she relaxed. Glancing at the sun, it was hard to believe she'd slept a little over two hours; it felt more like two minutes. But even though every bone in her body ached, she knew she had to be on her way. A pleasing thought entered her mind. For the first time in her life, there were no chores, and there was no one to answer to.

The sun glistening on water suddenly caught Jessy's attention. It seemed like weeks since she had bathed. Surely a fast dip wouldn't cause too much delay. The water might even serve to soothe her aching body, and what with the creek curving away at both ends, the small area was perfectly secluded. Her mind made up, Jessy undressed.

As she stepped into the water, her feet caused the soft dirt to swirl beneath the surface, and small fish darted in every direction. Though the water was warm, it felt invigoratingly cool against her hot body. Slowly she worked her way out until she could finally sit on the bottom with the water reaching her chin. Like a child, she laughed with delight, and using her heels, she turned herself in circles while splashing water in her face. Suddenly, her cupped hands stopped in midair. Standing by the water's edge stood the gunman, his right thumb looped over his gun belt, his left arm extended in the air. Her clothes hung from his fingers.

"Would you like to come out and discuss the money you owe me?" he asked.

"I'll do no such thing!" Jessy sputtered. "You can just get the hell out of here, because I'm not moving until you leave!"

"I'm in no hurry." He turned and walked to the mule.

To Jessy's horror, she watched as he quickly unhobbled the animal then gave it a hard slap across the rump. The mule took off as though it had seen a rattlesnake.

"What are you doing?" Jessy yelled.

The stranger sat, then leaned back on his elbows. "How long do you plan to stay out there?" he asked casually.

Furious, Jessy refused to answer. How in the world would she get to Atchison without the mule?

By dusk Jessy's teeth were chattering, and gooseflesh covered her body. She didn't know how much longer she could hold out, and leaving the water's protection seemed less and less intolerable. She longed to sit by the small warm fire the stranger had built, and the delicious aroma of brewed coffee was almost more than she could bear.

While distant coyotes raised their voices in an eerie serenade, Jessy bemoaned her plight. Considering everything, she knew she had no choice but to get out, but the knowledge certainly didn't make the doing any easier. Staying in the water had accomplished nothing except making her skin wrinkle like a dried apple. There was no doubt about it. The gunman had no intention of leaving. Oh, he had disappeared a few times, but she'd had a gut feeling he could see her even though she couldn't see him. And he was never gone more than a few minutes.

Other than unsaddling the dappled gray stallion, building a fire and drinking the coffee he'd made, the stranger had spent most of his time relaxed at the water's edge lying on her clothes. With his hat tipped over his eyes, it was impossible to know if or when he slept.

It galled Jessy to know he'd won the standoff. She had to get out. She might have tried to escape without her clothes, but she refused to leave without the carpetbag and its contents.

"The water looks inviting," the gunman said suddenly as he pulled off a black boot. "It's been a hot day. Since you're not going to come out, I think I'll join you. I could use a good cooling off." He removed the other boot.

"No!" Jessy yelled, throwing her hands up as if to ward him off.

He stood and removed his vest.

Jessy thrashed wildly at the water, but it only served to hamper her progress. She glanced back. He was unbuttoning his shirt.

"All right!" she declared. "I'm coming out!"

"Then make it quick, lady!" he barked at her.

"You have to turn your back!"

"I think not, Jessy dear. I've earned my moment of pleasure."

Jessy stood and rushed forward, trying to cover her shaking body with her arms.

"So the mermaid finally leaves her hiding place," the man drawled, his eyes raking her naked form. "I must say, seeing you like this is almost worth the wait."

As soon as she was close enough, Jessy dove for the blanket. In one fluid motion, she reached under the edge for the derringer. Nothing! Frantic, she ran her hand across the ground, but the gun wasn't there. Hearing him laugh was almost as mortifying as having him see her naked. Quickly she drew the blanket around her, blessing its warmth.

"Go to hell!" she said.

"My, my. Such harsh words from such lovely lips. And a preacher's daughter at that."

His words snapped Jessy into action. Burying her head in her hands, she began sobbing loudly. "Oh . . . you're right. My father would turn over in his grave if he heard me say such things. But just how much can a woman take?" Jessy bit hard on her lip to bring tears to her eyes, then looked at him. "You must admit, you've pushed me to the end of my endurance. Please leave me alone, mister. I have no necklace." Jessy almost choked when he began clapping his hands.

"You do that very well," he stated simply, "but your talents are wasted on me."

She watched him go to the fire and pour some coffee. To her amazement, he returned and handed her the metal cup. That was followed with jerky and hardtack, which he retrieved from his saddlebags. After eating and drinking two more cups of the hot brew, Jessy felt almost normal.

"I'll take my clothes now," she said sarcastically to the man sitting on a stump a few feet away.

"I think not, Mrs. Turner. You'll have to settle for the blanket tonight. I don't trust you."

Jessy curled her toes in aggravation. There had to be a way to outsmart this man. At least he hadn't found the necklace and the money, or he would have already left.

"I've told you everything I know," she stated flatly. "Why don't you believe me and leave?"

His eyes narrowed. "Because you've done nothing but lie from the moment we met."

"That's not true!"

"Lady, I've about had it up to my ears with you. Let's get a few things straight. Your father was certainly no preacher. And as for your poor-little-me-act, forget it. You've pulled just about every female trick there is, except one. I'm surprised you didn't try to take me to your bed in hopes of changing my mind."

"No one talks to me like that! You are a—"

"I don't like people who try to do me out of what's mine. The fact that you're a woman makes little difference to how I decide to handle this."

The tone of his voice and the look in his cold brown eyes left no doubt in Jessy's mind that the man meant what he was saying. Still, as frightened as she was, she refused to give up what she considered rightfully hers. She lifted her chin.

"Kill me, if that's what you have in mind," she said bravely. "You'd probably do it anyway even if I did have what you want."

An evil grin played at the corner of his lips. "Oh, there's more ways of dying than death."

"What ... what do you mean?"

He stood and walked to the water's edge. While his back was turned, Jessy searched desperately for something to protect herself with. She found a good-sized rock and tucked it inside the blanket just as he faced her again.

"Do you really want to know?" he asked.

"No."

"Very well." He rubbed his hand across the stubble on his cheek, his eyes never leaving hers. "The people in town were certainly right about you, Mrs. Turner."

"But that—"

"Be quiet and let me finish. You are as dishonest and conniving as any woman I've ever met, and you use your beauty to get out of trouble." He rested his hand on the butt of his gun.

"Oh! You're a fine one to talk. What are you? A gunman and a gambler!" Sitting on the ground with a blanket wrapped around her was definitely not to her advantage.

"I know you have nothing of value because I searched your things," he said, ignoring her. "So why did you sneak out of the house and why are you headed toward Atchison?''

It came as a shock to know he had followed her. She'd been so cautious, and had thought the meeting had happened by accident! Maybe if she told him *some* of the truth, he'd start believing her. "I'm running away from BJ."

He laughed. A deep, hearty laugh that ground on her already raw nerves. "What's so funny?" she challenged.

"A falling out among thieves? I give you credit, Jessica Turner, you've got nerve," he stated. "How many others are on your trail?"

"None."

"I believe that about as much as your telling me you're running from your lover, BJ."

If she'd had a means, Jessy would have gladly strangled the offensive man.

"Now lie down," he ordered.

"What?"

"I said lie down. Tomorrow I'll decide what I'm going to do with you."

Jessy considered refusing, but thought better of it. Besides, she might be able to escape while he slept. Obediently she lay on her side, facing away from him. The next instant, an arm circled her waist and a body hugged her back. She tried to jerk away, but he had too strong a hold on her "What are you doing?" she demanded.

"I'm making sure you stay right where you are for the night. Now go to sleep."

"Get your filthy hands off me!" Jessy tried to kick her feet and swing her arms, but the blanket impeded her efforts. Just as she managed to get one leg free, he swung his leg over hers, effectively pinning her down. Still she struggled, but the harder she fought, the tighter he squeezed. In no time, her breathing became labored.

"If we continue this much longer, Mrs. Turner," he whispered in her ear, "we'll be spending the night in more enjoyable pursuits. Or maybe that's what you want."

Panic and fury engulfed her. Her hand suddenly touched the rock she'd hidden. With great effort, she calmly said, "I have to go to the ... well, you know what I mean."

There was a long pause. "All right," he finally said, "but make it quick." Exasperation threaded his words, but he released her. "Don't try running away. You know I'll find you."

Jessy sat up. Palming the rock, she marshaled her strength and swung. The stone hit his head with a sickening thud, and his arm slid to the ground. He remained motionless.

"My God!" she whispered. "I've killed him!"

Jessy placed her hand on his chest, almost giddy with relief as she felt a strong heartbeat. He wasn't dead, just knocked out. She scrambled to her feet.

As fast as her shaking hands would permit, Jessy dressed then saddled the horse. As she grabbed the carpetbag, the stranger moaned and rolled onto his side. Jessy jumped on the horse and rode off.

During her life, Jessy had spent little time atop a horse. She found out that handling the big stallion wasn't going to be an easy task. It took all her strength to pull the reins and slow him down to a jarring trot, but in no time, she discovered a walk was far more comfortable.

Since the gunfighter had guessed her destination, Jessy changed direction and headed south. She'd catch a train out of Topeka.

Nothing had gone right since Jonathan's death. Now she was forced to add more miles to her travels. Even though he'd pretended innocence, the gunman's accusations made sense. She had heard the rumors that she had bedded BJ and helped BJ and Jonathan in their crooked deals. But she

hadn't realized that her mother's necklace had been used to
further their schemes. It was the only thing left to remind
her of her family and better times. Jonathan had promised
never to gamble it away, and it had never occurred to her
that he would use it as bait. She should have known better.
But there was nothing she could do about it now. She had
always thought of the rubies and diamonds as fire and ice.
Calling it fire and ice now seemed very appropriate.

By the time Jessy could see Topeka in the distance, she
was hungry, tired and dirty. Though she had carefully ra-
tioned the food in the stranger's saddlebags, it had run out
the day before. Moving the horse at such a slow pace had
taken its toll.

Just outside town, she pulled the horse to a halt among a
group of tall trees. She was anxious to be rid of the filthy
pants and shirt and put on a clean dress. But when she
eagerly opened the carpetbag, she discovered it was empty.
Her clothes were gone! Frantically she checked the hidden
compartment. The money and necklace were still safely
tucked inside.

Jessy plopped down on the ground, and for the first time
since Jonathan's death, she allowed her anger its freedom.
"Damn, damn, damn!" she yelled, hitting her fist on the
ground. "He had no right to take my clothes!"

It took some time for Jessy to regain her composure.
Though still angry, she climbed on the stallion and headed
for town.

She had never been in a large town before, and Topeka
left her awestruck. By the time she turned the stallion onto
Kansas Avenue, her eyes were large pools of lavender. The
street stretched out before her, a hundred and fifty feet wide,
filled with fast-moving carriages, wagons and horses. She
was fascinated with the men and women hurrying in and out

of the many stores. She wanted to take a closer look at what the women were wearing, but her head kept moving back and forth as she tried to take in everything at once.

As she continued down the wide street, Jessy caught sight of two men standing in front of the Topeka Bank. Upon seeing her, they suddenly began pointing their fingers. At first Jessy thought it was because of the way she was dressed, but the men seemed to be concerned about something. Troubled by their interest, Jessy urged the stallion on at a faster pace.

Two blocks from the bank, she saw the Gordon House. Knowing clothes and a place to stay were her first priorities, she headed toward the hotel.

Jessy pirouetted in front of the mirror in her room, admiring her new green linen traveling dress. She was not particularly fond of the bustle, but fashion was a must. At least that's what the woman at the store had said. Fondly, she scooped up the ball gown she'd bought and returned to the mirror. It had been her one extravagance, but she excused it by dreaming of dances held in beautiful homes.

She glanced at the bureau to assure herself the train ticket was still there. Tomorrow she would leave for Kansas City. Though she had spent more money than she'd planned, the clothes and shoes would stand her in good stead. But she'd have to be frugal.

A loud thud against the door caused Jessy to jump. Another followed, and wood splintered as the door suddenly flew open and banged loudly against the wall. Standing in the doorway was the gunman, his brown eyes black with fury. His clothes were covered with dust, and he had a large, vivid black and blue bruise on the side of his dirty face. Jessy's mind told her to run, but her body had become paralyzed with fright.

She said the first thing that came into her head. "Did you bring my clothes?"

"Mrs. Turner, men have been killed for less than what you've pulled," he growled as he slammed the door shut. "Did I bring your clothes?" He sneered, looking her up and down. "I would say you've taken care of that problem all by yourself. Where did you get your money? In a poker game? Or perhaps you shared your bed for the funds!"

Jessy couldn't speak. She was having a hard time trying to breathe.

"Sit down," he barked.

She immediately collapsed onto a chair. "How did you find me?" she whispered.

It was several moments before he answered. "Friends recognized my horse." His words were cold and clipped.

"You live here?"

"That's right, Mrs. Turner. I live here."

Of all the blasted luck! Jessy thought. Why did I have to choose Topeka? Without thinking, she glanced at the bureau and her ticket to freedom.

Horrified, Jessy watched as he snatched up the piece of paper, glanced at it and tore it into small pieces. With a flick of his fingers, he scattered them across the room.

Finally regaining control of herself, Jessy bolted for the door. She wasn't fast enough. A strong hand on her arm brought her to an abrupt halt.

"Sit back down, Jessy my dear, we're going to have a talk."

His voice was low, threatening, and Jessy did as she was told.

The gunfighter sat in the other chair, but Jessy wasn't fooled by his relaxed demeanor. He now had the good beginnings of a beard, and though his face had the drawn haggard look of the face of a cowboy after days on the trail, his eyes were very alert.

"Please, mister—"

"By all means, call me Cort." He released a chuckle. "After all, we've become such close friends."

"I'm sorry about hitting you, but what was I supposed to do? Let you have your way with me?"

He continued to stare at her.

"Damn it, I'm not responsible for my husband's debts!"

Still nothing.

Jessy sank back in the chair. "All right! If you're so hungry for blood money, I have some I'll give you." Jessy didn't plan on giving him all the money, but even so, she'd probably end up having to hock her necklace until she could get back on her feet. "And as soon as I make some money in Kansas City, I'll send it to you."

"I don't want money you've suckered some poor man out of. The money you pay me will be earned by the sweat of your brow. And forget about Kansas City. It will be a long day in hell before I let you leave town."

He stood and moved the short distance to where she sat. Placing a large, sun-browned hand on the arm of her chair, he leaned down and looked her straight in the eyes. "*Mrs. Turner*," he said, his tone low and deadly, "I'll give you three choices as to how you're going to pay me back. You can work as a Harvey Girl...or you're welcome to be my maid. I've always wanted a pretty little thing attending to my *very* need." He stood, an evil smile forming on his lips. "Or perhaps you'd prefer to paint your face and work at my saloon? It's a profession you'd probably enjoy. You're a beautiful woman, and I'm quite sure you'd get out of debt quickly. I may even decide to test your pleasures myself."

Furious, Jessy jumped to her feet and kicked him on the shin. She rejoiced as he grabbed his leg and yelled, but the next instant she fell down, moaning and holding her toes. She hadn't stopped to think that her shoe leather was soft.

"What do you know about me?" she finally managed to say. "Nothing! I will never be your *maid*, and I will certainly never be seen dead in a saloon!"

"Then I guess you've chosen Fred Harvey's place," he snapped at her.

Standing, Jessy put a safe distance between them before she turned and faced him. His eyes expressed his fury as he rubbed his shin. "I suppose Harvey's is some fancy bordello!"

"It's a very reputable eating house. At this moment, I'm not even sure you'd meet the requirements!"

"Well, I'm sorry to disappoint you, Mr. Almighty, but have no intention of working for anyone. I'm leaving Topeka!"

"That isn't one of your options, lady. I'm going to count to three, then you'd better come up with an answer. But before I start, I'll say one other thing. If I decide to have you work in my saloon, I'll personally deliver you there, and it'll be a long day in hell before you see daylight again!"

"You can't make me do it." The words didn't come out nearly as strongly as she'd intended.

"One!"

Jessy couldn't think of the name of the place.

"Two."

"All right!" she blurted out. "I'll eat!"

"You'll what?"

Jessy rubbed her throbbing temples. "I'll work at that eating house," she mumbled. She wanted to scream and dig her nails into his chiseled face. Men! First there was BJ, then Jonathan, now...Cort. Her life would never return to normal until she was rid of them all.

"Your wages will go to me, unless I deem otherwise," he continued. "And if you should do anything to lose your position at the Harvey establishment, you will work at the saloon. And don't try to escape. You'll not only be watched, but I also have acquaintances who work there who would be perfectly willing to keep an eye on you for a certain fee. This time you won't get away with your shenanigans. You'll pay your debt."

"What makes you think you're God?" she yelled. She clasped her hands together, trying to regain control. "I'm telling you the truth," she pleaded. "I am not guilty of your accusations."

"Spare me the drama. Get packed. We're leaving."

Jessy had never known such a feeling of defeat.

Jessy sat uncomfortably propped in front of Cort as he guided the dappled gray stallion toward the railroad track. She had sent a boy to purchase her train ticket, so she hadn't seen this part of town. Her eyes nearly popped out of her head when she saw a train. Though she'd heard about them, never in her wildest dreams had she thought the iron horse would be so big. Smoke poured from the black spout on top of the engine, and steam billowed around the huge wheels. The words Atchison, Topeka and Santa Fe were printed on the side.

As Cort brought the stallion to a halt at the end of a long two-story frame building, Jessy saw men of every size, shape and age milling around. Fear gripped her as one after another turned and looked. There were smiles as men began to call, yell and whistle at her. Most of the men she recognized as being from the boiled-shirt civilization she'd come to know so well in western Kansas. Some were hardworking, while others were loafers and had probably never bathed in their lives. Jessy's hands began to shake. Was this to be her future?

"This is the train depot," Cort said as he slid off the horse.

Seeing Jessy's white face, he glanced over his shoulder at the men. "Afraid?" he challenged.

Jessy squared her shoulders and raised her small chin. "Not in the least," she replied as he lifted her to the ground.

After untying the bags from the pommel of the saddle, Cort guided Jessy toward the men. "The entrance is around the side," he informed her.

Jessy only half heard what he said. Any moment she expected one of the men to reach out and grab her. To her surprise, they separated, leaving a clear path. They're probably afraid Cort will gun them down, she thought. Still, she kept her eyes lowered and refused to listen to their comments. Once they rounded the corner, Jessy let out a sigh of relief.

"Remember my warning, Mrs. Turner," Cort snapped. "I don't make idle threats. I'll do all the talking."

He opened the heavy door, and as they stepped inside, Jessy found herself in a large room full of tables and well-dressed customers. It really was an eating house!

"Hello, Mr. Lancaster," an attractive brunette greeted them. "We haven't seen you in some time. Will you be dining with us?"

"Not today, Emma. I've just arrived in town, and as you can see, I'm not properly dressed. I came to see Miss Cragshaw."

Emma glanced at Jessy then immediately looked away. "I'll tell her you're here."

A few minutes later a tall, bone-thin woman with a hooked nose and a sallow complexion arrived. If this is Miss Cragshaw, Jessy thought, her name certainly fits.

"Mr. Lancaster," the woman said. "What may I do for you?"

"Miss Cragshaw, I'd like you to meet Jessica Turner. Mrs. Turner's husband recently passed away, and she's badly in need of work. I know how strict Fred Harvey is about his girls, but I'm sure Mrs. Turner will meet all the requirements."

Jessy had the distinct feeling Miss Cragshaw had been put in an awkward position. Why didn't the woman just tell Cort no instead of letting him intimidate her? Jessy started to speak her thoughts then remembered Cort's threat of having her work in his saloon.

"Actually, Mr. Lancaster, several of our girls have just left for Florence. Mr. Harvey has opened a new hotel there," Miss Cragshaw said proudly. She looked at Jessy. "In order to be a Harvey Girl you must sign a contract stating you will not marry for one year." She glanced at Cort then at Jessy. "Will this present a problem?"

"No," Jessy hastily replied. "Not at all. I have no desire to marry again. I had such a wonderful husband. I doubt any man could ever take his place." She chose to ignore Cort's raised eyebrow.

"Fine," Miss Cragshaw said, her smile softening her pointed features considerably. "I must tell you, Jessica, we maintain strict rules concerning hours and beaux. Everyone must be in by ten at night, except on special occasions, and the men the girls go out with must be of good character. We set a high moral standard here, and all are expected to maintain it."

The men must be of good character? Jessy wondered why Miss Cragshaw was showing respect for the likes of Cort, a gambler and gunfighter. The woman had the tongue of a snake—forked.

"You will be paid $17.50 a week," Miss Cragshaw continued, "plus room and board. The girls are allowed to keep their tips."

Jessy groaned inwardly. At that rate it would take a lifetime to pay Cort off.

"Is that agreeable to you?" Miss Cragshaw asked.

"Yes." Anything to get away from this man, Jessy thought.

"Good. I'll take you upstairs."

"There is one other thing, Miss Cragshaw," Cort said as he handed over Jessy's bags, "Jessica wants all her wages to go to me so I can invest them for her."

Jessy bit her tongue to keep from calling Cort a liar.

"Well, Jessica, you certainly couldn't have picked a better person. I think it's a very wise move."

Obviously the woman has delusions where Cort is concerned, Jessy told herself. He'll take my money and gamble it away just like Jonathan did before he started cheating.

"Come this way, dear," Miss Cragshaw said as she headed for the stairs. "I'm sure you're going to enjoy being a Harvey Girl."

Chapter Three

Cort felt the dappled gray stallion, Emperor, tug at the reins, eager to run now that they had reached familiar territory, but he held the horse to an easy lope. He glanced at the cattle grazing peacefully to his left, and one of the wranglers tending the large herd tipped his hat in recognition and called, "Good to have you back, boss."

Cort nodded his head and continued on. After being in the saddle for nearly five months, he was anxious to get home and climb into a tub of hot water. His trip was over.

Topping a small hill, he brought the horse to a halt. Nearly a mile away sat a large, two-story white frame house. Tall green trees grew on either side, and numerous barns could be seen farther back. Home. Cort twisted in the saddle and looked over the land. Farther than the eye could see was Lancaster land. His land.

His chest swelled with pride. All things considered, he thought, life's been pretty good to me. He nudged Emperor forward.

Sheila managed to contain her excitement as Cort entered the large salon. Bored, she'd been looking out the window for some time and watched her brother ride up to the house. "At last," she said, "the wandering son has returned."

"Looks like you spent some money while I was gone. Isn't that a new outfit?"

Sheila turned ladylike circles so Cort could have a good look at the very properly cut pale blue day dress.

"Do you like it?" she teased.

Cort studied her, making a point of giving the dress proper consideration. "It shows off your blue eyes and makes your hair shine like raven's wings."

She watched the corners of his full lips twitch with humor.

"I think you should go straight upstairs and change," he said with mock seriousness. "You already have every man's attention for a hundred miles around."

Unable to contain her excitement a moment longer, Sheila ran to her brother and threw her arms around his neck. She quickly withdrew. "You smell." Playfully she placed her fingers on her nose.

Cort chuckled. "I followed those rustlers all the way into Mexico. There weren't too many opportunities for bathing."

"Did you get our cattle back?"

"No, but I assure you, the guilty men won't try again." He leaned down and kissed her fondly on the cheek.

"I've missed you so much, Cort." Her eyes sparkled with pleasure.

Sheila watched Cort go to the oak sideboard and pour himself a healthy shot of whiskey. A quiet sigh escaped her lips. Why do I have to have such a handsome brother? she asked herself. Because of him I'm still not married. No one can fill his shoes. Every male I meet is afraid to lock horns with the great "King" Lancaster.

"Do you have any idea how dull it is when you're gone?" she asked as Cort turned around.

"I'd think my being gone would come as a relief to everyone."

"I don't care about anyone else." Sheila pouted. "When you're not here, Mother insists I act like a lady, which means—"

"I know what you mean." He winked at her. "How would you like to go riding with me tomorrow?"

"She'll do no such thing."

Cort looked toward the trim-figured woman entering the room. His eyes turned cold. As always, Marie wore a black dress, and her brown, gray-streaked hair was parted in the center and twisted into a bun at the back of her head. The large diamond brooch pinned to the high neckline of her gown and the diamond drop earrings gave evidence of the family wealth.

"How nice to have you home, Cortland." Marie's tone of voice belied her words. She refused to call him Cort or King, a name his fellow ranchers had bestowed on him several years ago. "Your manners are unforgivable. You know how I feel about wearing a gun in the house, and you could have bathed and changed out of those filthy clothes before entering the salon. I hope you plan on retiring to your rooms soon. I have friends due to arrive for tea in an hour." She sat on her favorite burgundy velvet chair, her posture rigid. With thin lips compressed and hands properly folded in her lap, she glared at her stepson. "You are always such an embarrassment to me. I have long since tired of making excuses for your behavior."

"You never give up, do you, Marie?" Cort slammed the glass down on the side table. "You truly tempt me to stay and greet those biddies you call friends. But because I long for a hot bath, I'll save you from having to make excuses."

"Shall we expect you for dinner," Marie asked coldly, "or will you be taking off to town for your usual... escapades?"

"Jealous, Marie?" Cort let out a low, humorless laugh. "It's been my experience that people who frown on such behavior are usually wishing they could partake."

Marie's hard expression didn't waver. Over the years she had become used to his bawdy remarks. "Though you care nothing for me, I'd think you would have the courtesy not to speak that way in front of Sheila. You are a rogue, Cortland, and you'll never be anything else."

"That's not fair, Mother," Sheila spoke up.

"Hush, Sheila," Marie snapped. "You'd do well to remember just what your brother is really like. Only a rogue would send for a mail-order bride when he could have his pick of any daughter of wealth and good breeding from Kansas to the Atlantic Ocean."

"Oh, Cort, you're not really going through with that, are you?" Sheila asked.

"As a matter of fact, I'll be picking her up at the train station in Topeka about a month from now. And, if we're agreeable, we'll marry."

"I simply cannot believe you would have the nerve to bring a nobody into my house. I'll be the laughingstock of Kansas!" Marie spit out.

"Oh, you know I have the nerve, dear stepmother," Cort replied evenly. "I'm marrying because I want a son. But I'll make damn sure my wife is never allowed to henpeck me the way you've done Father. She'll know her place and learn to jump at my every command. Something Father should have taught *you* a long time ago."

Marie returned his steady gaze. "You or your father would have nothing if it weren't for me. You'll do well to remember it's my money that bought this land."

"The first hundred and fifty acres, Marie, but you've spent your money a hundred times over since then."

Sheila watched her mother's hands curl into fists as Cort left the room. "Why must you fight him, Mother?" she asked softly, her eyes lowered. Marie seldom showed affection, but Sheila loved her just as she loved Cort. Though the two women were not related by blood, Marie was the only mother Sheila had ever known. It hurt terribly to always see the two fighting.

"I should have put my foot down when I married Arthur and never allowed that boy into my life!" Marie practically whispered the words, the faint quiver in her voice testifying to her anger. "He was fourteen and already making trouble. He'd fight anyone who so much as looked at him the wrong way. Now he's nothing but a worrisome thorn in my side."

Marie reached over and removed her embroidery from the sewing basket sitting beside her chair. Deftly she threaded red floss through the needle's eye. "If only I could think of a way to be done with Cortland once and for all."

Sheila felt her cheeks redden with anger. She wanted to remind Marie that if it weren't for Cort, they wouldn't be living in this fine home Marie called her own. Through hard work and a keen business sense, Cort had doubled their money many times over. It was Cort who had run the ranch and had bought all the land that made them the powerful family they were today. That was why everyone called him King. Though she had heard her mother make the same comments a million times, they still rankled. But Sheila refrained from saying anything, knowing to do so would only cause more arguing.

"Don't forget, Sheila, tomorrow the women will be over for our weekly quilting session," Marie reminded her.

"Where is your needlework? A woman's work is never done if she's to have all that's needed to start a new household."

Sheila flinched. Mother still hopes I'll marry Terrance Wilkens, she thought, even though I've turned him down an uncountable number of times. "I left it in my room," she finally replied.

"Well, run upstairs and get it. Idle hands make idle minds."

Sheila left the room, happy for an excuse to get away.

Cort sat in the copper bathtub, a long cigar clenched between his white teeth and a glass of whiskey sitting on the low table within easy reach. Byron, his valet—the only one of Marie's ideas that Cort had learned to appreciate—stood by the door.

"Will there be anything else, sir?" Byron asked, his friendly black face creased with pleasure at Cort's return.

"Sure you don't want another drink?"

The old man laughed. "I think I've had enough. If the mistress smells my breath, I'll be sorely put to explain. She already accuses me of stealing from the liquor supply."

Cort gave Byron a lazy smile. "And do you?"

"Yes, sir."

"Good for you. I'm glad to see you haven't changed since I've been gone."

"I've laid your clothes out on the bed, sir. Will you be wanting my help to dress?"

"No, I'm fine. I just want to sit here and relax." Cort looked at the well-educated, gray-haired man from the East. Byron hadn't been a young man by any means when he came to work for them over ten years ago. Yet he was still spry. Many a time Cort had felt the older of the two, especially when he'd been riding for days.

"Then I'll see that your traveling clothes are properly cleaned."

As Byron silently closed the door behind him, Cort blew a smoke ring and watched it trail upward. After depositing Jessica Turner at Harvey's, he'd stopped by the Belly Up Saloon and told his partner, Tim Riley, to pay some men to watch the Harvey place. He hadn't said anything to anyone who worked at the restaurant. He doubted it would be necessary. Jessy had an imagination, and she'd suspect everyone of spying on her.

Cort closed his eyes and sank back in the tub, a smile tugging at the corners of his lips. The hot-tempered Jessy would have already left for Kansas City if he hadn't threatened to deposit her in the Belly Up Saloon. Tim had stated many times he'd never have any girls working in the place, and Cort respected the man's wishes. Tim was an old friend of Cort's father's who, due to his age, could no longer work with cattle. Cort had given him the money to open a small saloon. His intention had been to sign it over to Tim, but the old man had insisted they remain partners.

Silently, Cort cursed himself for getting involved with Jessy. In fact, he wished he'd never put a boot in the town of Binge. He raised a wet hand and touched the bruise on his forehead. Most of the tenderness had left.

It seemed like months since he'd decided to collect his IOU and had returned to the dingy saloon to find out where Jonathan lived. He had stuck the toe of his boot on the brass rail and tossed his money on the long bar. "Whiskey," he had said to the bartender, named Buck.

"Ain't you the feller who took that signed paper from Jonathan Turner at the poker game last night?" Buck asked as he plunked down a small glass and filled it. Instead of placing the bottle on the shelf behind him, he set it on the bar.

"I'm the man."

"I reckon you know Jonathan got shot and died."

"No. I didn't," Cort replied with a sigh. Well, no need to stay around here any longer, he thought as he tossed down the drink. But the bartender's laughter made him pause.

"Good thing you left when you did, stranger," Buck said, humor shining in his normally dull eyes. "Made me feel right good seeing them two get taken. You left just in time. They always let strangers win, then they change decks. They'd have won back everything they lost, plus all your money."

"I doubt that."

"That's their game, you know. All three of them are as crooked as snakes."

Cort shoved the shot glass forward and watched Buck fill it. "Three?" he asked.

"Hell, yes. Jonathan, BJ and Jonathan's wife, Jessy. Now that's a woman I'd like to bed. A real looker, she is, but I ain't about to fight BJ Johnson for her. Besides being mean, he's plum loco."

"BJ has an eye for the lady, huh?"

"Hell. You gotta be joking. I know BJ shares her bed. Now whether Jonathan knew it might be a different story."

"How do you know?"

"BJ talks about it all the time."

"Who has the necklace?"

"I imagine Jessy Turner. That belonged to her ma, and she ain't about to part with it. She flashes it around all the time. Thataways, Jonathan and BJ can use it as bait."

"And you think she's in on all this?"

"Just between you and me, I figure she thought it all up. She's the only one who's got any brains. Hell, she can even read and write. Her folks was right smart and taught her. They come by wagon train from Tennessee right after the

Civil War, you know, headed for California. The train left at the wrong time of the year, and rather than get caught in the mountains come winter, they decided to wait here in Kansas. Come spring, some headed west, but a lot of the families, including Jessy's folks, stayed.''

"You seem to know a lot about the woman."

Buck gave him a grin that showed rotted front teeth. ''I was on that wagon train. Many a night I spent playing poker with Thomas Revington. That was Jessy's pa. Lost a good deal of money to him. He was smart when it came to cards.''

Cort had never liked being played the fool, especially by a woman. "So you think because her father was a gambler, she learned from him and passed it on to her cohorts?"

"Well, now, I can't say as I'd call her pa a gambler, he just liked playing cards. Nope, he was a real gentleman, and from what I heard, he had a lot of money before the war. Him and the missus worked real hard on that farm of theirs before they got killed. But the rest of what you said I'll go along with. Even as a young pup, Jessy used to like to sit and watch her pa play cards.''

"Then I should be able to collect my IOU from her," he stated flatly.

"I'd think so. They've taken a lot of money from strangers over the years, and Jonathan sure never spent it paying bills. He owed everyone in town. Now BJ, he used his money to run off farmers and buy their land. Owns practically everything in the area, and what he don't own, he soon will. The man's land hungry, but he wants Jessy more. Wouldn't surprise me none if they got married real soon.''

"How do I get to Jessy's place?"

"Don't have to. She's across the street at the funeral parlor right now."

Cort had been standing outside the saloon when Jessy left the small log building across the street. She was certainly not what he had expected. Her silver hair had glistened in the hot sun, and her beautiful flawless face looked white against the high-collared black dress. When she fainted, he wasn't so sure the bartender had told the truth about the lady. It seemed apparent at the time that she was overcome with grief. He decided to make some quick inquiries around town while Jonathan was being buried.

Most of the stories he'd heard collaborated Buck's statements. The fact that BJ drove the lady home added to the story's credibility.

That night, as he stood in the shadows of a dilapidated barn, Cort still had doubts. Then he saw the wily woman sneak out of the house. It amused him to watch her go from spot to spot giving a good imitation of a weasel.

Over the years, he'd done a lot of tracking, so following her hadn't presented a problem. The fact that he had allowed her to get the better of him at the river, however, was an entirely different story. It had made him angry as hell to know he'd underestimated the woman. His anger became worse as he began walking, and if he hadn't found her donkey, he would have been up a creek. Fortunately, a rancher near Atchison had accepted the mule and some money in exchange for a horse. Once he had a worthy animal, it occurred to him that if Jessy was smart, she wouldn't go to Atchison. That left Topeka.

Cort heard a light tap on his bedroom door. "Who is it?" he called.

"Sheila."

Grabbing a towel, Cort lapped it across the tub so only his torso could be seen. "Come in."

Watching his eighteen-year-old sister back into the room gave Cort cause to smile.

"Mother will have a fit if she finds out where I am." Sheila giggled softly while making sure the door was firmly closed. Turning, she spied Cort comfortably reclined against the back of the copper tub. "Oh, cannonballs, Cort! You must be dead set on getting me in trouble. Surely you take after our real mother, because you're nothing like Father."

"Don't get prudish with me," he said, still smiling. "You're beginning to sound like Marie. When you were just a little tyke, you used to wait until I got in the tub to have talks with me, knowing I couldn't escape. And you've certainly seen me bare-chested before. But, in deference to the lovely lady now sitting on my bed, I shall make myself respectable." Reaching to the floor, he picked up his wide-brimmed black hat and placed it on his head. "Now, is that better?"

Sheila cupped her hands over her mouth to keep her laughter from ringing out.

"Mother's right," she said after catching her breath. "You are a rogue."

"You wouldn't have me any other way."

As he reached for his glass and took a healthy swig of whiskey, Sheila noted the wet ends of her brother's dark brown hair curled sleekly at the base of his strong neck. His muscled arms and chest testified to his tremendous strength. Glancing at his face, she met his brown eyes watching her.

"What's his name this time?" he asked softly. That his sister compared him to other men was no secret. He and Sheila had always been close, more like father and daughter. Almost from the time she could walk, Sheila had confided in him.

"Terrance Wilkens."

Cort roared with laughter as a picture of the thin, pimpled-faced kid came to mind.

"It's not funny, Cort." Sheila jumped off the huge four-poster bed. "Mother wants me to marry him."

Still laughing, Cort slid down into the water while tipping his hat forward until the wide brim practically covered his face.

"All right, have your laugh," Sheila said in a huff. "But you wouldn't find it so funny if you were in my shoes. She's always thinking of ways for us to be together, and she's always telling him what a good wife I would make."

Cort tipped his hat back, and though a broad smile still peeked through his beard, Sheila knew she had his attention. "Mother is determined I will wed Terrance." Seeing Cort's eyes narrow, she was satisfied. He'll help get Mother out of my hair, she thought.

"Has he asked you to marry him?"

"Quite a few times. And I always tell him no." She sank down on the bed.

"Then why doesn't he turn toward other pastures?"

"Because Mother keeps telling him I'll see the error of my ways and consent."

Noticing Cort's glass was empty, Sheila immediately rose again. After filling his glass, she set the whiskey decanter beside it.

Cort gave her a grateful grin. "I thought I had made it quite clear to Marie that you would not be pushed into marriage. Do you want to marry him?"

"Heavens, no! I could never put up with that mother of his, let alone him. She leads him around by the nose, and probably even tells him when to spit."

Cort chuckled. "Don't worry your pretty head, I'll put an end to this nonsense."

"Thank you, Cort. I knew I could count on you." Sheila leaned over and started to kiss him on the forehead, but stopped. "Heavens, what happened to your face?" she asked worriedly.

A glint of orneriness lit his eyes. "I saw a beautiful woman, but she became offended and hit me with a rock. Very embarrassing story, but my head is fine."

"Obviously, you're not going to tell me the truth. I'd kiss your cheek, but I'm sure that scruffy beard would scratch. You will shave it off, won't you?"

"I haven't decided. I've grown rather fond of it and I should probably keep it so Marie can have something to complain about. I swear, the woman's only happy when she's unhappy." He rubbed his hand over the thick growth. "Now get on out of here before Marie comes looking for you."

When Sheila left Cort's room, she headed for her bedroom to retrieve her sewing. She'd have to hurry. Her mother would never believe she couldn't find it.

After shaving and putting on fresh clothes, Cort went downstairs to let his father know he had returned, and to check on the old man's well-being. As he entered the large study, a cloud of smoke assailed him. His father sat in one of the soft leather high-backed chairs by the window, reading a book and smoking one of his favorite Cuban cigars. The room reeked of tobacco, and of the beeswax on the freshly polished furniture. Shelves lined the walls, laden with every description of reading material.

Engrossed in his reading, Arthur Lancaster didn't hear his son enter, and Cort took the opportunity to study him. It came as a shock to see how much his father had aged in the short time he'd been gone. Deep wrinkles lined the old man's face, and his pink scalp could be seen through his thin white hair. Arthur was two inches shorter than his son, and he had always been slender.

For the last ten years or so, Arthur could be found in this room day or night. This was his world. His books. Cort had once asked why he preferred reading to being outdoors.

"It's really quite simple, son," he had replied. "I never could ride a horse worth a damn, and much preferred walking. In fact, I couldn't even handle a buggy properly." His father had laughed. "Your mother did all the driving. I've never been a brave man, and unlike you, the thought of getting into a physical fight is almost nauseating. But through books, my imagination allows me to be anyone wish. I can travel to different countries, ride the seas, harpoon whales, fight wars. I'm virtually free to do whatever please."

"But that's not really living, Father," Cort had replied.

"When I was married to your mother, I had fifteen glorious years. When she died giving birth to Sheila, my life would have ceased had it not been for my love for you. didn't even have the strength of character to say no when Marie nagged me into marriage. At the time I excused it by telling myself I needed someone to raise your sister. My books, you and Sheila are all I have now, but I'm content." Cort had shrugged at his reply. If his father was happy, that was really all that mattered.

"Hello, Father," he said softly, so as not to startle the old man.

Arthur lifted his head, causing his wire-rimmed glasses to fall down his nose. Marking his place in the book, he smiled. "Hello, son. I hope you haven't come to chastise me for smoking," he said, a bit short of breath. "I know what the doctor says, but an old man should be able to keep some of his pleasures." He dropped the stub of the cigar into the copper spittoon strategically placed by the chair.

"No, I stopped in to see how you've been doing while I was gone." Cort propped himself on the corner of the large mahogany desk.

"I wondered why you hadn't been in to see me." Arthur started to reach for another cigar, but thought better of it. He'd wait until his son left. "I'd forgotten about you leaving, and Marie never tells me anything. Of course that also has some good points. I see less of her. I'm sorry, son, but lately my memory sometimes fails me. How long have you been gone?"

"Not long. About a month." Telling his father the truth would serve no purpose.

"Time passes so quickly these days." Arthur adjusted his position in the big chair. "Have you spoken to Sheila? Marie wants her to marry that Wilkens boy."

"Yes."

"Most ridiculous thing I've ever heard. You'll put a stop to it, won't you?"

"Yes, Father. I'll talk to Marie tonight."

"Good. I told Sheila you'd handle it. Marie hasn't said a thing about the will. You know, it's hard to believe we pulled that off without her knowing. She always has her nose stuck in everything. Of course, it's only been a week since I signed the papers."

The will had actually been drawn up and signed over a year ago, but Cort said nothing.

"Making that will was the smartest thing I've ever done. After all, if it weren't for you, we'd be broke by now. This place belongs to you, no one else. But you have to keep your promise not to tell Marie about any of it. I know I'm a coward for not wanting her to know, but if she were to find out, she'd nag me to my grave."

"You needn't worry, Father. I'll say nothing."

"And you have to take care of her when I'm gone. She may have been put on this earth as the devil's tormentor, but she is my wife and she has raised Sheila."

"She'll be taken care of."

Arthur suddenly bent forward and began to cough and wheeze. Grabbing a medicine bottle, King held it to the old man's lips. When the coughing subsided, Arthur stuck his tongue out. "Ugh! That stuff tastes horrible!" He leaned back in his chair and immediately drifted off to sleep.

After removing the book from his father's lap, Cort silently left the room.

Those were the last words Arthur spoke. Only a short time later, a servant found the gray-haired gentleman dead in his chair, a peaceful smile on his face.

"You're not serious!" Marie snapped sharply. "That can't be Arthur's will!"

The remaining members of the Lancaster family gathered in the parlor of Cort's house in Topeka. Though Marie sat properly on the edge of the seat with her back straight, for once she couldn't hide her emotions. She was livid. "Arthur and I discussed this many times, and he assured me I would receive everything! Any of my friends will testify as to what a rogue Cortland is. I am sure if you check into it, Mr. Parson, you'll discover Cortland has forged Arthur' signature."

Mr. Parson, who had chosen to remain standing, winced. He had just finished reading the part of the will that stated Cort was to receive all his father's holdings. The lawyer had tried to prepare himself for the woman's sharp tongue, even going so far as to put off reading the will for a week longer than necessary. There was gossip in Topeka that when Arthur Lancaster died, Marie had every intention of kicking her stepson out.

"Mother," Sheila whispered, "Cort would never do such a thing."

Marie looked at her stepson. The heels of his booted feet rested on a footstool, and he appeared not to have a care in the world. The black band circling his arm was his only concession to his father's death.

"Oh, yes, he would," Marie accused.

"Please, Mrs. Lancaster," Mr. Parson spoke up. "This is a perfectly legal document, incontestable. The will was prepared exactly as Arthur requested, and your accusations are unfounded. I personally witnessed his signature."

Marie tried to compose herself. "Very well, skip over everything, and read what Arthur left *me*."

Pulling a lacy handkerchief from his sleeve, Mr. Parson mopped his damp forehead. "I'm afraid he left you nothing, Mrs. Lancaster," he replied.

Marie glared at the attorney, her face ashen. "What did you say?"

Marie's words were spoken softly, but Henry Parson had no trouble deciphering them.

"He said you have nothing, my dear stepmother," Cort answered.

"That can't be possible! How am I supposed to live? If it weren't for my money—"

"Don't worry, Marie, you will always have a place in *my* home." Cort smiled.

"Never! Sheila and I shall move out and live off her money!"

Mr. Parson coughed, effectively gaining everyone's attention. "Whatever Miss Lancaster receives as an allowance will be determined solely by Cortland Lancaster. He has been appointed her guardian. A trust has been set aside, but Miss Lancaster is not to receive it until she is twenty-two."

"Do you expect me to believe any of this? This whole thing is a farce! A lie! Mark my words, Cortland, you won't live long enough to enjoy your fruits. Before long, everything will be rightfully mine!"

Cort maintained a casual demeanor, though inside his blood was at the boiling point. "It will never be yours, dear stepmother. I'll see to it."

"And just how do you plan to accomplish that?" Marie asked.

"My son will inherit everything."

"Hogwash! With your wild living, someone is going to shoot you down in the street before you get the chance. And how do you expect to accomplish this overnight? You ridicule me about never bearing a child. What if that mail-order bride can't have children? And who's to say you'll have a boy?"

Cort ground his teeth together. He would not let Marie see how much she had angered him! "Marie," he said nonchalantly, "are you going to let this man finish reading the will?"

Marie marched toward the door. "Come on, Sheila," she called over her shoulder. "There has been enough underhandedness today. We'll see another lawyer!"

Sheila looked at her brother questioningly.

"Go with Marie," he said softly. "Everything is going to be all right. Don't go filling that pretty head of yours with concern." He winked at her.

Sheila grinned, her step sprightly as she took off after her mother. For the first time since her father's death, she felt happy and relieved. With Cort head of the family, all would remain secure.

Cort let his feet fall to the floor and stood. "Thank you for coming, Henry." He shook the man's hand.

The lawyer placed the papers in a leather case. "You'd better watch out for Marie, King," he said, using the name most familiar to the locals.

"I will," the younger man replied. After seeing the lawyer out, Cort retired to the study, where he knew no one would disturb him, and lit one of his father's Cuban cigars. He considered Marie's threat. Was the woman planning to do him in? He was tired of keeping his guard up and hiding the pain he felt at the loss of his father. But it was necessary. If Marie or any business rival saw a sign of weakness in his character, they'd jump on it and use it to their advantage. God, how he missed the old man. He had known his father had been in bad health, but he hadn't expected the sudden death. Having to stand quietly and watch the dirt shoveled over his father's coffin was the most difficult thing he had ever experienced. Now, the only family he had left was Sheila. But the day would come when some man would claim her heart, and she'd leave.

Since returning to Topeka, he had spent most of his afternoons catching up on business. But after years of hard work, his holdings were pretty much self-sustaining, and he was able to enjoy the fruits of his labor. He had an excellent foreman to handle the ranch, which ran smoothly. Still, if Marie ever got her greedy hands on any of it, all his efforts would fall to ruin.

Damn it! he thought bitterly. I need a son!

Chapter Four

From a safe distance, BJ watched the fire rise high in the air and lick the night sky, gaining momentum as its insatiable appetite made a meal of the wheat field. Dark figures, silhouetted against the flames, were running back and forth, trying to put the fire out. BJ laughed. He knew they wouldn't succeed. The crop would be destroyed. He wasn't worried about the fire spreading. The surrounding area had been freshly plowed.

He turned the big gelding around and headed down the dirt road for home. Tomorrow he'd return and purchase the farmer's land for next to nothing.

All his life he'd been obsessed with the need for land, money and power. As a boy, he'd wanted Thomas Revington's land. The family had always treated him like dirt beneath their feet. When he grew older, he dreamed of seeing them beg for mercy when he took over their holdings. They would have had no choice but to give him their daughter's hand in marriage. Unfortunately, that was before BJ had learned how to gain land the easy way. The old man and his wife had been killed by marauders, and Jessy had married Jonathan.

More than once BJ had devised a plan to do away with Jonathan, but the man seemed to have nine lives. Then fate stepped in, and Jonathan was dead. BJ was determined that this time he would make sure the uppity Jessy became his. But she'd slipped away, making him look like a fool.

Jessy. Just thinking about her made him ache. She should already be with child, his child, and cleaning his boots and floors while thanking him for taking her in. What made her think she was so much better? Soon he'd own everything for miles around. She would rue the day she had left. He'd hired two men to track her, and he waited impatiently for their report.

BJ's thin lips curled in anger. "Can you hear me, Jessy?" he yelled. "You'd better watch out 'cause I'm coming after you. You'll be mine yet, and I'll make your life a living hell!"

Jessy's uniform consisted of a plain black dress with a white Elsie collar and black bow, black shoes and stockings and a white heavily starched apron. She was required to wear a white ribbon neatly tied in a bow at the nape of her neck.

Because of its superb food, the Harvey restaurant was very popular with the Topeka residents. But Jessy quickly discovered that the main purpose of the establishment was to service the railroad passengers. She learned to serve a full meal to sixteen people in twenty-five minutes as was necessary to maintain the train schedule.

Side by side with the other girls, Jessy polished and inspected the English cutlery, made sure the linen tablecloths and napkins from Ireland were fresh and showed no signs of wear, checked the china cups for nicks and removed any broken toothpicks from the tables. Above all, she was never to converse with customers while a train waited.

The upstairs of the large building housed the girls. The area was kept immaculate. Comfortable beds sat between the windows lining either side of the room, and behind the beds were closets for each girl to keep her clothes and personal articles, as well as a small washstand and mirror. A very comfortable arrangement, but even so, Jessy considered the place a labor prison. For the first few weeks, her legs and arms ached miserably, and it was all she could do to undress, drop into bed and silently curse Cort for bringing her here.

Though she chatted with everyone, Jessy's closest friends were Kathleen and Lora, who were housed on either side of her.

Several times Jessy accompanied the two women into town, to see if Cort was really having her watched. To her exasperation, on all occasions they were followed. Escape wasn't going to be easy. But she had discovered that the harder she worked the more customers she had, and the more customers she had the better the tips. She was already developing a sizable purse. At this rate perhaps she could collect enough money to bribe a guard to turn his head, and still not touch the money in her carpetbag. That goal gave her incentive.

As the days slowly passed, Jessy began to look forward to seeing her prison warden. She knew it was only a matter of time before Cort would make an appearance, and she longed to spit out the words of hate that festered within her. But as one week blended into another, she realized the futility of such action. So far, temper and pity had gained her nothing. Obviously a different approach was necessary.

Jessy knew her nemesis had finally decided to honor her with his presence when a smiling Miss Cragshaw informed her she had a guest in the sitting room. Jessy was ready.

"Good evening, Jessy," Cort greeted her as she entered the Victorian-style room.

As far as Jessy was concerned, his slow smile and black clothes painted an intimidating picture. She'd chosen to remember him as a snake slithering on the ground, and had managed to forget just how tall and handsome he was.

She gave him an amiable smile. "You're looking well, Cort. I wondered when you would come to see me."

"Oh? Have you missed me?"

She widened the smile just a fraction. "Quite the contrary. I've actually wanted to thank you for getting me this position as a Harvey Girl."

Jessy enjoyed the look of confusion that momentarily crossed his lean face. "Though you have wrongfully judged me," she continued, "I now realize there is nothing I can do to change your mind. Actually, I'm quite happy here, and the tips allow me to purchase what few things I need. I've never liked being idle."

As Cort made himself comfortable on one of the brocade chairs, Jessy couldn't resist saying, "A gentleman isn't supposed to seat himself until the lady is seated."

"Oh, I admit you're a lady, and a very beautiful one at that. Even in your uniform." His dark brown eyes traveled blatantly over her from head to toe. "But who said I'm a gentleman?"

Jessy refused to let him bait her. "Certainly not I," she said flippantly as she sat on the sofa across from him.

Cort chuckled. "I had a long talk with Miss Cragshaw."

And collected your blood money, Jessy thought.

"She said you've turned out to be one of her best girls."

"How nice."

Cort couldn't help but wonder why she was acting so complacent. This certainly wasn't the fiery female he'd met before, and he seriously doubted she could change in so short a period. Obviously she needed to be reminded of her situation. "It's going to take you a long time to pay me off."

"I realize that."

"So you're content to spend years working here?"

Jessy quietly smoothed the skirt of her black dress then looked him straight in the eye. "Yes. As I said, I'm quite happy."

"And what about men?"

"I beg your pardon?"

"What will you do when you long for a man to share your bed?"

Cort's brown eyes held hers, and Jessy was surprised at the effort it took to look away. "Only a man would ask such a question," she hastily informed him. "I have no need for a man, nor do I desire one."

"Are you telling me you're a woman of ice?"

Jessy resented his broad smile. "I don't appreciate barroom conversations, Mr. Lancaster." She rose from the sofa, but before she could make it to the door he had blocked her path.

"You're a mature woman, why can't you answer my question?"

Jessy felt her temper rise. The conversation had gotten entirely out of hand. She had intended to make him think she was satisfied with her fate, but as usual, he'd successfully thwarted her efforts. "Very well. I do not like having a man paw me. Now, does that answer your question?"

"Not even Jonathan or BJ?"

"Least of all Jonathan, and certainly never BJ!" Jessy wanted desperately to escape, but he refused to move.

"How interesting."

"Now, would you please let me pass?"

Before Jessy realized what was on his mind, Cort drew her into his arms and lowered his mouth to hers. His kiss was harsh and demanding. Furious, she pulled away. "You—"

He twisted his fingers in her silver mane, and holding her head in place, kissed her again. His lips assaulted hers, but the hard, unyielding kiss became softer yet more passionate. His tongue caressed her mouth, then he gently nibbled her lower lip. Jessy tried to fight the strange, delicious wanting that was starting to build in her. When his hand caressed her breast, desire shot through her entire body. She had never experienced such a feeling. Suddenly he released her, and Jessy felt both foolish and vulnerable.

Seeing desire lingering in her lavender eyes, Cort smiled. "Either you're telling lies, Mrs. Turner, or you've been with the wrong men."

"Oh!"

"Make sure you remember we have a bargain and don't do anything foolish. I can still put you to work in my saloon." He studied her haughty look. "What happened to the necklace, Jessy?"

His voice had turned cold, and Jessy wasn't sure whether to stick to her story or not. On a hunch she told him the first thing that came to mind. "I don't know. Jonathan must have taken it. The night he was shot I searched the house, but it wasn't there."

Cort stepped aside and allowed her to leave. Jessy certainly had a way of making herself appear misjudged. The kiss had proven what he'd suspected all along. She was a very passionate woman. She was also a very determined one, and would never allow any man in her bed unless she chose to, including BJ. Acting as if she hated the man was quite brilliant. But Cort knew they'd shared a bed, and right under her husband's nose. He looked at the empty doorway and rubbed his chin. The woman was incapable of telling the truth. As sure as the sun rose and set, Jessy would eventually try to run. She was only biding time until she could figure a way to escape. He couldn't expect her to spend the rest of her life paying him back, but he was going to make damn sure she paid a goodly portion before he let her go. Maybe she'd think twice before she tried taking another man's money, but he doubted it.

Sheila was in a great hurry this particular morning. She was so determined to be on time that she had even managed to get out of bed earlier than usual and had dressed herself. Ready, she sat on the windowsill, waiting impatiently for Cort to leave.

Sheila liked Cort's house in town because it allowed her easy access to parties and friends. He'd bought the place several years ago and, wanting all the comforts of home while attending to business in Topeka, he maintained a well-trained staff. Even so, with the exception of the social aspects, she didn't like it as well as the house on the ranch where she had been raised.

Finally hearing Cort's bedroom door close and his booted feet going down the stairs, Sheila waited several minutes before following after him.

"When did Cortland say that *woman* would be arriving?" Marie called as Sheila passed the doorway to the parlor.

Sheila slumped her shoulders in disappointment. She'd hoped to pass unseen, but maybe her mother wouldn't delay her too long. Accepting her fate, she entered the room. "You mean his mail-order bride?" she asked innocently.

"Of course."

"This morning, Mother. In fact, I believe he left a few minutes ago."

"Are you just going to stand there?"

Sheila pursed her lips as she lowered herself onto a high-back chair.

"I suppose your brother plans to bring the hussy straight to the house?" Marie asked.

"I don't know. He's said nothing about it to me. Mother, I'm sure Cort is not going to marry a woman he'd be embarrassed to introduce to our friends."

"Why not? He doesn't care what people think. He certainly makes no secret of his affairs, and Lord knows there have been many."

Sheila had seen many women turn to jam after casting their eyes on her handsome brother, but she seriously doubted that all the stories circulating about him were true. Besides, she had a feeling the affairs people didn't know about were far more interesting. But her mother loved gossip, especially if it confirmed Cort's worst qualities, so Marie's friends were always bending the older woman's ear.

"Why other men admire him is beyond me. But that's neither here nor there." Marie brushed a piece of lint off her black sleeve. "Nothing is going to change his unforgivable conduct, and certainly not this woman he's shipping in. He'll continue his carousing and use her to get the son he wants. The rest of the time he'll leave her at the house under my feet and expect me to take care of her and his brat."

"Maybe she won't want to marry him," Sheila said, trying to appease her mother.

"Oh, be serious, Sheila! Any woman would jump at the chance to marry a man with so much money. I'd think you would be more concerned about this whole affair. After all, he's only doing it to get a son and keep me from getting what is rightfully mine, as well as yours in time to come. Well, I for one refuse to be here when the trollop arrives. I'm going over to visit with Mrs. Commers."

Sheila swallowed her elation at discovering her mother wouldn't be home to ask questions later. Now all she had to do was make it to the depot on time. "I absolutely agree,

Mother," she said, rising to her feet. "I was also leaving for that very same reason." Never good at telling a lie, Sheila thought she'd handled that quite well.

Since returning to town, Cort had spent a good many nights in the arms of supposedly upstanding Topeka women. This morning he'd arrived home just before dawn, and what with having to meet the early train, he was plain tuckered out.

He'd dressed in buckskins so his potential bride wouldn't suspect he had money. Leaning against the hitching post at the train depot with his hat pulled low so as to rest his eyes, Cort contemplated any problems he might encounter with getting her to sign the papers waiting at the lawyer's.

More than once he'd silently questioned the validity of bringing Amy Rothchild to Kansas. Admittedly, he cared nothing for a wife; he wanted a legitimate son. And whatever it took, he'd damn well have one. After taking everything into consideration, he still felt his actions were justified. The women he knew were well aware of his wealth, and none would be willing to settle for what he had in mind. Maybe he wasn't being fair to Amy, but he had told her in his letters he wanted a child. When that was accomplished, he'd set her up in a fine home somewhere out of Kansas, and leave her with a sizable bank account. That should be enough to make her content. Obviously she had problems or she'd never have agreed to come West.

If Amy proved as good as her picture, he'd marry her straightaway. She had a pretty little face, looked intelligent and healthy, could read and write, and twenty was a respectable age for bearing children. The possibility that she might not choose to marry him never entered his mind.

Upon hearing the train whistle, Cort moved forward. He didn't see his sister standing at the other end of the building.

Sheila stood motionless, waiting. She had to be careful. Cort would be angry if he discovered her there, but her curiosity had overcome any rational thinking. She couldn't imagine what kind of woman would marry a man sight unseen, and if the woman turned out to be a painted lady with bright clothes, she would simply die of laughter.

As the passengers left the train, Sheila's blue eyes continually shifted from female passengers to her brother. A particularly fat woman had trouble getting down the metal steps of the car, and Sheila giggled. Could this be the one? But Cort didn't move. How will he know her? Sheila wondered. Finally there were no passengers left, and Cort still hadn't moved. Where was the woman? Seeing her brother start to turn, Sheila quickly ducked behind the side of the building. Could the woman possibly have thwarted the great King Lancaster's plans? Could Cort's mail-order bride have changed her mind? Sheila broke out laughing as she climbed into her buggy.

Though Sheila didn't know it, Cort was wondering the same thing. As he headed for the depot, a scowl crossed his sun-browned features. When he set something into motion, he didn't like having things go astray. Not one damn bit! He hoped Amy Rothchild had merely missed the train.

After checking to see if Amy had sent a telegram, Cort left word with the stationmaster to send a boy to his house if a woman arrived later. Angry, he mounted Emperor and headed home. The twit probably cashed her ticket in for the money, he told himself. If that was what she had done, he was flat out of luck. He doubted that she would remain at the address where he'd sent the letters. If she was smart enough to pull such a stunt, she was smart enough to move to where he couldn't get his hands on her. If she didn't show up by tomorrow, he'd have his answer. He cared less about the money than he did about having a woman play him for a fool.

Sheila impatiently tapped her fingers on the arm of the sofa. She had rushed home, picked up her embroidery and sat herself sedately in the salon to await her brother's arrival. She was beginning to wonder if her hurried efforts had been in vain when she heard the front door open and close.

"Is that you, Cort?" she called sweetly. She tried to look relaxed even though the laughter within her breast threatened to explode. That quickly disappeared when she saw the thunderous look on Cort's face as he stood in the doorway.

"What are you doing home?" he asked, leaning against the door frame. "I thought you'd spend the day shopping."

Though she knew he was angry, Sheila couldn't control her sense of humor. "No, I decided to stay home. Isn't your bride-to-be supposed to arrive today?" she asked innocently, keeping her eyes on the needle so as not to give herself away.

Cort's eyes narrowed. "You weren't by any chance at the station, were you?"

Sheila suddenly had trouble keeping her hands steady.

"One of these days, Sheila, you'll stick that little nose into something that is none of your business, and someone is going to cut it off."

"Now don't be cross with me, Cort." She pouted, setting her needlework aside. "I had to see, didn't I? I'll bet you would have done the same thing when you were my age. What if I were to advertise for a mail-order husband?"

"I wouldn't advise it."

Sheila stifled a giggle. "You'll have to admit, it would be pretty funny."

"I don't think Marie would find it very funny. Did she tell you I'm taking you to Harvey's for dinner?"

"Yes, and I can't wait. I'll be ready promptly at seven." As he started to leave, she said, "Wait! What about your mail-order bride? Why wasn't she on the train?"

"I have no idea. When I find out, *if* I find out, you'll be the first to know."

"Oh, Mother's going to love this."

Cort's eyes hardened, and Sheila knew she shouldn't have verbalized her thoughts. "Cort, if the woman doesn't come, are you going to try again?"

"I haven't decided."

Sheila glowed with pride as she sat eating raw oysters in the dining room of the restaurant. Of course her mother had been furious at the whole idea, saying it wasn't safe for her to be out alone with a rogue like Cortland. That Cort hadn't asked the older woman to go with them certainly didn't make matters any better.

Through lowered lashes, Sheila watched various women trying to catch her brother's eye. She couldn't blame them. He looked so handsome in his white linen shirt, light trousers and black frock coat.

Jessy, when she had a moment, was also watching Cort. She knew he had deliberately sat at one of her tables. She had never seen him dressed in such a gentlemanly manner. The lady with him was very lovely, and her clothes and jewelry left no doubt as to her wealth. He was probably out to get all her money, too!

By the time Jessy had served dessert, she was seething. It didn't bother her that Cort showed no signs of recognition—it probably wouldn't set well with his lady friend.

What made her angry was the way he constantly gave orders, treating her as if she was below him.

Upon completion of their meal, Sheila left the table to say hello to an old friend also dining there. Taking advantage of her absence, Cort motioned for Jessy to come to the table.

"I hope you enjoyed your meal, sir," she said sarcastically, "and will return to Harvey House soon."

"As a matter of fact, the service and food were excellent. However, I won't be leaving a tip. I'll subtract it from what you owe me."

His words were the last straw. "I understand perfectly." Jessy smiled sweetly then deliberately knocked over a glass. The water landed directly on Cort's lap, the material of his light pants quickly absorbing the liquid.

"What the hell—"

"Oh! I'm so sorry, sir." Jessy grabbed a napkin but on second thought decided not to dab the area. "You can add the cleaning bill to what I owe you."

Cort collected Sheila and, stopping only long enough to toss some money to the cashier, stormed out of the place.

For the next week, Jessy's thoughts centered mostly on Cort. She had devised a plan of escape. A week from Friday, Fred Harvey was having a party for the girls, and that was when she would set her plan into action.

Jessy had long since recovered from Cort's kiss, but that she had even reacted to it was unforgivable. She had always been self-reliant, and the sudden discovery of weakness in her armor came as quite a shock. She considered herself immune to that sort of thing, and had never wanted to feel another man's hands on her again. Why Cort, of all people? He was nothing but a black-hearted gunman! But she'd make sure those feelings were never allowed to creep out again.

"Thank you, Mike," BJ said as he handed over the money agreed on. "You did a good job. You say Elmer is staying in Topeka to keep an eye on her?"

The man with the pox-scarred face nodded.

Chapter Five

The girls had helped to make the party an enjoyable affair by hanging streamers of every imaginable color across the dining room and moving the tables and chairs to allow plenty of room for dancing.

A small, smartly dressed Englishman with a mustache and goatee stood by the front door greeting people as they arrived. Frederick Henry Harvey looked nothing like the godlike figure Jessy had pictured in her mind. Miss Cragshaw stood beside him, busily collecting tickets, checking for neatness and sobriety and making sure the men deposited their shooting irons and any other weapons in a basket by the door.

Some of the young men wore new clothes direct from the mercantile store, crease lines intact. The suave, more experienced men wore fine, tailored clothes, which complemented the women's beautiful gowns.

Everyone was in a festive mood except Jessy, who stood with the other girls, nervously wringing her hands. Her blue watered silk dress had a low neckline, and the tight corset had pushed her full breasts up so that she felt exposed. She had never worn anything that left so little to the imagination. Small sleeves draped over her shoulders, leaving them bare, and the fine material hugged her tiny waist then billowed out into a full skirt. A matching fan hung from her wrist. Her mother's necklace would have added the perfect touch, but she hadn't dared to wear it.

As the musicians began playing a Virginia reel, Jessy watched the men hurry forward, ready to claim the first dance. She could smell the bay rum liberally splashed on the faces of those who had visited the barbershops and bathhouses.

Jessy's anxieties quickly faded as she danced with merchants, railroad men and cowhands, many of whom were badly in need of dancing instructions. They certainly hadn't been informed that the waltz was supposed to be a graceful dance. She grimaced when they stepped on her toes and felt like a water pump as they moved her arm up and down to the beat of the music.

Being whirled around the floor by her various partners left Jessy breathless. She was grateful that little conversation was required on her part, and a simple nod or smile was quite sufficient. They did the talking, and in no time she knew their life histories. The men flirted openly, declaring their love and even asked for her hand in marriage.

Cort knew Jessy was unaware of his presence as he stood in the background, talking to other businessmen who were seeking his opinions. His eyes followed her around the room. Every man in the place seemed to be vying for her attention. Several overzealous men had already stepped outside, deciding to settle their claims with fists.

Cort had no quarrel with their preference. Jessy was a very beautiful woman, and the dress she wore showed off her creamy skin while allowing a titillating view of firm, white breasts. It was interesting to see how appealing she was, yet she maintained a certain aloofness.

When her current dance partner started to lead her toward the punch bowl, Cort decided it was time to make his presence known. He stepped forward, meeting the couple halfway.

"Excuse me, but I believe this next dance is mine," he informed the hapless man as he watched the fire leap into Jessy's lavender eyes.

Jessy sucked in her breath. She should have known Cort would show up. Her displeasure increased when her current partner dropped her arm as though it was a hot branding iron and said, "Yes, sir, Mr. Lancaster," before disappearing.

"Mr. Lancaster," Jessy said with an overabundance of sweetness, "I'm surprised you were even allowed in. You must have dearly resented having to check your gun. Oh, but I forgot. You're a personal friend of Miss Cragshaw's."

Cort smiled and offered her his arm. "If you've finished, shall we dance?"

"I think not." Jessy tilted her chin up, determined to be rid of him. "I'm thirsty and quite famished."

Jessy walked away, headed for the punch bowl, but Cort followed. "Good. I'll get you some punch and a couple of finger sandwiches and we can step outside for a breath of air. Besides, I want to talk to you." Jessy stopped so fast he almost ran into her.

"I have no intention of going anywhere with you! Need I remind you we have a deal?" she asked, furiously fluttering her blue fan. "I've kept my end of the bargain, and there was nothing said about me having to put up with you. I still have my job, and you get your money every week." She turned aside, refusing to look at him. "If you persist in staying, find some other woman to pester."

"You seem to be a bit confused, Mrs. Turner," Cort said calmly. "There was no bargain, I gave you an ultimatum."

Realizing people were starting to turn and look at them, essy lowered her voice. "Well, call it what you may, I've ill held up my end."

Seeing Lora watching her, Jessy nodded her head in recgnition. It suddenly occurred to her that some of the other rls were also staring. The foolish women are probably mitten with Cort's handsomeness, she thought.

"Shall I get you that drink?" Cort asked.

"Don't bother. I'd prefer someone else fetch it, and I have o intention of going outside with you."

"Yes, you will."

Jessy faced him, her determined eyes clashing with his. No, I won't!"

"What if I started a fight and swore you caused it?"

"You wouldn't dare!" Jessy gasped.

"You underestimate me, my dear."

To Jessy's horror, Cort reached out and tapped the entleman beside him on the shoulder. As the man turned, is jaw met with Cort's hard fist.

"What's going on there!" Mr. Harvey began pushing his ay toward them.

Seeing the man lying on the floor out cold, Jessy shook er head in disbelief. How could Cort seem perfectly noral one minute then turn around and pull something like is?

Cort raised a dark eyebrow. "Well, do we go outside for at talk?"

"This is blackmail!"

"You'd better make up your mind quick."

Mr. Harvey was almost upon them. "All right," she hispered angrily, "I'll go outside. But only for a moent!"

Cort turned and helped the dumbfounded man off the floor. "Sorry," he said as he dusted the fellow off. "I thought you were someone else."

Rubbing his aching jaw, the man assessed Cort's size. "That's quite all right," he grumbled. "We all make mistakes."

"King! What's this all about?" Fred Harvey asked as he reached them.

Cort noted the astonished look on Jessy's face when Fred called him by name. He smiled sheepishly at Fred Harvey. "Sorry, someone insulted Mrs. Turner."

"Who?" Fred glared at the man Cort had socked.

"I saw him go out the door just as I hit the wrong man."

Jessy had thought to tell Mr. Harvey exactly what had happened and be rid of Cort. But they appeared to know each other, and Mr. Harvey was believing the lies Cort was telling him. Her hands were tied.

Fred laughed. "Well, if you see him come back in let me know, and we'll help him out. No one insults one of my girls."

"My feelings exactly." Again Cort extended his arm to Jessy. "Shall we go outside for a breath of air?"

Jessy came within inches of saying she had a headache and wanted to go upstairs, but what would it accomplish? She knew, one way or another, Cort would have his talk. As crazy as he was, for all she knew he might even follow her upstairs! Wasn't it better to be done with it? She turned and headed for the door.

Jessy's mind was spinning. Was this really the same King Lancaster she'd heard so much about? No wonder the girls had been staring at her. Practically every one of them had expressed a desire to marry the man who owned so much of the area. This had to be some kind of mistake. Maybe Mr. Harvey was confused, and Cort was a relative or a brother.

As they stepped outside, Jessy took a deep breath of clean night air. Then she saw her guard propped against the building. As he tipped his hat and said, "Good evening, boss," Jessy stuck her tongue out at him. Not a ladylike thing to do, but at this point she didn't care.

"Good evening, Bud," Cort replied. "I won't be needing you for a few minutes. Why don't you go get a drink?"

"Sure thing, boss."

"You must be awfully worried about me," Jessy said as she watched Bud fade into the shadows. She had to say something to clear her thoughts.

"I don't trust you, if that's what you mean." Cort pulled a cigar from his vest and lit it.

"How many men do you have watching me?"

"Enough."

"So you're actually using my money to pay for them."

"I guess you could say that."

"And maybe some of your money as well? So what purpose does it serve to have two men always watching me, Mr. Lancaster?"

Two men? Cort wondered. He'd have to check into that. "The purpose hasn't changed. But we can do away with all this if you'll agree to an idea I have."

Jessy slapped her fan against her skirt. "I'm sick and tired of your ideas!" Her curiosity couldn't stand it a moment longer. She had to know the truth. "Why did Mr. Harvey call you King?"

Cort took her by the elbow. "Let's take a stroll."

Jessy jerked away. "No! Just answer my question."

Jessica Turner was without a doubt the most stubborn woman Cort had ever met. "Very well," he said smoothly. "King is the name most people call me. My friends call me Cort."

"Well, I'm certainly not your friend! You've taken my hard-earned money while deliberately letting me think you were a gambler and a gunfighter!" Jessy threw her hands in the air. "If you have so much money, why do you want mine? You are the lowest form of cad!"

"I don't think you have any room to cast stones, my dear." He threw his cigar away. The moon lit the area well enough for Cort to see Jessy clearly. Her small jaw was firmly set, and her generous lower lip was extended a fraction. He had trouble keeping his eyes from straying to her breasts, which rose and fell with her angry breathing.

"I have a business proposition for you. I want a son." Cort enjoyed the look of shock on her face. "And in order to get a son, I'm willing to pay handsomely."

"I'm going inside!" Jessy hissed. His strong hand gripped her arm so tight, she knew there would be bruises tomorrow.

"Damn it, you'll stay and hear me out! When I'm finished you can go in."

Jessy didn't move, and he released her arm.

"In order to get a son, I'm willing to marry under certain provisions. If you agree to become my wife, I'll consider your debt paid, and as soon as I have a boy, I'll buy you a home in Kansas City. You'll have a large enough bank account that you will never have to soil your hands again."

"Without the child, of course. Are you finished?" she asked loathingly. Jessy couldn't believe what he'd just said. Never in her entire life had she received such a cold-blooded proposition! The man had to be rattled in the head. She needed to get out of town, and soon!

"I don't expect an answer, I just want you to think about it." He gave her a sly grin. "What have you got to lose? You'll be a very wealthy woman, Jessy Turner, and you'll never see my face again."

"I don't want to see your face now! Have you ever had it slapped?" she asked.

Cort chuckled softly. "Quite a few times, and I must say I handle it very well. Do you want to try?"

"I find nothing humorous about this! You have just insulted me, and I can give you my answer right now. No! Now, may I leave?"

"Be my guest. But the offer is still open should you change your mind."

Jessy didn't rejoin the party. Instead, she went directly upstairs. To her aggravation, Kathleen and Lora joined her a few minutes later, their faces lit up like candles. From their heavy breathing, Jessy could only assume they had run all the way up the stairs.

"Oh, Jessy," Kathleen said excitedly, "we saw you come back in."

"Tell us what he said." Lora collapsed on the bed.

Jessy stared at her two friends. Kathleen, a woman of medium height with mousy blond hair, tended to be a bit giddy. Jessy could understand her reaction to Cort's handsomeness. Lora, however, was tall and regal and never got excited about anything, until tonight.

"We just went outside for some fresh air," Jessy replied. "Lora, would you please undo the back of my dress? I have a terrible headache." She leaned back so Lora could reach it.

It suddenly occurred to Jessy that this was the ideal opportunity to put her plan of escape into action. Cort inadvertently had given her a perfect excuse. "Mr. Lancaster is the most obnoxious man I have ever met. He was simply awful, and I had a terrible time getting rid of him."

"I don't care what you say," Kathleen insisted. "I think having the great King Lancaster fight for your honor is quite thrilling."

Jessy let her dress fall to the floor and stepped away. "No one insulted me, Kathleen. Cort made the whole thing up so he could get me outside. I tell you, he's a dangerous man."

"Cort? My, my. From what I've heard, he has quite a reputation with the ladies." Kathleen began preening in front of the mirror. "I certainly wouldn't mind being one of them."

"Why do you say he's dangerous?" Lora asked.

Having undressed, Jessy slipped a white cotton nightdress over her head then joined Lora on the bed. It allowed her time to get her story straight. "I met Cort...King many months ago when I was heading toward Topeka after my husband's death."

"How exciting," Kathleen said as she joined them.

Seeing she had both women's attention, Jessy continued. "On the trail, he told me he wanted to get married and have a son. After the child was born, he would send the woman away to some city with enough money to last the rest of her life."

"What does that have to do with you?" Lora asked.

"He's determined to have me bear his child, and he won't accept no for an answer. Now he's having me watched constantly so I won't run away." Jessy sniffed. "I'm so frightened. From everything I've heard, he's very powerful, and I'm afraid he's going to find a way to force me into it."

Lora shook her head. "I don't understand. Why would he want you to have his child?"

"Who knows? That's my point. I'm about convinced he's rattled in the head."

"No decent woman should be treated like that," Kathleen said angrily, "or marry a man under those circumstances."

"And to make matters worse," Jessy continued as she reached over and removed a handkerchief from the nightstand, "I think I'm in love with him. He is such a handsome, no-account devil."

As she watched both women nod in agreement, Jessy felt guilty. But she had to get away, and this was the only way she knew to accomplish it, short of telling the truth. "I have to think of a way to get on a train without being seen." She dabbed her nose effectively.

"Maybe we can help," Kathleen offered. "Or, Miss Cragshaw might know what to do."

"No," Jessy said sadly. "She thinks he's wonderful and would probably tell him."

"Oh. Then what about the girls? If we all put our heads together, surely we can come up with a solution."

"That would probably work, except for one thing. Cort is paying one of them to spy on me, and I don't know who."

"My heavens," Kathleen said, glancing around the empty room. "He certainly is determined!"

Lora rose to her feet and began pacing as she thought. "I can go to the depot and buy you a ticket, but getting you out of here unseen presents a problem."

The two women became quiet, each trying to think of a scheme. After allowing what she considered an appropriate length of time, Jessy spoke up. "I've thought of an idea that might work, if you're willing to help. Kathleen is about my height. What if she put on one of my dresses, a bonnet to cover her blond hair and a veil?"

"I see what you're saying," Lora said. "And whoever is following will think it's you trying to hide."

"Exactly. Then all I have to do is slip onto the train, and no one will ever know who helped me."

Kathleen smiled. "I'm willing. When should we do it?"

"Thursday. I've already checked the train schedule."

"This is going to be so exciting," Kathleen whispered.

Caught up in the adventure, they all started laughing.

By Wednesday, Jessy awoke a tired, nervous wreck. With the tension building within her, she'd had little sleep. She hoped that tomorrow it would all be over, and she could proceed with her life. But try as she may, she couldn't stop worrying about Cort. Every morning since the dance, he had eaten breakfast at the restaurant. He didn't always sit in her area, but he made a point of cheerfully greeting her or saying good day when he left. All the girls in the dormitory thought it was very romantic, and teased her unmercifully.

Lora had already obtained the ticket, and other than to pack her few things, Jessy was ready to leave. This time she placed the ticket in her drawer, making sure there would be no repeat of what happened last time.

Dressed in her black uniform and white apron, Jessy went downstairs ready to start serving customers. Miss Cragshaw made a comment about how thin she was looking but Jessy excused it by saying she hadn't felt well. As the morning passed, Jessy was relieved that for once, Cort didn't make an appearance.

Caught up in serving breakfast, which consisted of a thick steak smothered with eggs, a six-high stack of large wheat cakes with syrup and a platter of hash brown potatoes followed with apple pie and coffee, she managed to push her worries aside. She was in the process of delivering food to a fresh table of customers when she heard a familiar high-pitched laugh. Thinking it coincidental, she ignored it. But when she heard the laughter a second time, she turned and looked for the source. It wasn't difficult to spot the carrot-red hair. Seeing BJ's beady eyes boring into her, Jessy dropped a plate of food.

"Look what you've done!" a lady said as she jumped up from the table. "You spilled food all over me!"

Jessy's head began to spin. Where was Cort...? He was the only one who could protect her... No... That was wrong... One of the men Cort had hired to keep her from escaping was now sitting with BJ... Cort must have been working with BJ all along... Of course... It all made sense now... That's why Cort had followed her from Binge.

"Jessy... Jessy..."

Jessy slowly lifted her eyelids and saw Miss Cragshaw leaning over her.

"How do you feel, dear?" The older woman placed a cool, damp cloth on Jessy's forehead.

It took a moment before Jessy realized she was lying on her bed. "All right, just a little groggy." Suddenly remembering BJ, she jerked into a sitting position. "How did I get here?"

"One of the men carried you."

"Who?"

"One of the customers. He wanted to take you to a doctor, but I insisted he bring you up here. I didn't like the man. When I came back with a damp cloth, I caught him going through your things. Never did trust a redheaded man."

Though her drawer was closed, Jessy knew instinctively BJ had seen the train ticket. A moan escaped as she clutched at the older woman's hand. "Please, Miss Cragshaw," she whispered, "don't let anyone take me away from here."

"Of course no one is going to take you away without your permission. I've ordered some soup to be brought up, and I want you to eat every bit of it and rest." Miss Cragshaw sat beside her and placed her arm around Jessy's shaking body. "Ever since you arrived, you've been a loner. There is very little I don't know about most of the girls that come here. I

have broad shoulders to lean on, and I think you're very
frightened. Why don't you tell me about it?''

Cort entered the cheap hotel room and took a quick
glance around. The bed, covered with a blue chenille bed-
spread that should have been thrown away years ago, sank
in the middle. The wooden floor was well worn, and the
walls probably hadn't seen a coat of paint since the place
was built. Then he looked at the woman who had let him in.
His mail-order bride.

"This is a surprise," he stated casually. There were crow's
feet at the corner of her green eyes, her jaw was beginning
to sag just a fraction, and her light brown hair had no lus-
ter. Amy Rothchild was considerably older than her picture. Even so, she was still an attractive woman, and her
subdued calico dress could not hide a well-endowed figure.
"When you didn't arrive on the train, I thought you had
changed your mind."

"To be truthful, I almost didn't come. It's not easy to
leave your home and go to a strange place." She gave him a
teasing smile. "I know I'm not what you expected, Mr
Lancaster, but you are certainly not what I had expected
either."

"Call me Cort."

Amy studied him from head to toe. "My, my, I wish I
were younger, but at this time in my life I honestly don't
think we have much in common. From your clothes, it isn't
difficult to tell you are a man of means."

When Cort received the message that a woman wanted to
see him, it hadn't occurred to him that the woman would be
Amy Rothchild.

"You're far too handsome for my liking," Amy continued. "I want a man I can be sure will come home every
night. And I don't believe I'm what you're looking for in a

wife. I haven't the experience of mixing with wealthy people—'' she grinned ''—nor the youth to keep up with a young buck like yourself.''

Cort laughed. He liked her straightforwardness.

''I think I can speak for the both of us. A marriage is out of the question. I'll catch the next train back.''

''Just out of curiosity, Amy, why did you come to Kansas?''

''To find a husband. Our farm was already in debt when my husband died two years ago. I tried to stay above water but I finally lost everything.''

''And you have no family?''

''No.'' Amy lowered her eyes. ''I know you said you wanted a child in your letters, and I'm not past the childbearing age. I didn't lie about that. I just had this crazy notion that only old men sent for mail-order brides.''

''I may not be the right man, Amy, but believe me, there are hundreds of men in Kansas looking for a good woman. Females are scarce.''

''I haven't the means to stay, Mr. Lancaster.''

''But I do,'' Cort said cheerfully. ''Come on. We're going to find a good boardinghouse for you. You're a fine looking woman, Amy Rothchild, and I'm sure some man will be smart enough to win your hand in marriage.''

''Why would you want to pay for me to stay here?''

Cort smiled. ''Let's just say that when I sent for you I wasn't exactly playing with a straight deck of cards, either. In all honesty, be grateful you aren't going to marry me. You may not realize it, but I owe you one.''

Hours later, Cort paced the small Victorian room waiting for Jessy. The kerosene lamps had been turned low, and his shadow followed him across the walls. Though he had thoroughly enjoyed his day with Amy Rothchild, getting her settled had taken longer than he'd expected. He'd also gone by his sister's favorite dressmaker to inform the woman to put Amy Rothchild's bills on his account.

From the frosty look Miss Cragshaw had given him, and the "I'll see if Jessica's willing to talk to you," Cort had the distinct feeling Jessy had told the older woman everything. Or at least her version of it.

After their talk Friday night, he'd become even more determined to marry her. This entire affair had certainly taken on a strange twist. Before, he hadn't wanted his mail-order bride to know he was wealthy. Now he depended on Jessy knowing he could take care of her financially. Why he was so obsessed with marrying her was no longer a dilemma. She was a challenge, and he had never been able to turn his back on a challenge. That was one of the secrets to his success. One way or another she would marry him. He just needed to figure out what it would take to accomplish his goal.

"You wished to speak to me?"

Cort turned and watched Jessy enter the room. Though her face seemed drawn, she was as beautiful as ever. Her lavender dress matched the color of her eyes, and her silver hair was twisted on top of her head with tendrils escaping and caressing her face. She sat primly on the sofa.

"I have checked into a few things," she said, folding her hands. "What should I call you? Cort, King or Mr. Lancaster?"

Cort smiled. "Whatever suits you."

"Well, Mr. Lancaster, here is what I found out. To begin with, you cannot force me to do anything, including giving you my wages. Should you try to take me to a saloon, Miss Cragshaw will report it to the sheriff."

"If they can find you and prove I was behind it."

His reply stopped Jessy cold. As usual, this was not the reaction Jessy had expected. She had been prepared to lay down the law. Didn't he fear anything? But she needed to consider what he had just said. It not only applied to him, but BJ as well. She would never be able to leave the building. One of them would be waiting to pounce on her! She'd already dismissed the possibility of catching the train in the morning.

Cort watched various emotions play across Jessy's face. "Have you given any thought to my proposal of the other night? Unlike you, I do stand by my word." He watched her eyes turn to dark purple fire. She was a very desirable woman. Even at this moment he had a wicked desire to remove the pins from her hair.

"Mr. Lancaster, try to understand something. I don't want your money. And I am not going to have your baby, then take off to live in luxury while you raise it. My life has already gone to ruin since you butted your nose in my business." Jessy fought back the tears that were threatening to escape. She took a deep breath and counted to ten before saying, "If it wasn't for you, I'd be in Kansas City, living a normal life."

"Spare me the dramatics, Jessy."

"No." She slammed her fist on the seat. "For once you're going to listen. There is a man I hate even more than you, and I was running away from him when you came along. Now he's caught up with me, and I don't mind telling you I'm scared half to death. He's crazy. I refuse to even think what will happen if he gets his hands on me."

"Who's the man?"

"BJ Johnson," Jessy whispered.

Cort leaned back in his chair and studied her. She had told him this more than once. Could she actually be telling the truth? He thought back to when he'd first confronted her at the sod house. He'd watched her talking to BJ, but hadn't heard what they were saying. He'd also seen her spit on the ground and call him a bastard, but at the time he'd dismissed it as a lovers' quarrel. And the bartender had said the man was loco.

Jessy squared her shoulders. "I have a reason for telling you this."

"Oh?"

"It's your interference that has allowed him to discover where I am, and I think you owe me protection."

Cort let out a sadistic laugh. "Lady, I did not cause the trouble between you and BJ. You did that all by yourself."

"I swear to you, I have done nothing." No matter what happened, Jessy refused to beg, especially from this man. "That's what makes this so unbelievable. Mr. Lancaster, there were a lot better men in Binge, and I could have had my pick of any of them! BJ is the one who spread the lies that I belonged to him, because that's what he wanted to believe."

"And what do you want me to do about it?"

"You are the only one I know who can help me. Today I saw one of your men having lunch with BJ. I didn't even know BJ was in town until then. Miss Cragshaw felt sure I'd jumped to the wrong conclusion."

Remembering her comment about two men watching her, Cort stood and strolled to the window. As he pulled the curtain back and looked down, he saw a cowboy standing across the street. The man looked up, and upon discovering Cort was watching him, pulled his wide-brimmed hat down and walked away. "What conclusion?" Cort asked as he let the curtain fall into place.

"I thought you and BJ were in cahoots. I've now decided that BJ has bought off one of your so-called faithful men." As he turned toward her, Jessy could see the muscle in his jaw twitch.

"What changed your mind?"

"Miss Cragshaw. She said you have quite a reputation, but the one thing she has heard over and over again is that you are your own man. She doesn't think you would ever fool with the likes of BJ."

"Smart woman."

"If you protect me, I will give my word that I'll not try to escape, and you will continue to receive my salary." There, Jessy thought, I've finally said it. She held her breath, waiting for his answer.

"I have a better idea. Marry me."

Jessy stood. "You haven't heard a word I've said! I knew this conversation would be futile!" She pointed a shaky finger at him. "I would never marry any man under your conditions—"

Cort moved toward her. Jessy backed away, but she was too close to the sofa. The back of her legs made contact, causing her knees to buckle. She fell down, with Cort standing over her like an avenging giant.

"Consider this," he said, his voice low. "As my wife, BJ wouldn't dare do anything to you. You'll have every luxury and a solid position in society." He straightened and moved to the window, but didn't bother looking out. "After I have my son, you can either leave or stay. I won't push it." He was watching her eyes and facial expressions, and he knew he was finally hitting the right chord. He pressed his point. "If you decide to stay I'll leave you alone if that's what you want. You can lead your life, and I'll lead mine."

"Aren't you afraid I'll embarrass the great Lancaster name?"

"I doubt there is anything you can do that I haven't done twice already."

Jessy couldn't believe it. She was actually considering his offer. "Would I have to remain under guard?"

"No. I'll accept your word that you won't leave. You'll have the freedom to come and go as you please. But don't fall under the delusion that I'm becoming soft. I assure you, if you try to run before I have my child, I'll follow you to hell. And if you think BJ is dangerous, make damn sure you never see my bad side."

"I'll give you my answer tomorrow," Jessy hedged. If I decide to marry you, she thought, we'll just see who has the stronger will!

When Cort left the building, he moved silently toward where the cowboy had disappeared. The man was in the process of rolling a cigarette when Cort slipped up behind him and snatched the gun from the man's holster.

"What the hell . . ."

"Turn around nice and easy or I'll pull the trigger."

As the cowboy turned, he brought his fist around ready to land a punch. Cort ducked and planted a solid blow to the stomach. The man doubled over in pain.

"What's your name?"

"Elmer." The word was more of a grunt.

"Elmer, I'd better not see your ugly face around here again, because if I do, you're a dead man. I don't know what BJ's paying you, but I'm sure it's not worth dying for. Do you understand?"

"I ain't got no quarrel with you!"

"That doesn't really matter, does it? What I said still stands. And while you're at it, give BJ a message for me. Tell him that King Lancaster says if he causes Jessy Turner any more trouble, I'll come looking for him. And if he doesn't believe it, he can ask just about any man in town about how mean a bastard I can be. I intend to marry the woman, and there's not a thing he's going to do to stop it. Now get out of my sight."

"What about my gun?"

"Mister, you're just damn lucky you're still alive."

Jessy remained in the sitting room for some time, deliberating. She would marry Cort, but she wouldn't have his child. On their wedding night she would refuse to sleep with him. If that didn't work, she'd have to tolerate his lovemaking. But she'd survived it before, and she could do it again. Then she'd handle him just as she had Jonathan. She'd start throwing tantrums and swear she'd kill him in his sleep if he ever touched her again. Other than that, she'd do all the things expected of a wife. Once they had an understanding, the situation should prove quite acceptable.

When Jessy informed Kathleen and Lora of her decision, they were shocked. But Jessy covered it over by saying Cort had declared his love.

Miss Cragshaw was an entirely different matter. Though she could understand Jessy's need for protection, she wasn't sure the girl had made the right decision. However, she did let Jessy's mind at rest when the girl expressed concern over the contract she'd signed upon becoming a Harvey Girl. Jessy learned that very few of the girls remained over six months without getting married. Fred Harvey was already getting a reputation for furnishing the best food and the finest women in the West.

By the time Jessy returned to the dormitory, the other girls knew of the forthcoming marriage. They all rushed forward with congratulations, and Jessy was hard put to maintain a happy demeanor. When the girls returned to their preparations for bed, Kathleen and Lora were still busily discussing how wonderful everything had turned out. Bone-tired from lack of sleep over the last few nights, Jessy didn't want to become involved in a conversation that had the appearance of continuing all night.

"Kathleen," she suggested, retrieving her nightdress, "why don't we change beds for tonight? Then the two of you can talk until the rooster crows."

"Aren't you too excited to sleep?" Kathleen asked.

Jessy smiled. "I could probably sleep in a graveyard, I'm that tired."

The two women changed beds.

Though the lanterns in the big two-story building had been turned off for some time, BJ continued waiting in the shadows. Mike had been hiding inside the restaurant since before it closed and would soon be opening the door to let BJ in. Another man held the reins of the horses, in readiness for a quick getaway. After delivering the warning from the man named King Lancaster, Elmer had wanted to take off like a scared dog. But he had served his purpose, so as he'd turned, BJ had shot him in the back.

The guard Elmer had told BJ about was now gagged and tied at the back of the building. BJ knew Jessy had no intention of marrying Lancaster. He'd seen the train ticket in her drawer and knew she was planning to take off in the morning. That's why he'd have to grab her tonight. She was only leading the man on, the same way she'd done him by making promises she had no intention of keeping.

BJ heard the door open before Mike stepped out and motioned him forward. The other man had his instructions. Stand guard in front, and have his gun ready if anyone tried to interfere.

The moment BJ entered the doorway, he made straight for the stairs. This morning he had put to memory every detail and obstacle to and from Jessy's bed. Now it was just a matter of being quiet. Although he slowly took one step at a time to keep his spurs from jingling, the stairs creaked each time he placed a big boot down on the next tread. The noise seemed to echo throughout the big rooms, and BJ felt sure the women would hear it. But all remained quiet.

As soon as he reached Jessy's bed, BJ stuck his rough hand over her mouth then scooped her up with his other arm. She struggled, but he had a firm hold. He didn't try to be quiet as he headed down the stairs and out the door.

BJ shifted his limp burden to a more comfortable position as the men rode their galloping horses out of town. Jessy had bitten his hand several times, and when he removed it, she screamed. He ended up knocking her out with his fist.

BJ finally brought the group to a halt. "All right, mister," he announced, "you've done your job. Mike will pay you, and you can head back to town." BJ's sorrel gelding pranced around, eager to move on. "Mike, I'll meet you in Binge!" BJ jammed his spurs to the animal's sides.

Only after covering several miles of flat land did BJ slow his lathered horse. Assured no one was following, he looped the reins around the pommel, leaving his hand free to roam over Jessy's body. Feeling her soft flesh against him created beautiful, agonizing pain.

Thunder rumbled in the near distance, and BJ silently cursed the dark rain clouds rolling overhead that hid the moon. He'd wanted to see the look of fear on Jessy's face when she discovered she was in his grasp.

Unable to stand his discomfort a moment longer, BJ brought the horse to a halt under a lonely, majestic tree. He climbed off the saddle dragging his captive with him, then dropped her to the ground. Hearing her moan, BJ hastily tied the reins around a thick limb.

As Kathleen came to and saw the big man standing over her, fear clutched her entire being.

"This time you won't escape me, Jessy," BJ snarled as he began unbuttoning his pants. "I'm going to take what I've waited years for!"

Though she couldn't see his face clearly, Kathleen could hear the hatred in his voice. She tried to roll away, but he landed a big boot in the middle of her stomach and pressed down. He started laughing, a sickly, high-pitched laugh.

"Please," Kathleen begged, "don't hurt me. I'm not Jessy. Please, let me go."

BJ was so wrapped up in pleasure at hearing her beg, it took a few moments for her words to sink in. A bolt of lightning suddenly lit the sky, affording BJ a quick look at the woman. Furious at being tricked again, he was about to kick her in the face when a deafening clap of thunder caused his horse to start rearing. Other than the horse's frantic snorts, everything became deadly quiet. Then BJ heard a low roar. He knew it was a tornado. The woman started screaming, but he didn't care what happened to her. The wind began to pick up, getting stronger with each passing moment, and it was all BJ could do to untie the reins and leap into the saddle as the horse swung free.

Chapter Six

Jessy had to admit it was a brilliant August morning, and Cort did look magnificent in his gray frock coat and trousers, black waistcoat and gray shirt. His strong hands easily handled the reins of the prancing gelding. The horse's glossy coat matched the shiny black buggy with its thickly cushioned seats.

As they traveled down the street, Jessy paid scant attention. The words "Till death do us part," spoken less than an hour ago, kept ringing in her ears. What will life be like as Mrs. Cortland Lancaster? she wondered. I know nothing about my husband. I don't even know if he has a family. And if he does, why didn't they come to the wedding?

The wedding had been a simple affair, with only the Harvey employees attending. Jean-Claude, the French chef, had baked a beautiful cake for the occasion, and other than her black and blue jaw, Kathleen looked none the worse for wear after her ordeal. A couple of cowhands, out checking to see what damage the tornado had done, had found her clinging to the big tree. Fortunately, the tornado had lifted before reaching her. Although Kathleen remained her cheerful self, saying what a story she'd be able to tell her children in years to come, Jessy couldn't rid herself of her guilt. She was the reason all this had happened.

"We're almost to my house," Cort lightly informed Jessy. "I don't expect my stepmother, Marie, to be there, but I know my sister is waiting on pins and needles to meet you."

"And your father?" Jessy asked while checking to be sure her ruffled bonnet was still in place.

"He passed away a while back."

Had she detected a note of sadness in his voice?

"My sister's name is Sheila. She will soon be nineteen, and is curious about everything. She'll probably want to know your life history."

"And just what have you told your family about me?" Jessy asked, suddenly taking note of the fine homes in the area.

Cort brought the horse to a halt beneath a large shade tree and turned toward her. A smile twitched at the corner of his lips. "Nothing. You're free to make up any story you like."

"Then I guess I can tell them I'm a dethroned queen!" she snapped at him.

Cort let out a deep, hearty laugh. "And shall I refer to you as Your Highness?"

Laughter gave the hard planes of his face an almost boyish quality. Jessy couldn't help but smile. Cort was a most beguiling devil.

"Now that's a pleasant change," she said softly. "You should smile more often, it becomes you." Cort admired her mauve street dress, lavishly adorned with lace and elegantly draped, which complemented her figure to perfection. "You're a beautiful woman, Jessy Lancaster." He rather enjoyed watching her face turn a bright shade of pink.

Jessy couldn't hide the blush. It wasn't that she hadn't received compliments before, quite the contrary. But coming from Cort the compliment seemed so different and personal. Unable to look into the depths of his warm brown eyes a moment longer, she bent her head. "Don't you think we should be getting on if your sister is waiting?" Jessy dreaded the thought of meeting his family, but it had to be done, and she wanted to get it over with.

"We're not in that much of a hurry. I just wanted to give you a few moments to adjust to the idea of being Mrs. Lancaster. Are there any questions you want to ask?"

Jessy looked at him suspiciously. "Why are you being so nice?"

"That's a fair question," he said, propping his foot on the front of the buggy. "I look at it this way. We both want something out of this marriage. I want a son, and you want protection. Not necessarily the best reasons for getting married, but I've seen marriages arranged where the two parties don't even know each other. We have one thing in common, Jessy dear. We're both ungiving and selfish."

Jessy flinched.

"Now we can kick this marriage off trying to be friends or enemies." His eyes lost their warmth. "Which is it going to be?"

"You ask too much," Jessy stated flatly. "How can I be friends with a man who wants me to..."

"Have my son? I assure you I'll do everything to make our time together as enjoyable for you as it will be for me."

Jessy sneered at him. "I don't intend to gain pleasure by being bedded, Mr. Lancaster."

"You really should get used to calling me Cort. But consider how much you're receiving in return. As of today, you're a wealthy woman with no worries except those you create in your own mind."

"You expect me not to worry? I'm supposed to share a bed with a man I don't even like! And how do I know you'll be able to keep BJ from me? Do you honestly think he'll give up because your name is Lancaster?"

"I'll worry about that. Now, what is it going to be, friend or foe?"

Jessy clicked her tongue in disgust. The man always skirted her questions. "I'll try to be friendly, but I guarantee nothing!"

Cort chuckled, suddenly thinking about Marie and Jessy in the same house.

What does he find so damn funny, Jessy wondered.

"By the way," Cort said as he put his foot down and flicked the reins, "I bought this horse and buggy for you as a wedding gift."

"Mine?" Her face lit with joy. "I've never had anything so beautiful!" Jessy couldn't help but run her hand across the fine leather seat.

"You can drive it, can't you?"

"Of course I can."

Cort had deliberately refrained from telling Jessy that ever since BJ had invaded Harvey House a week ago, he'd spent day and night looking for the man. He'd also sent one of his ranch hands to Binge to see if BJ had returned, and others to search the area around where Kathleen had been found. Cort knew BJ was holed up somewhere, and eventually he'd find him. When that time came, BJ wouldn't bother anyone again.

When Cort drove the buggy onto a circular driveway and stopped in front of the house, a young man was already there to take the reins.

"Thank you, Tod," Cort said as he helped Jessy down. "I'd like you to meet your new mistress..."

Sheila stared out the window in shock. Fortunately the curtains hid her from view. Cort had refused to describe his new bride, so she had tried to prepare herself for anything. The beautiful woman standing in front of the house, how ever, far exceeded all her expectations. The woman looked familiar, but Sheila couldn't place where she'd seen her.

Running to the clothes hooks in the entry hall, Sheila quickly checked her appearance in the mirror, then turned to face the door and wait. Would the woman like her?

When the door opened, Jessy was surprised to see the raven-haired girl standing there. Jessy recognized her immediately as the woman Cort had brought to the restaurant.

Cort walked over, placed an arm around his sister and made the introductions.

The rest of the morning passed quickly, with a leisurely tea being served by Sheila. Jessy was grateful when, shortly after noon, Cort said he had to return to town because of business, but he'd be back in time for supper. Jessy wondered what Sheila thought about Cort leaving, or if she'd consider it strange that he didn't kiss his new bride goodbye.

As soon as Cort had departed, Sheila introduced her sister-in-law to the servants and took her upstairs to show Jessy the bedroom that would henceforth belong to her.

Jessy couldn't contain her joy upon seeing the brightly lit room. It had been a long time since she'd had a room all to herself. The two large windows had been raised, and the sheer white curtains fluttered in the gentle breeze. The room was as large as her entire sod house had been. Knowing she wouldn't be sharing Cort's room also helped add to her feeling of giddiness.

"I'm sorry Mother wasn't here to greet you," Sheila apologized, "but she's spending the night with friends." She wasn't about to tell Jessy the real reason her mother was gone. Jessy would find out soon enough. "May I ask you a question?"

Jessy gave the girl a broad smile. "Your brother said you were inquisitive." Opening the clothespress, she discovered her things had already been neatly put away, and with a sigh of relief saw her carpetbag sitting on the top shelf. "Since we are now related, you have every right to ask me questions. I know you're curious. It's plain to see how fond you are of Cort." She pressed her hand down on the bed and felt the thick feather ticking beneath the white satin spread.

"Are you in love with my brother?"

Caught off guard, Jessy turned and sank down on the bed. This wasn't what she'd expected. Seeing the concern on Sheila's face, she knew she couldn't lie to the girl. Sheila had every right to know the truth, and maybe by knowing she'd come to accept. "No, I'm not," she said softly.

"Does Cort love you?"

"No." Jessy hated seeing the hurt in the girl's blue eyes.

"It's because he wants a son, isn't it?" Sheila's words were almost a whisper.

"Let's just say that the marriage was advantageous to both of us."

A tear formed in the corners of Sheila's blue eyes. "You're doing it because of the money? I had always hoped that some day Cort would find a woman he could really love, and she would make him a good wife."

Jessy suddenly felt so old. Rising, she went to the girl and cradled her in her arms. "Sheila, I didn't marry your brother for his money, and I'm going to try to make him a good wife. I truly hope some day you will wed a man you love, but unfortunately not all marriages are love matches."

Sheila leaned back and looked at Jessy, a smile beginning to form on her pink lips. "But love can grow, can't it?"

"Well . . . yes, of course it can."

Sheila giggled. "I just know that's what is going to happen with you and Cort. You're so perfect for one another. Come on, I'll show you the rest of the house."

Jessy was amazed at how quickly Sheila's spirits lifted. Oh, well, she thought, let the girl have her dreams.

Supper proved to be a trying affair for Jessy, with Sheila and Cort keeping up a light conversation about Sheila's younger days and all the mischief she'd gotten into. Though the food was cooked to perfection, Jessy hardly ate a thing. Before long, she would be expected to go upstairs and consummate her marriage. She wasn't looking forward to giving Cort her ultimatum. What had seemed like a perfectly simple way to handle a bad situation didn't seem so simple now. To make matters worse, she had discovered one of the doors in her bedroom opened to his rooms. She'd braced a chair against it, but remembering how he'd kicked down the door at the Gordon House, she seriously doubted it would do any good. However, she assured herself, with Sheila and the servants in the house he surely wouldn't do it again.

After supper the threesome retired to the salon. They had hardly sat down when Thomas, the butler, appeared at the doorway holding a cape.

"Your carriage is waiting, Miss Sheila," he announced.

"Thank you, Thomas, I'll be right there."

"Your carriage?" Jessy asked worriedly.

Sheila blushed.

"She's spending the night with a friend," Cort spoke up.

Jessy looked at her husband sitting relaxed on a beautiful Queen Anne sofa. "But . . . there's no reason for her to have to leave," she insisted. She tried to hide the panic that was rapidly building.

"Jessy, dear, you're embarrassing Sheila."

How can he act so casual about something like this! Jessy thought. She started to protest again, but Cort stood and went to his sister. "You have a nice time, dear, we'll see you tomorrow." He kissed her forehead.

Jessy felt a strong need to lean against the back of the wide silk chair for support, but her horsehair bustle prevented it.

When Sheila left, Cort resumed his seat, but said nothing. His eyes, however, were warm and unwavering. Jessy's hands began to shake, and she quickly twisted them together to keep it from showing. "I have something to say," she finally blurted out.

Cort cocked a dark eyebrow but remained silent.

"I do not want you in my bed." She gave him a hard, determined look. "I told you once before, I never want to feel a man's hands on me again."

"May I remind you, playing coy and innocent isn't necessary now."

"I'm doing neither."

"But we had an agreement," he quietly reminded her.

"I never agreed to anything. You did all the talking, and I would have done anything to get away from BJ." Cort just sat there silently looking at her as if reflecting on something. Why didn't he yell, or at least do something!

"And if I insist?"

Jessy stood, ready for battle. "Oh, I'll survive if you force yourself on me, but if you do, you'd better not try it again because I swear to God, I'll kill you in your sleep."

Cort laughed. "Now that's an interesting twist. I never could refuse a challenge."

He moved so fast that he took Jessy completely off guard. The next thing she knew, he'd picked her up in his arms and was heading up the stairs, two at a time.

"Let me down, you bastard!" she seethed. Hitting her fists against his hard chest accomplished nothing except to serve as an outlet for her anger.

In what seemed like less time than the batting of an eye-lash, they were in his room. After swinging the door shut with his foot, he placed her none too gently on her feet. The moment he removed his arms, Jessy ran for the door connecting their rooms. She tried opening it, but the damn chair she had put there earlier held it closed!

Hearing a click, Jessy whirled around. He'd locked the door, and she was trapped. She wanted to make a grab for the key as he stuck it under one of the pillows, but instead she remained where she stood. Cort had a glint in his eyes that told her he'd like nothing better than for her to try.

"I want out," she demanded, "and I want out now!"

Cort casually removed his coat and tossed it over the back of a chair, his eyes never leaving Jessy's. The coat was followed by his vest.

"If you don't unlock that door, I'll scream, and every servant in the house will hear me!"

When he removed his shirt, Jessy sucked in her breath. She knew she should turn away, but Cort wore no long johns, and his muscled torso was absolutely magnificent. Jonathan had always undressed after the candles had been snuffed, and had slept in his long underwear.

As if mesmerized, Jessy watched Cort quickly shed his shoes, then lie on the huge bed. She stiffened her shoulders, determined to stick to her resolve. She wasn't going to make it easy for him.

"Do you plan on standing there all night?" he asked with a bored tone of voice.

"If I have to."

"I think not. Come over here and lie down." He patted the bed beside him.

"No."

Cort crossed his arms beneath his head and considered the woman standing at the other end of the room. She ap-

peared pious in her pale blue, high-necked dress, her posture rigid and determined. Was it all an act? Somehow, he
didn't think so. Unless... "Tell me, Jessy, dear, is it cruelty
that ignites your passion?"

"Of course not!"

He gave her an evil smile. "Then I suggest you come over
here, or that's what's going to happen." She hesitated. "I
really prefer women to come to my bed willingly, but I'm
not beyond forcing the issue."

Jessy shuddered. "You may beat me, but I will not fall
into your bed willingly! And if you force me into this, you'd
best remember my warning and keep your doors locked at
night."

There was anger dancing in her lavender eyes, but in the
last few moments Cort had discovered something very interesting about his wife. He knew, without a shadow of a
doubt, Jessy had yet to discover how pleasurable bedding
could be. He also knew that forcing her wasn't the answer.
There were other ways of handling the prickly lady. Cort
reached beneath the pillow and pulled out the key. "I've
tired of this little game of yours. Here. Take the key. I've
decided I'm really not in the mood. In fact, now that I think
of it, I'm not even sure you're my type."

Jessy hesitated. Was he serious, or was this a trick? She
knew his outward appearance never gave any indication as
to what was on his mind. Though she would not give in to
him, a strange disappointment engulfed her. Was it actually possible she'd wanted him to make love to her? No,
of course not! Well, she just couldn't stand there. Cautiously, she moved toward the bed and extended her hand.
He gave her the key.

Still keeping an eye on him, Jessy unlocked and opened
the door. Feeling safe and proud of herself for winning the
first round, she turned toward her tormentor. "You're not

fooling me," she sneered. "You needn't try to hide the real reason you're letting me go. I'd think twice, too, if someone threatened to kill me in my sleep. And believe me, I was quite serious!" It wasn't true, but she wanted to get her point across so she wouldn't have to put up with another night like tonight.

When Jessy saw Cort leap off the bed, she knew she'd pushed her luck too far. Lifting her skirts, she ran down the hall and threw open the door to her room. Cort's hand prevented her from closing it. Seeing his bare foot, Jessy jammed her heel down on his toes. As he withdrew cussing, she shut the door, turned the bolt and leaned against it for support. Would this night ever be over? she wondered, trying to catch her breath. The next instant, the crash of her bedroom door sent her flying across the room to land on the floor.

Angered beyond the point of thinking straight, Jessy ignored her skirts, which now billowed around her waist. Reaching up, she grabbed a vase from a small table and hurled it in Cort's direction. Before she could get to her feet, Cort was on top of her, crushing her to the floor, her bustle jabbing her in the back. She tried to scratch his face, but he effortlessly held her hands at bay.

"You damn little wildcat," he uttered, his voice husky. "This is to let you know just how concerned I am by your threat!"

Knowing he was going to kiss her, Jessy tossed her head back and forth. But his lips came down on the base of her neck, sucking and nibbling, then moved down to her breast. Gently he bit her nipple, and she could feel it through her clothes, almost as if she were naked.

Jessy continued to fight, but now it was more from fear. She didn't want and had never experienced the desire that threatened to claim her. It wasn't until a glorious tremor shot down her stomach and ended with an aching throb between her legs that she began accepting defeat. Her mind said one thing, but her body wasn't listening. Then his mouth was on hers, devouring her resistance, claiming her very soul. She felt him untie the strings of her pantalettes and move his hand inside. Her palms became moist as his hand slid down, stopping momentarily to caress her flat stomach, then slowly down farther . . . farther.

Cort knew the moment Jessy was his for the taking. What had started out as nothing more than an effort to teach her a lesson was rapidly turning into something more serious. He raised his head and looked at her half-closed lavender eyes. God, she was a beautiful witch. Then he noticed her bowed back, and the cause. Whoever invented bustles should be shot! Reluctantly, he removed his hand and stood, raising her with him. A look of disappointment and confusion crossed her lovely face.

Standing on her feet, Jessy began to regain her senses. What was happening to her? "You've put a curse on me!" she accused.

Cort chuckled softly. "If desire is a curse, my love, then our souls are certainly entwined." Reaching up, he slowly pulled the pins from her thick, silver hair, letting it fall to her hips. "I've wanted to do that for some time." He ran his fingers slowly up her neck, but she jerked away. "Don't fight me, Jessy. You know you want me to make love to you. You have a desire, and I can satisfy it."

"No," Jessy moaned. His hands cupped her slender neck while his thumbs moved along the line of her jaw. Everything he touched turned to fire. Jessy felt lost in the depths of his dark brown eyes. She couldn't look away, and her breathing had become labored. Slowly he lowered his head, and when their lips touched, Jessy knew she wanted his kiss and the feel of his hands on her body again. Falling deeper nd deeper into the abyss of desire, she didn't protest when e unbuttoned her dress, pushing it off her shoulders so that t fell on the floor around her ankles.

Cort reached over and turned down the kerosene lamp.

Jessy awoke, stretched lazily and smiled. Warm, early unshine poured in through the open windows onto the vhite bed cover, causing the satin to shimmer...white? Jessy at bolt upright, disoriented. It took a moment to remember that this was her room, and that she was actually married. Jessy moaned as memories of last night flooded her mind. Quickly glancing around the room, she felt a momentary sense of relief. She was alone. She was also quite naked. Immediately she clutched the bedsheet to her chin, hen over her head as she fell back against the pillows. You acted like a whore last night, letting Cort do whatever he vanted with your body! she silently chastised herself. Still, ust remembering was already causing her skin to turn warm with desire. She could almost feel his strong body beneath her hands...his mouth on her nipples...driving her insane as he thrust deep within her...holding her breath, afraid he would stop as he took her higher and higher until everything exploded... "Stop it, Jessy!" she said aloud as she sat up. "It wasn't your fault!"

Jessy climbed out of bed, dragging the sheet with her for fear someone would look in the broken door. She quickly washed, then put on a white pleated blouse and a gray and blue striped skirt. During her preparations, she came to the conclusion that Cort had put something in her food last night. Jonathan had told her of such things happening and knowing Cort as she did, she certainly wouldn't put it past him. Mentally berating Cort with every foul word she could think of, Jessy checked to be sure her carpetbag was still on the shelf, then went downstairs. He was going to get a piece of her mind, but she'd wait to do it on neutral ground.

Jessy found only the servants busy with their cleaning. After eating a big breakfast, she was at a loss as to how she would spend the day. As a Harvey Girl, she'd become used to a busy schedule. Now she had nothing to do and no one to talk to, and time seemed to drag. Obviously Cort was still in his room catching up on his sleep.

The feeling of being closed in suddenly became over whelming, especially since she knew that going anywhere was out of the question. She certainly wasn't going to help BJ get his hands on her. But surely a stroll around the yard would be safe, and most beneficial.

Circling the brick house Jessy discovered an iron gate and opened it. It creaked loudly, testifying to its lack of use. To her delight, she discovered a huge flower garden badly in need of attention. Weeds and tufts of grass were sprouting up everywhere. Carefully she plucked a perfect red rose and raised it to her nose. The sweet aroma reminded her of the roses her mother had grown so long ago. As she continued along the path, she saw flowers of every description, a tiny herb garden and a bricked off area in the center with a small gazebo. It was badly in need of painting, but appeared to be structurally sound. Jessy entered and sat on the circular wooden seat.

"Jessica?"

"I'm in the gazebo," Jessy called upon seeing a tall, trim-figured woman dressed in black headed in her direction. The lady had a very stern look, and Jessy had the impression she did little laughing. Her eyes were large and round, but cold. Though the woman was well along in years, few wrinkles marred her face.

"My dear," Marie said sweetly as she joined Jessy on the seat, "I'm Cort's stepmother, Marie. I guess you can consider me the matriarch of the family."

Jessy felt uncomfortable with Mrs. Lancaster's air of superiority, but at least the woman appeared to be friendly.

Marie's attitude would have been considerably different had she not heard the servants gossiping about the speculation that Mr. Lancaster had forced his wife to his bed. Realizing she might have found an ally, Marie had decided to try to win the woman's confidence.

"Why in the world would you want to sit out here?" Marie asked, holding a handkerchief to her nose. "I for one have never cared much for flowers. They make me sneeze."

"I'm sorry, perhaps we should return to the house," Jessy suggested. She started to stand, but the older woman raised a hand to stop her.

"No, no. This will do fine. At least we're alone and will have an opportunity to get acquainted. Cortland's servants listen to everything."

Remembering last night, Jessy felt more than a little embarrassed.

"With Cortland and Sheila gone, we can enjoy this rare time to ourselves."

"I thought Cort was still in his room." Jessy looked down at the rose in her hand.

"I only arrived a few moments ago, but the servants said he left earlier this morning. They weren't sure when he would return. Didn't he say anything to you?"

"No, he didn't."

"How very thoughtless of him, but Cortland has never been considerate of anyone but himself. He sets his mind to something, and no matter who he hurts, nothing will stop him." Marie suddenly realized she was about to let her true feelings show. Not a wise idea until she found out what Jessica thought. "I understand you were a Harvey Girl. A most reputable establishment. The women are known for their poise, grace and elegant manners, and quite envied by the women of Topeka, if they'd only admit it."

"So I've heard," Jessy said softly. The woman's cold black eyes seemed to bore into her.

"I must say I quite approve of Cortland's choice of a bride. Heaven knows what his mail-order bride would have looked like. Thank the good Lord she didn't arrive. It's one time Cortland's plans never came to be."

"Mail-order bride?" Jessy asked, astonished.

Marie let out a snort. "I suppose he said nothing about that, either. Did he say anything about wanting a son?"

The woman certainly doesn't hedge, Jessy thought. "Yes, he did."

"Don't be embarrassed, my dear. At my age I've long since learned to say what I think. It serves to keep things less complicated. Having been married twice, and being much wiser and older, I feel you could use a friend. I don't mind telling you that Cortland has never been anything but a rogue, and I certainly do not envy you for being his wife. I hope you haven't been unfortunate enough to fall in love with him?"

"No," Jessy whispered, "it is a marriage of convenience."

"Good!" Marie let out a sneeze, followed by two more.

"Are you sure you wouldn't like to move?" Jessy asked as she tossed away the rose.

"I do not wish others to hear what I have to say." Marie blew her nose loudly. "I'm glad you don't love Cortland, because the man will never be faithful to you. You may not like hearing that, but knowing the truth about him will only serve to fortify you. You said a marriage of convenience. Am I to assume you are agreeable to giving him a son?"

Jessy looked at the woman sitting bone-straight on the seat, and caught a momentary glimmer of expectation in her eyes. She doesn't want me to have Cort's child! she suddenly realized. Why? "Mrs. Lancaster, I get the feeling you do not like your stepson."

Now that she knew what Jessica's feelings were, Marie felt no hesitancy in telling the woman the truth. "You're right, I don't. He has stolen everything that's rightfully mine, and usurped my authority, even down to what is best for his sister."

Jessy was shocked by the venom in the woman's voice. There was something about her that reminded Jessy of BJ, and she was hard put to stop the shiver that wanted to run through her body. All of a sudden the older woman's expression changed, and she actually smiled.

"I'm frightening you," Marie said kindly, "and I apologize. What's between Cortland and me has been going on for years. You needn't concern yourself." She reached over and patted Jessy's hand. "You didn't answer me about the son."

"I haven't decided," Jessy said cautiously. Whatever her decision, she wasn't at all sure she wanted to share it with Marie.

"I see. Well, perhaps you would be interested in using some herbs I know of until you make up your mind."

"Herbs?"

"Yes. It's an old Indian remedy that prevents you from conceiving. They're common herbs, but put together and boiled, they have the desired effect. Come, I'll show you." Marie stood and headed toward the garden.

After leaving Jessy's bed early this morning, Cort had decided to head for the ranch to see if anything had been turned up about BJ.

As Cort guided Emperor over the land, his thoughts turned to the woman he'd left in peaceful slumber. A smile tickled the corners of his mouth, and the next minute he broke out laughing. His romp with Jessy had proved to be quite an enjoyable experience. The lady was definitely a tiger in bed.

Jessy was very naive in the art of making love. The first time he'd had to guide her along, placing her arms around his neck and moving her hands along his body. But once that had been accomplished, she had held nothing back, which only served to confuse him. Having seen her act out various parts in the past, he couldn't decide whether or not she was doing it again. In all truthfulness, he doubted it. Or was it just his own pride that wanted to believe that? One thing he did know. His dear wife had never been sexually fulfilled. So what had she done with Jonathan and BJ? What the hell difference did it make? he asked himself. All I'm interested in is a son. Now that I know every curve of Jessy's body and how to ignite her fire, I'll have no trouble bedding the witch. She's mine now, and there's not another damn soul that can change it. Once I take care of BJ, everything will proceed according to plan.

Hearing a snap, Cort's reflexes took over. In one fluid motion, he kicked free of the stirrups and jumped off the horse's back. Fortunately he landed upright with a rein still held in his hand. His saddle lay on the ground beneath Emperor's feet.

"Whoa," Cort said, trying to settle the stallion down.

It took a few moments before Cort was able to check the saddle. The cinch had been cut, leaving only enough to keep the saddle secure until a sudden movement of the horse had completed the break. Cort could have been seriously injured. Someone was out to do away with him. The first person that came to mind was BJ Johnson. It infuriated

Cort to know the man had been right under his nose, and he still couldn't get his hands on him.

If he hadn't been preoccupied, or if he had let Tod saddle the horse, the cut cinch would probably have been found. He was going to have to be more alert. If BJ had tried once, he'd try again.

Grabbing Emperor's mane, Cort swung himself up onto the bare back. The horse was still spooked from the incident, but Cort held him to an easy trot and continued on his way.

Chapter Seven

Jessy was relieved when the seven elderly women were ready to depart. For almost two hours she'd watched them sip tea, eat cookies and cake and gossip. She was glad she knew none of the people the old busybodies were raking over the coals. Several times one of them had started talking to Marie about Cort, but quickly changed the subject upon remembering his new bride was in the room. It had been embarrassing enough when the ladies had asked questions. Was she happy?... Where was Cortland?... How long would the happy couple remain in town?... When Marie told her friends Cortland had pulled one of his unforgivable stunts and had left the day after the wedding, Jessy saw the pity leap into their eyes. She would have liked nothing more than to tell them all to mind their own business, but of course she didn't. To make matters worse, Marie had taken the opportunity to add, "Poor Jessy had no idea the type of man she'd married." The women shook their heads knowingly.

"When will Cortland be returning?" one of the biddies asked.

"Who's to say?" Marie sneered. "He's already been gone four days."

When the ladies finally departed, Jessy went outside and headed straight for the flower garden, not trusting herself to say a word. She was furious with Marie, and the thought of shooting Cort was most appealing! It had been bad enough with the household treating her like some lost soul. Now everyone in town would know Cort had taken off after their wedding night. Not that she really cared, in fact she was glad to be rid of him. But having people whispering behind her back was an entirely different matter.

Spying a rusty hoe among the weeds, Jessy leaned over and picked it up. Without thinking, she started chopping around the flower bushes. I'm tired of having to remain in the house with nothing to do except read, eat and talk to Marie and Sheila, she thought. If I knew BJ wouldn't show his ugly head, I could go shopping with Sheila, or to the opera. Jessy had never attended the opera, but listening to Sheila go on about the beautiful singing and the many costumes had created a deep desire to witness it. Of course Sheila had asked her to go, but as usual Jessy had to refuse with some lame excuse.

Suddenly Jessy let the hoe fall. A coarse laugh escaped her lips as she realized what she had been doing. "I'll never be rid of the farmer instinct," she mumbled bitterly. "If I'm going to work as a laborer, I might just as well live in a sod house." She returned to the house.

"Good heavens!" Marie exclaimed upon seeing Jessy enter the foyer with dirt on the skirt of her lovely yellow day dress. "What have you been doing?"

"Digging in the flower garden," Jessy replied, still angry with Marie.

"Well I hope you won't be doing it again. I certainly wouldn't want people to know we would lower ourselves to that level. We'd be the laughingstock of the town. If you want the garden cleaned out, I'll hire someone."

Rebellion ran through Jessy like a hot poker. She ha spent most of her life as a farmer's daughter, and suddenl she was proud of it. Her family were good, hardworkin people, and she wasn't about to let someone like Marie pu them down. "No. I'll work in the garden, and if it embar rasses you, just keep your friends away." Jessy marched t her room.

Sheila sat quietly for some time watching her sister-in-la hoe the garden weeds with a vengeance. The skirt of Je sy's faded blue muslin dress was almost brown from th rich, dried dirt clinging to it. Finally, Jessy let the hoe dro and placing her hands at the small of her back, sh stretched. As if her thoughts were miles away, she slowl mopped the perspiration from her brow and neck with th red bandanna that had been tied around her head. He damp bodice served as a testimonial to the hot sun and har work. A long braid hung down her back, and she imp tiently pushed back the damp, silver strands of hair that ha escaped to cling tenaciously to her neck and face.

Sheila couldn't understand why Jessy persisted eve though she'd been told they would hire someone to do t work. But there was very little she understood, and no o seemed inclined to enlighten her. She didn't know why Co had been gone for over a week, nor why, after her moth had been so angered about the marriage, the two wom were on such friendly terms.

"Aren't you about ready to quit, or do you plan to co tinue until you drop?" Sheila asked.

Jessy looked up at the sun and smiled. "I'm ready to qu for today," she said, joining Sheila in the gazebo. "It's ge ting too hot."

"Shouldn't you be wearing a bonnet?"

"You sound like my mother. She used to scold me about not wearing a bonnet, or clothes that covered my entire body. 'You have to keep your skin looking beautiful,' she would say."

"Mother says the same thing." Sheila studied her hands. 'I fail to understand her reasoning. At the rate I'm going, I'll die an old maid."

"Nonsense. Isn't that nice-looking Carlton Chalmers I met the other day coming to take you for a buggy ride?"

"Yes, but I'm not interested in him."

"Well, you're much too pretty to die an old maid. Someday, when you're least expecting it, just the right man will come along."

"I doubt it."

Jessy suppressed a smile and looked at the flower garden. It aggravated her to see how little progress she'd made at cleaning out the weeds. Maybe she should let Marie hire someone to help after all, but she refused to let someone else do all the work. She needed something to take her frustrations out on, and the work kept her mind and body occupied. The same mind and body that wouldn't let her forget her night with Cort and how he'd taken her to heights she never dreamed of or even knew existed. Damn Cort. By teaching her the meaning of desire, he'd made her vulnerable.

"Jessy, do you think Cort will be back in time to take you to the ball?"

Jessy caught herself before coming back with an unkind remark. She would love to go to a ball. Just to get away from the house would be worth it. "I would be the last to know what Cort has on his mind. I haven't seen him in days," she replied, trying to keep the bitterness out of her voice. "Anyway, I'm not planning on it."

Sheila decided she should change the subject. "I've been sitting here wondering if you enjoyed being a Harvey Girl."

Jessy watched Sheila smooth back the sides of her shiny black hair. It was really amazing how little she looked like Cort. "Not at first. My arms and legs ached as bad as when we came West by wagon train."

"I didn't know you were on a wagon train," Sheila said excitedly. "What was it like? I've always thought it would be so wonderful."

Jessy brushed off her skirt then straightened the folds. "I didn't consider it wonderful at the time, though actually the children in the train fared the best. Even though their work was never ending," she said, warming up to the conversation. "They cared for the babies, cooked, sometimes drove the oxen and did any other chore necessity demanded. When we reached the plains, wood became scarce, so the children had to gather buffalo chips for the fires; not one of my favorite tasks. But even though I considered myself grown at almost ten years of age, it didn't make me exempt. My father made sure I carried my load of the work. Never having done manual labor in my entire life, I balked more than once, but to no avail."

"Why did your arms and legs hurt? Didn't you ride in the wagon?" Sheila asked, mesmerized by Jessy's story.

"I can honestly say I walked from Tennessee to Kansas and now that I think about it, I'm quite proud of the accomplishment. But I wasn't the only one. Unless you were lucky enough to be driving the wagon or too old or sick, you walked. There was simply not enough room inside."

Sheila shook her head in disbelief. "I would have never survived."

"Oh, you'd be surprised what you can do, especially you have no choice."

"Why did your family come West?"

"We lost everything after the war. Our plantation was snatched up by carpetbaggers because we couldn't pay the taxes. At least that's what my parents told me. I was too spoiled to pay attention to what was happening, and my mother and father kept a lot from me at the time."

"Sheila! Didn't you hear me calling?" Marie asked as she rushed forward. "Carlton is here."

Sheila let out an exasperated grunt and rose from the bench. "I'm coming, Mother."

Jessy watched the two women disappear, then glanced at the hoe on the ground. The idea of work didn't appeal to her. Her thoughts were still in the past.

She could still remember the miles and miles of monotonous terrain, the blistering sun and the buffalo grass that had made walking so difficult. More times than she'd cared to count, she had caught the toe of her boot in the thick undergrowth and fallen. She had especially hated the grasshoppers that hid in the grass and clung to her clothes.

The only thing that changed was the weather. One week not sun, the next rain.

Jessy suddenly remembered a particular day when she hadn't noticed the wagon train moving slowly to her right. Occasionally a man's whip would crack in the air as he urged his team onward, or a baby would cry from inside one of the wagons, but these were all familiar sounds. Her attention had been riveted to the ground so she could avoid mud holes. The rain had been bad enough, but in her young mind, the light drizzle that had plagued them for the past two days proved to be even worse. She was fed up with the nightly routine of scraping off the thick mud caking her boots and of cleaning the filthy mess from the bottom of her skirts. All she wanted was to return to Magnolia Manor instead of watching the water drip into her plate and turn the food to mush. Of course, there were plenty of dried apples but she hated apples.

Jessy had pulled the heavy, dark blue shawl tightly around her and quickly crossed her arms around her waist in an effort to hold the wool material in place. Though the dress and hat were of the same warm wool fabric, they did little to protect her from the dampness. She had glanced up at the sky in hopes of seeing a break in the low, gray clouds. Nothing. Not even one *tiny* ray of sunlight.

Continuing on, she placed one booted foot in front of the other, trying not to stumble on a rock or step in yet another mud hole. That morning she had had the sniffles, and Mammy Mae had placed an asafetida bag around her neck to get rid of them. The gumlike substance was wrapped in a muslin bag, and in order to get her mind off the vile odor, Jessy concentrated on the muddy earth sloshing beneath her feet. At least by now her legs were stronger, and she no longer fell on her sleeping mat at night, fighting back tears because of the painful ache of sore muscles.

"Hey, Jessy!" BJ taunted as he pulled his horse alongside her.

Jessy kept her head down and tried to ignore him. Even then she hated the redhead. Being fourteen, he thought he knew everything. He and his friends were always giving her a hard time.

"Your ma's looking for you," Billy said, a wide grin spreading across his thin lips. "She and your old man must have some mighty fine times in the back of that wagon. No sense in them havin' all the fun. When you goin' to let me show you what it's like?"

"You go to hell, BJ!" Jessy yelled. Reaching down, she grabbed a handful of mud and flung it at him.

Laughing, Billy nudged his horse in the ribs. The animal leaped forward, kicking mud on her clothes.

"Damn you!" she hollered after him. During their journey, Jessy had learned a whole new vocabulary.

"Jessica. Wait up and I'll walk with you."

Jessy heard her mother's words, but didn't stop. She merely slowed her pace while trying in vain to brush off the mud BJ's horse had splattered on her.

"What was that all about?" Elizabeth asked after catching up with her daughter.

"Nothing. BJ's just up to his usual ornery tricks," Jessy hedged. Her shawl had slipped and again she adjusted it.

"You should try to stay away from the likes of him," Elizabeth scolded gently.

Jessy had thought to remind her beloved mother that BJ had approached her, but remained silent.

And since that time, so many years ago, what have you accomplished? Jessy asked herself. You've married twice and BJ is still after you. Besides the money and necklace that you don't dare tell anyone about, there's Cort, whom you haven't even seen for days!

"I'll never forgive him for not telling me he was leaving," Jessy mumbled. "It certainly would have saved me nights of walking the floor and waiting for him to enter my room so I could tell him off." Jessy expelled a soft moan. What difference did it really make? Threats didn't work, and he paid no attention to her demands to be left alone, so why did she keep fighting him? From the time they'd met, he'd had his way. "Damn him! I won't let him treat me like a brood mare! Maybe this isn't a normal marriage, but as long as we reside under the same roof, he should treat me with respect." Jessy stood and headed for the house.

"Jessy, dear," Marie called upon seeing her daughter-in-law start up the stairs to her room.

"Yes, Marie?" Jessy turned, her hand on the thick oak banister.

"After you've cleaned up, I want us to go into town."

"Do you or Sheila have something to pick up?"

"No, my dear. I'm taking you to the dressmaker's shop to be measured for a wardrobe. As a Lancaster, you have a certain image to uphold. Heaven knows, Cortland would never take that into consideration."

"But I don't need any clothes, Marie."

Marie walked to the bottom of the stairs. "You need summer and winter clothes, not to mention ball gowns. You certainly can't wear the same dress twice to a ball! Everyone in Topeka would laugh at us."

Jessy wanted to go into town, but did she dare? What if BJ decided to take advantage of the situation? She wouldn't stand a chance unless...

"Yana has your bath prepared, and I'll see that some food is sent up. I'll expect you to be ready in an hour and a half." Marie turned and headed for the kitchen.

As soon as Jessy entered the bedroom, she made straight for the door connecting her room with Cort's. Unfortunately, Byron was there.

"Is there something I can do for you, Mrs. Lancaster?" Byron's black face wrinkled into a friendly smile. He gave Jessy his full attention.

Jessy returned his smile. "Yes, there is. Sometime back, I gave Mr. Lancaster my derringer for safe keeping. Would you happen to know where he put it?"

In a matter of moments, Byron produced the gun from a drawer. "Is this the one?" he asked.

"Yes. Thank you, Byron," she said as he handed it to her. "You've been most helpful."

After getting little sleep for the past week and watching for BJ all the way to the dressmaker's, Jessy was exhausted by the time they finally arrived. She did feel a little safer with the man driving the carriage, but not much. Her hand had remained close to the reticule, which contained the small gun.

As she and Marie entered the small shop, a bell hanging over the door announced their arrival.

"Good afternoon, Mrs. Lancaster," a petite woman of about fifty whispered as she rushed forward. "I'm going to be with a customer for a few minutes. Perhaps you'd like to do some shopping and return later."

Before Marie could reply, an attractive woman, dressed in the latest fashion, stepped from behind a curtain. Mrs. Simon hurried toward her.

"If that will be all, Miss Rothchild," Mrs. Simon said, trying to hurry the woman out of the shop, "I will have your dress delivered in time for the ball."

Miss Rothchild picked up a hand mirror and checked to be sure her hat sat properly on her head. "And you will be sure Mr.—"

"I'll attend to everything," Mrs. Simon interrupted.

"Mr. Lancaster has paid my other bills, hasn't he?" Amy asked as she replaced the mirror.

Mrs. Simon's face turned beet red as she quickly glanced at the two women standing near the door. "Yes, he has."

"Let's leave this place!" Marie snapped. "There are other equally fine seamstresses in town!"

Marie turned and marched out the door with Jessy right behind her.

Once in the carriage, Marie gave instructions to the driver then settled back in the seat. "I warned you that Cortland would never take his marriage vows seriously, Jessica," she said in a hushed, angry voice. "He's probably been with that woman ever since he left the house. Well, it was bound to happen eventually, and better now than later. At least you have proof that what I say is true. Cortland is the most worthless type of man. If you ever decide to leave him, I'd certainly understand."

Jessy was furious at coming face to face with Cort's mistress. How many more embarrassing episodes was she going to have to face? But if she left, she'd not only have to be looking over her shoulder for BJ but also for Cort.

"This is just another example of what I've had to put up with over the years," Marie said. Actually, she was quite pleased with what had happened. It had presented a perfect wedge to drive between Jessica and Cortland. As long as she could keep a thorn in their marriage, she had nothing to worry about. With Jessica taking the herbs, she would never get pregnant, and Cortland could always be counted on to turn to greener pastures. Once she had established a deep friendship with Jessica, Marie would have no trouble controlling the younger woman. Jessica would be easy to manipulate, which was probably why Cortland had married her.

By the time they returned to the house, Jessy wanted nothing more than to take a long nap. Her head was throbbing, and every joint in her body seemed to ache. But to her aggravation, Cort had returned, and he wasn't in a pleasant mood. He met them in the entryway.

"Where have you been?" he demanded of Jessy.

The words served as a fuse to Jessy's temper. "You have a nerve to ask me such a question!" She reached out and slapped him across the face.

Pleased, Marie left the two alone.

"And suppose you tell me just where you've been for almost a week! With Miss Rothchild?" Jessy could see her red handprint on his cheek, and his eyes had turned black with anger. "You once told me you handle a slap quite well," she reminded him. "Now you have your chance to prove it! I'm going to my room."

Cort raked his fingers through his thick dark hair as he watched Jessy run up the stairs. He wasn't about to explain his whereabouts to any woman, let alone the unreasonable female he now claimed as his wife. If she thought he'd been with Amy, fine. It worked out a lot better than her knowing he'd spent most of his time at the ranch listening to his men say they'd learned nothing about BJ Johnson. Finding the man had become an obsession. He had everyone looking, but it was as if the man had vanished into thin air. Then, to make matters worse, he returned home to discover Jessy and Marie had taken off unescorted. Byron had told him about Jessy getting her gun, but what damage did she honestly think a small derringer could do unless she shot someone in the face?

"Hell," Cort mumbled, heading up the stairs to his room to change. Before he left the house, he would make damn sure that when *Miss Jessica* decided to take off again, she'd have company!

Jessy heard Cort come up the stairs, and grabbing her gun, she pointed it at the door. But he didn't come in. She sat on the bed waiting. A while later she heard him go down, then the front door slammed shut. She let out a self-mocking laugh. She was so weak, she probably couldn't have even pulled the trigger.

I need sleep, Jessy told herself. Her head pounded so badly she wanted to cry, and her stomach was beginning to cramp. Quickly slipping out of her clothes, she didn't even try to pick them up off the floor. Instead, she pulled on her white nightdress and collapsed on the bed.

Cort arrived home much earlier than he'd planned, and in a considerably better mood. He had spent the afternoon visiting Amy Rothchild. Cort was pleased to discover Amy was being wooed by a wealthy banker. It was through her that he had found out what had happened at the dress-maker's shop. Amy had been quite upset about causing trouble between him and his new bride, but Cort had assured her there had been no harm done.

After leaving the boardinghouse, the thought of spending an evening in the arms of one of his lady friends held no appeal. He had stopped at a saloon, but after one drink he was ready to leave. Restless, he decided to return home and confront his lioness in her den.

As Cort entered the house, he heard soft sobbing. He found Sheila curled up on the sofa crying.

"What's the matter, little one?" Cort asked tenderly.

Seeing her brother, Sheila jumped up and ran into his arms. "Oh, Cort," she sobbed, "something is wrong with Jessy."

Cort gently pushed her back and asked, "What do you mean something is wrong with Jessy?"

Though the words came out slowly, his tone of voice told Sheila he wanted an answer immediately. "She's sick, Cort. I was so afraid you wouldn't come home."

Cort left his sister and went up the stairs two at a time. He reached the top level just as Marie came out of Jessy's room.

"What's going on here," Cort demanded.

"I'm sure it's nothing to worry about," Marie said calmly. "I was just going to send for Dr. Mattson."

"How long has she been sick?"

"About an hour after you left, Yana came to help her dress for supper and found her in bed."

"You mean to tell me it's been that long and you're just sending for a doctor?" Cort stormed.

"May I remind you, Cortland, I raised your sister, and you can at least give me credit for knowing what I'm doing!"

"Who's watching her?"

"Yana. I suppose you're going in her room?"

"Of course I'm going in her room!"

"Then I suggest you remember that some people handle pain poorly."

"Send for the doctor, Marie," Cort said through clenched teeth.

Cort stood in front of Jessy's door several moments before finally opening it quietly. What confronted him twisted his gut. Jessy had her knees pulled tightly against her stomach, and her hands were gripping her head. A low, raspy moan escaped her lips as she twisted from side to side. Her face was covered with perspiration, and her gown clung to her wet skin. Her silver hair was everywhere; in her mouth, around her neck, her face, and twisted around her body.

Furious, Cort looked at Yana, who was sitting in the rocker looking out the window and humming.

"What the hell are you doing?" Cort had trouble keeping his voice lowered.

"Oh!" The black-haired girl jumped to her feet and headed for the bed. "I'm taking care of Miss Jessica."

"Get out of here, and never set foot in this room again! Did you hear me?"

The girl rushed from the room, sobbing.

Tossing his jacket across a chair, Cort rolled up his sleeves as he leaned over the bed. He couldn't help but notice Jessy's short breaths had a peculiar odor. "Jessy, can you hear me?"

Jessy became still. "Mama, I love you and Papa so much... Some day I'll grow up and be beautiful just like you and marry a handsome man like Papa." She started clutching her stomach again.

Cort went to his room and quickly returned with a large hunting knife held firmly in his hand. The sharp blade cut through the white nightdress, making it easy for him to remove Jessy's damp gown. He placed several cloths in the bowl of water by the bed, then began the difficult task of rinsing and drying her face and body. More than once he was tempted to cut off her hair.

Fortunately, even though Jessy remained incoherent, she stopped tossing. She began to mumble, but he couldn't understand what she was saying.

"I demand you leave this room immediately," Marie stated as she entered the doorway. "It's not decent for a man to be in a woman's sickroom."

"Instead of standing there bellowing like a bull elk, Marie, come over here and do something with Jessy's hair."

"You've removed her clothes!" Marie exclaimed when she reached the side of the big four-poster bed.

"Of course I've removed her clothes," Cort barked out quietly, dropping the rag in the water.

"But... but the lantern's lit and she's lying there unclothed... What I mean is, this is women's work and you shouldn't be in here."

If the situation had been different, Cort would have roared with laughter. Instead he said, "Well, I certainly didn't see anyone else attending to it!"

"Yana was supposed to be keeping a cool cloth on her head."

Cort stood up and glared at his stepmother. "Damn it, Marie, the girl was sitting in a rocker looking out the window. What is she doing here anyway? I certainly didn't hire her. Now go find a clean gown."

To Cort's amazement, after Marie produced the nightdress, she helped him dress Jessy, then parted her hair and tied it back with a ribbon.

"Pick her up," Marie commanded, "and I'll change the wet bed clothing."

Cort lifted Jessy into his arms, and though her body remained limp, she was as light as a feather. It seemed strange that this woman who had fought him at every turn now needed his help. An uneasiness stirred within him as he realized how much he wanted to see that challenging look return to her lavender eyes, and just how worried he was about her condition.

"You can lie her back down now," Marie said as she finished.

Watching Cortland place Jessy gently on the bed, Marie was feeling a strong twinge of guilt. Could the herbs she'd told Jessy to take have possibly caused this sickness? She had never heard of such a thing, but how was one to know?

"Did you send for Sidney?" Cort asked as he squeezed the water out of a cloth and placed it on Jessy's forehead.

"Yes. I hope he'll be here any time now."

Cort was surprised to hear a small note of concern in Marie's voice, but said nothing.

"I shall release Yana immediately. I only hired her to be Jessica's personal maid, and since she seems incapable of handling the task, I see no reason to keep her."

"I agree. How is Sheila holding up?"

"She's better. This was just too close to Arthur's death, and she was convinced Jessy was dying." Marie's voice had turned cold and detached again.

As the doctor and Cort left the bedroom, a calm Sheila went in to help her mother take care of Jessy.

"What did you discover, Sidney?" Cort asked.

Dr. Mattson ran a hand over his bald head, letting it come to rest on the back of his neck. His clothes were rumpled, and he was tired. Since early this morning, he'd been with a woman in labor. The baby had been born dead. Now he had another dilemma on his hands. "King, would your wife want to take her own life?"

Cort's dark brown eyes narrowed. "No. What are you getting at?"

Sidney slowly shook his head, thinking. "And your wife seems too young to be concerned about her looks."

"Sidney, what the hell are you talking about?"

"Your wife's been poisoned, King."

"Are you sure?"

"Yes."

Cort moved to the thick oak railing and leaned his hands against it, his muscles tight. "Is she going to be all right?"

"I'm not sure. Depends on how big a dose she took."

Though he didn't outwardly show it, Cort was consumed with fury. His own house had been invaded, and now neither food nor drink were safe. On the other hand, no one was sick except Jessy. BJ? For what purpose? Revenge? He couldn't exclude the possibility of Marie, either. She'd do anything to keep him from having a son. Cort turned and looked at the man who had doctored their family for years.

"This isn't the first one of these cases I've treated. As you know, we have a lot of Gypsies come through here. Everyone rushes out to their camp to get their fortunes told. The Gypsies also sell a potion that they claim will lengthen life and keep you from aging. If taken in small doses, it's harmless, but a large amount can be lethal. In all the cases I've treated up to now, the person thought that taking more than they'd been told to take would work even better."

It suddenly occurred to Cort that Yana could very well be a Gypsy. Her coloring and name would certainly indicate as much.

"The poison has a sweet taste," the doctor continued, "but strangely enough, it leaves an indescribable odor on anyone's breath who has taken it."

Cort remembered how Jessy's breath had smelled.

"That's how I knew what had happened. The headaches and cramps go along with it."

"I would prefer no one know about this, including my family."

Sidney nodded just as Marie came out the door.

"Marie, is Yana still downstairs?" Cort asked.

"No, she left right after I released her."

It was a long night. After she delivered some coffee, Cort sent Marie downstairs. He didn't trust her.

By dawn, Jessy was resting easier.

"Well," Sidney said as he rose from his chair, "I believe I can finally go home. I'll leave some bitters to be sure the poison gets out of her system." He checked Jessy again. "She's going to be just fine, King. Weak for a couple of days, but your wife will be up and around in no time." He stretched. "I'm going home and get some well deserved sleep. I'll be back late this afternoon."

Cort pulled himself off the chair and wondered if he looked as haggard as the good doctor. "You're welcome to stay here, Sidney."

"No, thanks, King, I sleep better in my own bed." He closed his black case.

Cort accompanied Sidney down the stairs of the quiet house, and a few minutes later Tod brought the doctor's buggy around front. The two men shook hands, words of thanks unnecessary between them.

Sidney chuckled as he climbed onto the black seat. "You know you're going to get a healthy bill from me?"

Cort grinned. "Wouldn't have it any other way."

Suddenly feeling hungry, Cort went inside and headed for the kitchen. The servants would be up, and he could use a big breakfast. The one thing he didn't want was coffee.

As he walked into the room, he could smell bacon cook ing, and a pot of grits sat on the stove. The servants were seated at the big round table busily talking. Cort heard the name Yana mentioned, and for some reason he stopped. Knowing he hadn't been seen, he stepped out of view and listened.

"I don't know why Mrs. Lancaster even hired her," a maid said. "I didn't like Yana, and I'm glad she's gone."

"Well, you noticed she only took the girl on while Mr. Lancaster was gone this week."

Cort recognized the voice of Mrs. O'Grady, the cook.

"She came out to the carriage house several times," Tod said. "She kept saying that if I wasn't nice to her she'd put a curse on me. I think she was plum loco."

Cort backed out of the room and headed for the study, his appetite gone. What he needed was a stiff drink.

Chapter Eight

In her dream, Jessy saw her mother working in the corn field while expounding Jonathan's wonderful qualities and saying how she hoped Jessy would accept his proposal of marriage. "Dear, thoughtful Jonathan," Jessy whispered, repeating her mother's words.

Jessy awoke, realizing she had been having a bad dream. Glancing around her room, her eyes came to rest on Cort sitting in the large chair at the side of her bed, his stubbled face expressionless. Except for one lamp turned low, the room was dark.

"How long have you been sitting there?" Still weak from her ordeal, her words were but a whisper.

"Long enough. How do you feel?"

Bits and pieces of things started drifting back to her. Pain, faces, strange images swimming in her mind. "Have I been sick?"

"Yes. Do you remember much?"

Why is he acting so cold, Jessy wondered, shaking her head.

"Two days ago you became quite ill." Cort watched her eyes light up with surprise. "The doctor said you had too much sun from working out in the garden, and something you ate disagreed with you. How do you feel?" Cort repeated.

"Hungry," Jessy said, her voice stronger. In fact, she felt quite ravenous.

Cort rose from the chair. "Would you care for some chicken broth?"

"Please."

Leaning down, Cort raised her high enough to place a pillow behind her back. Jessy's eyelids began to droop, and when she reopened them, Cort was holding a bowl in his hand. He raised the spoon to her lips.

After only a few spoonfuls, Jessy drifted back to sleep. Cort had just returned the bowl to the silver tray when there was a light tap on the door. Without waiting, Prudence O'Grady entered the room. Cort had assigned the cook's daughter the position of Jessy's personal maid.

"She'll be fine now," Cort whispered to the tall, attractive girl. "Just let her sleep. I want her to eat nothing unless it has been prepared by either you or your mother. If my wife becomes sick again, I will hold you responsible. Do I make myself clear?"

"Yes, sir," Prudence answered, her head lowered. She couldn't understand why Mr. Lancaster was requiring this of her, but it wasn't her place to ask questions.

Cort left and went to his own bed chambers. As usual, Byron was waiting.

"Will you be wanting to bathe?" the old man asked.

Cort moved to the window and stared out. The sky was starting to lighten. At the ranch the men would have already eaten and be preparing to go out on the range. Would Jessy be safer at the ranch? Cort wondered.

"Sir?"

Cort turned and faced him. "No," he snapped without thinking. "I'm going straight to bed. Get some rest yourself," he said in a softer voice, "you look like you could use some as well."

After Byron left, Cort remained standing by the window. So Jessy thought of Jonathan as dear and wonderful! Somewhere along the way he'd come to the conclusion she hated the man. Obviously dear Jessy had been acting all along. There was nothing about the woman he could trust. Although hearing her whispered words had rankled him, it had also served to remind him of the kind of woman he had married. Cort rubbed the stubble on his cheek. How could she possibly care for such a weasel? But that was just one of many questions he didn't have an answer for. He didn't like not having control over everything that touched his life, or wondering when the ax would fall. Where the hell was BJ, and who set Yana up to poison Jessy? BJ or Marie? Now he had someone else to track down, because only Yana could answer his questions.

A week later, Cort came home in a state of frustration. All his efforts had been in vain. Yana was nowhere to be found.

Entering the salon, he discovered Marie, Sheila and Jessy busily chatting.

"Cort," Jessy said upon seeing her husband, "you know I'm back to normal now, but Marie says you won't allow me to work in the garden. May I ask why? The man you hired has already torn up some of the flowers."

Cort forced a smile. "You're perfectly welcome to supervise."

"I can't be expected to sit around the house all day doing nothing! I don't agree with Dr. Mattson that working in the garden caused me to become ill."

Marie placed her embroidery in the basket and rose. "Cortland, has that boy brought my carriage around to the front yet?"

Cort finished pouring his brandy before answering. "Yes. He drove up just as I came in."

"Then I'm off for tea at the Wilkersons'. Are you sure you won't change your mind and come with me, Jessica?"

"No, but perhaps another time." Jessy glared at her husband. "Since we see so little of your stepson, I'd like to have a word with him."

Marie left, and a moment later Jessy heard the carriage drive off.

"Before you leave," Cort said casually upon seeing Sheila start to rise, "I have decided that Jessy should get out of the house. I think it would be a good idea if the three of us went to Harvey House for an early supper." Cort watched the pleasure leap into the two women's eyes.

"I'll go inform Mrs. O'Grady," Sheila said excitedly.

Seating himself on a brocade wingback chair, Cort sipped his drink. "And what were you ladies discussing when I came in?" he asked.

"Sheila and Marie were talking about the ball at the Wilmounts' next week. Cort—"

"And is your gown ready?"

"What?"

"I didn't stutter."

Jessy opened her mouth, but it took a moment for her to find her voice. "You haven't mentioned anything about my going," she finally said. He sat there calmly sipping his brandy, and Jessy had a strong urge to slap it from his hand. "But as I said before, I've hardly seen you. Are you sure you wouldn't care to take Miss Rothchild?"

"No, she's being escorted by Horace Bitman, a banker."

"I see. So now you've decided to take me."

Cort watched Jessy's hand toying with a small figurine on the table beside her. He was ready to duck if she sent it flying in his direction. "Quite the contrary. I had planned to take you all along. It's time you were introduced to the local society. I'm sure everyone is anxiously waiting to meet my dear bride. After all, I was once considered a prize catch."

"You pompous ass!" Jessy accused, rising to her feet. His handsome, chiseled face showed no concern at her accusation. "I suppose your mistress is quite disappointed at having to go with the banker."

"Probably."

"Well, you might as well take her, because I'm not going!"

Cort gave her a complacent smile. "Oh, but you are, my dear, even if it's in your nightdress. Now be a good girl and go upstairs and get ready for dinner. I'm really quite hungry."

By the time Jessy reached her room, she could think of nothing but strangling Cort. He was the most duplicitous man she had ever met. After hearing how he had stayed with her during her illness, she had wanted to thank him, but he never came home until after she'd gone to sleep. Now he was setting down rules for her to follow!

"I should be thankful to his mistress for keeping him out of my bed," Jessy grumbled, but she wasn't. "I'm nothing but another piece of furniture in his house."

She threw open the doors of the clothespress and yanked out a dress.

Jessy was still in a bad mood when they reached the restaurant, but her spirits lightened considerably as she talked to old friends while Sheila and Cort sat at one of the tables. She was delighted to learn that Kathleen and Lora were engaged to brothers who owned adjacent ranches. The two women would be neighbors.

Though the women were too far away for him to hear what was being said, Cort watched various emotions of pleasure play on his wife's lovely face. Who is the real Jessica? he wondered, not for the first time. She was like a chameleon, always changing color, depending on whom she was with.

As Sheila glanced around the room to see if there were any familiar faces, she spied a man headed toward their table. He was not what she would call handsome, but his blond hair, sun-darkened skin and aquiline features were very interesting indeed! He was dressed casually and wore one of the sober alpaca jackets furnished for coatless patrons. The gentleman certainly did not have her brother's stylish flair for clothes, but he had a self-assured stride that Sheila had seldom seen. She judged him to be several years younger than her brother.

"King Lancaster!" the man said.

Cort looked up and smiled. He placed his napkin on the table, then stood and shook hands with the man. "Tom Sterling. What brings you out this way? It's been . . . what? Two years since we last saw each other?"

"Just about," Tom replied. "I'm on my way to check on some land in Colorado. I planned on seeing you before I headed out." He looked at Sheila. "An acquaintance of yours, old friend?" he asked Cort while giving her a crooked grin.

Sheila stared into his green eyes, practically mesmerized. He's almost as tall as Cort, she thought.

"Excuse my bad manners. I would like you to meet my sister, Sheila. Sheila, Thomas Chandler Sterling III. I've done business with his father for years."

Sheila extended her hand. Tom hadn't taken his eyes off her, and when his lips brushed her knuckles, she felt a tingling sensation run up her arm.

"Why didn't you tell me you have such a lovely sister?"

Cort laughed inwardly. He'd have to be blind not to see the attraction these two felt for each other.

"Have you eaten?" Cort asked.

Tom finally took his eyes off Sheila. "No. As a matter of fact, I had just started to take a seat when I happened to see you."

"Then why don't you join us?"

"I'd be delighted. That is, if your sister doesn't mind."

"No, not at all," Sheila spoke up, a little too quickly. She knew she sounded a bit breathless, but couldn't seem to prevent it.

Jessy joined them, and Cort made the introductions. Tom had great fun teasing Cort about finally settling down and asking how he'd managed to pluck such a beautiful rose out of nowhere.

Jessy liked the easygoing man, and from all indications, so did Sheila.

After the manager had brought a huge platter of sizzling steaks and forked them onto their plates, the group settled down to eating the fine feast.

The evening passed quickly, with Tom and Cort discussing cattle, railroads, Indians and politics. Sheila was content to unobtrusively watch the man seated across from her. *I wonder if he's married?* she asked herself. *Does he think I'm as pretty as Jessy? Oh, cannonballs, no one is as pretty as Jessy!*

Over dessert and coffee, Tom asked Sheila if she spent much time in town. Listening to his long-time friend draw Sheila into small talk, Cort wondered if the man's wild days were behind him and if he was ready to settle down. He thought it would be a good match. Tom came from a wealthy, well-established shipping family. Last time Cort had seen Tom, the man had already begun to take control of his father's business holdings, which were extensive.

"Since you'll be staying in town a couple of days, Tom, I think you should stay with us. Don't you agree, Jessy?"

"I think it would be a fine idea."

Cort was curious to see if anything would develop between his sister and his friend. Sheila was obviously quite taken with Mr. Sterling, and he'd never seen her show so much interest in any man. She radiated pleasure and flaunted her charms. As for having a man like Tom in the house, Cort had no worries. Marie would look after her daughter like a hawk. Something did prick at the back of Cort's neck, however. Jessy also seemed to enjoy Tom's company.

"I'd appreciate that, King," Tom said in a jovial manner. "I'm tired of staying in hotels."

Amused, Cort nodded. "You can go home with us. I'll have someone come pick your things up later."

Sheila couldn't understand why her brother had been in such a cranky mood lately. For nearly a week he'd snapped at everyone, offering no explanation for his behavior. He seemed to be looking for a fight. For once her mother had enough sense to keep her mouth closed. Tom, on the other hand, simply shrugged his shoulders and stayed out of Cort's way, while Jessy appeared to not notice a thing.

Tom spent practically all his time with Sheila. But so did her mother, and most of the time Jessy did, as well. If they went on a carriage ride or to the Kaw River for a picnic, her mother went also. A walk? Her mother walked. A talk in the salon? Her mother sat in the room doing her stitchery. To make the entire situation even more unbearable, Marie constantly quizzed Tom. She asked where he lived, what his house looked like, the family background, what his business interests were, his age, if he had a wife waiting back home, why he had come to Kansas and, the final blow, if he was looking for a wife. With the last question, Sheila had turned absolutely scarlet with embarrassment.

It seemed that the one time Sheila truly needed Cort to intervene for her, he was unapproachable. Left to her own resources, she started looking at the situation from a different angle. Tom showed no apparent concern over the constant questioning. And on more than one occasion, he actually had her mother laughing, something Sheila had seldom seen in the past years. Many times during Marie's bombardment, he would glance toward Sheila while his mouth twitched in silent amusement as though the two of them shared a secret.

Sheila had, however, learned a great deal about their guest. She longed for them to spend some time alone, and as the days passed swiftly by, Sheila began wondering how his kiss would feel. Certainly not like Terrance Wilkens' slobbering attempts. Besides his attractive looks and personality, there was another quality that attracted Sheila. Tom wasn't the least bit intimidated by her brother, and would probably stand up to Cort should the occasion ever arise. Thomas Chandler Sterling III had nothing to prove. He was his own man.

Cort's view of the situation was entirely different. At meals, Jessy seemed to hang on Tom's every word. Other than going out to supervise the garden weeding or driving her buggy into town for dress fittings, she remained with the others. She did manage to thank Cort for the two armed riders who followed her wherever she went. The night Jessy discovered Tom had been to Kansas City many times had been almost more than Cort could handle. She became excited and began asking all sorts of questions. Cort didn't bother to tell her how many times he'd been there.

More than once Cort had started to claim his marriage right in Jessy's bed, but for some damn reason, he kept backing off, knowing a full-fledged fight would ensue. He'd been too long without the feel of a woman beneath him. He hadn't even visited any of his various lady friends. What he wanted could only be given by one woman. He wanted to feel Jessy's total surrender to him again.

The night of the ball, Jessy was nervous and excited as Prudence slipped the new gown over her head. The exquisite material had come from China, and was a fine blending of blue turning to almost jade green. It shimmered in the light. There were large puffed sleeves starting at the edge of her shoulders, then fitting snugly from the elbow down. The bodice formed a deep V in the center of her waist, and the many layers of material in the skirt draped gracefully to the floor. Dancing slippers had been made to match, as well as a full-length cape. That her chest was well exposed didn't bother Jessy. For the first time in years, she truly felt like a woman.

With Jessy's instructions, and after several tries, Prudence had pulled her hair straight back and twisted it into a huge knot at the back of her head, with one roped loop hanging down her long neck. She had thought to wear feathers in her hair, but upon seeing herself in the mirror, Jessy changed her mind. She preferred the simple look. She was so pleased with the overall effect she started laughing. She knew this new self-assuredness was all Tom's doing. He had the ability to make her laugh, feel special, and he always treated her like a lady.

Cort and Tom stood enjoying a glass of port while awaiting the women. Both men were in black evening dress and ready to depart.

"I'm looking forward to a grand evening," Tom announced. "With father sending me all over the country of late, it's been some time since I've had the privilege of attending such a grand soiree, and especially with two beautiful women."

Cort lit a cigar and let the smoke trail slowly upward. "I hope you don't fail to remember that one of those women is my wife and the other my sister."

Tom chuckled.

"You wouldn't happen to have designs on either of them, would you?"

"I have the distinct feeling the only woman we're really talking about is Jessica." Tom arched a blond eyebrow. "Is she available? You may be her husband, but you don't own her, my friend. And why all the concern? I doubt very seriously that you've given up your ladies fair, and I've certainly not seen any love between the two of you. In fact you act more like enemies than lovers. She's a beautiful woman any other man would be proud to have."

"Don't fool with what's mine, Tom," Cort warned, "I wouldn't take kindly to it."

Cort had just spoken the words when Sheila waltzed in, a fluff of pink. Her gown had fine lace around the bottom of the sleeves and across the top of her bodice. Pink bows with long streamers adorned her skirt. Her black hair was piled on top of her head, and Cort was quite proud of his sister.

"I thought I would be late, but I see neither Jessy nor Mother are here yet."

Tom rushed forward and, taking her hand, brushed his lips across her knuckles. "You look ravishing."

A moment later, Marie and Jessy arrived together. Neither one of the men paid attention to the older woman,
dressed in her usual black. Their eyes were riveted on one of
the most beautiful women either had ever seen. Everything
about her was perfection.

Sheila's self-assuredness dropped several notches.

"You're the picture of loveliness, my dear," Cort said as
he walked over to Jessy. Reaching inside his pocket, he
pulled out a small box and handed it to her. "I bought a little something for your first social outing."

Jessy gasped when she opened the box and saw the long,
sparkling diamond and ruby earrings nestled inside. The size
of the stones told her they were very valuable. "Thank you,
Cort," she uttered, unable to think of anything else to say.

"Permit me." He removed the earrings from the box and
placed them on her small earlobes. "They would have gone
well with your necklace," he whispered. "Don't you
agree?"

Before Jessy could make a reply, he said, "Now, if
everyone is ready, shall we be on our way?"

In the carriage, Jessy was itching to make some tart reply
to Cort's comment. It was Tom's and Sheila's jovial chat-
ter that finally made Jessy decide to forget it. She wasn't
going to let Cort ruin her evening.

Jessy felt like the belle of the ball. Cort played the perfect gentleman, introducing her to so many people she
couldn't possibly remember all their names. Everyone
seemed to want to meet her. She couldn't help noticing that
more than one female gave her the jealous eye, but she
didn't care. She knew Cort was the handsomest man there,
and decided to consider it a compliment.

Jessy danced the first few dances with Cort, and she
wasn't the least bit surprised at how smoothly he guided her

around the large floor. She was beginning to see that her husband was quite accomplished at everything he did.

It was while she was dancing with Tom that Jessy saw Miss Rothchild enter on the arm of a short, stout man. Then Cort joined them and shook the man's hand. Surprisingly, it hurt too deeply to see her husband's handsome face light up with pleasure as he and the woman laughed about something.

Refusing to watch a moment longer, Jessy looked at Tom and smiled. "I guess you will be leaving soon," she stated sweetly.

"Tomorrow, as a matter of fact."

"Sheila shall miss you."

"And you? Will you miss me?" he asked, his tone suddenly serious.

Jessy blushed. "Of course I'll miss you. We've all enjoyed your company."

"Spoken like the perfect wife. If I thought there was a chance, I'd ask you to come with me."

"And if I weren't married, I'd probably give it some serious consideration."

They both laughed. Almost from the beginning, their friendly bantering had drawn them into a close friendship.

"Can you keep a secret?" Tom asked after turning her in several circles.

"Depends on what it is."

"I'm seriously thinking about marrying Sheila."

"Oh, Tom, that's wonderful. Of course I won't say a word to anyone."

"I'm not going to ask her right away, I have work to do in Colorado. When I come back, I'll have more time to spend, and we can get to know each other better. Since I can't have you, I need to decide if I can make her a good husband."

"Oh, Tom, stop teasing about something so serious."

Tom refrained from telling Jessy he was quite serious. I would serve no purpose. He wasn't sure whether it was love or infatuation he felt toward this beautiful woman in his arms, and he needed time to sort out his feelings.

After leaving Amy and her beau, Cort went out on the long terrace for some fresh air and a smoke. Walking to the shadows in the far corner, he pulled out a cigar. The night was warm, and stars lit the heavens. From where he stood the voices of the guests and the sound of the music seemed far away. Cort felt a strong urge to climb on his horse and leave everything behind. The last time he'd felt this way was when he took off after the rustlers instead of letting his men at the ranch take care of them. From that, he'd ended up meeting Jessy, and his life had been in an upheaval ever since.

Cort threw away the partially smoked cigar. He knew why he was feeling this way. Part of it had to do with Jessy and Tom, but the other part was that he'd never been in a situation where all he could do was sit and wait. It was like trying to find a particular straw in a bed of hay. But he had no doubt that BJ would eventually make his presence known. The man had tried to kill him once, and he'd try again. How the man could stay hidden so long remained a mystery. As if one disappearance wasn't bad enough, Yana also couldn't be found.

"King Lancaster's wife is quite a beauty, don't you agree, Buster?"

Cort had been so absorbed in his thoughts he hadn't heard the two men come out on the terrace.

"I'd like to know how it would feel to have her in my bed," Buster replied.

Cort stepped out of the shadows. "Well, you're sure as hell never going to find out!" he said as he went inside.

Since Sheila and her mother were the only ones up early for breakfast, Sheila grabbed at the opportunity to speak privately with the older woman. "Mother, do you realize Tom is leaving today?" she asked.

"Of course."

Take your time, Sheila told herself, and don't act anxious. If you handle this right, maybe Mother will allow you to take Tom to the train station alone. "He's a nice man, don't you think?"

"Yes, he'll make you a good husband. I doubt that even Cortland will object to this union. I hope to get a commitment out of Thomas before he leaves."

Sheila nearly choked on her bite of egg. "Mother! You wouldn't!"

Finished with her meal, Marie placed her fork by her plate and dabbed her mouth with her napkin. "It says in the Book of Proverbs that a virtuous woman is a crown to her husband." Marie stopped a moment to consider. "I believe that's right." She waved her hand in the air, her large diamond ring sparkling in the light. "Well, you know what I mean. As your mother, I have every right to be sure Thomas understands what a wonderful crown you'd be for him. I shall also find out just what his intentions are. If Cortland was half the gentleman he should be, he would have already obtained the information instead of leaving the task to me. You always talk so highly of him, but as you can see, he has no intention of watching after his ward's interest. He thinks only of himself."

"Mother," Sheila said in a low, husky voice, "if you do this I shall be absolutely mortified! He has only been here a week!"

"Wasn't he supposed to leave town in three days? Why do you think he stayed longer? Certainly not to keep Cortland company, and I doubt that he's interested in me."

"Why are you so insistent that I marry?" Sheila aske[d] angrily. "Why can't you just let things take their natura[l] course instead of shoving me at every man who has th[e] misfortune to be rich?"

"I'll not have you talking to me in that tone of voice," Marie bit out quietly. "Go to your room, Sheila, until yo[u] decide to keep a civil tongue. If you had your way, you'[d] end up an old maid. Soon you'll be nineteen. You shoul[d] have been married when you were sixteen. But no! Cort[-] land has put a stop to every effort I've made to find you [a] proper husband with a good family background. Consid[-] ering your age, this may very well be your last chance. Yo[u] should be grateful to me for having your best interests a[t] heart."

Sheila jumped up so fast she nearly knocked the chai[r] over. "I will not marry a man I don't love!"

"Once you're married you'll discover that a good hus[-] band with a position in life is far more important than love Now I've heard enough of your silly prattle. Go upstairs."

Cort was about to leave his room when Sheila cam[e] bounding in. She ran straight into his arms. He didn't hav[e] to ask why she was crying. It had to be Marie. "What ha[s] the old war-horse done now?" he asked, holding her in hi[s] arms.

"Oh, Cort," Sheila sobbed, "Mother is going to ask Tom if he intends to marry me." She looked at his face. "How could she embarrass me like that?"

Cort pulled a handkerchief from his coat pocket an[d] wiped her tears. "Calm down," he soothed. "Things aren'[t] always as bad as they seem."

Sheila took the handkerchief and blew her nose.

"Everything will be all right," Cort said after a moment "Tom's been around the horn, he'll understand. I could tal[k] to Marie, but I doubt it would do any good. The woman i[s] obsessed with getting you married, and nothing is going to change her mind." Sheila had regained control of herself, so he gently sat her in a chair. "What you have to do, little sister, is accept the way she is and try not to let it bother you. She only makes a fool of herself. You wouldn't think she'd be such a fanatic about the subject, considering the way she talks about her husbands." Cort grinned. "But I'm not even going to try to second guess the woman's thinking."

Sheila giggled. "I suppose you're right. I've made more out of this than is called for."

"Tell me, why are you so concerned what Marie says to Tom? When she's pulled this with other men, you've been mad, but never upset."

Sheila started fidgeting with her hands. "I don't know."

Cort watched his sister with keen eyes. "Do you like Tom?"

"Of course I like him."

"How much?"

"Cort—"

"How much?"

Sheila lowered her head. "A lot," she finally whispered.

"I see. Sheila, Tom is not a man to tuck his tail between his legs and run. When he wants something, he goes after it. If he's interested, you can be sure you haven't seen the last of him."

Sheila stood, his words giving her ego a big boost. "You certainly know how to perk up a woman's spirits."

Cort let out a low, hearty laugh. "So I've been told. Now why don't you go and freshen up? You don't want Tom to see you've been crying, do you?"

Sheila shook her head. "Cort, may I be allowed to drive Tom to the train depot without Mother?"

"We'll see."

When Cort left his bedroom and walked down the hall toward the stairs, Tom also exited his room.

"Well, hello there," Tom greeted his friend, a broad smile splashed across his face. "I'm all packed and ready to leave." He gave Cort a mischievous look. "Too bad we didn't get to spend more time together, but I can't say I haven't enjoyed myself."

"Even with Marie dogging your steps?" Cort asked as they proceeded down the stairs.

"She is something, isn't she? Not very subtle. I feel like a fish that's been scaled and cooked and is ready to be served on a platter. When is she going to ask me to marry Sheila?"

Cort roared with laughter. When he could finally speak, he said, "As a matter of fact, this morning, as I understand it. Sheila was just in my room begging me to prevent it. She's quite embarrassed over the entire matter."

"Does Marie make a habit of this?"

Cort's eyes glittered with amusement. "I'm afraid so."

When the two men entered the dining room, Marie was still seated at the table. Her eyes expressed dissatisfaction at Cort's arrival. She had anticipated being alone with her future son-in-law. "Good morning, Thomas," she said, completely ignoring her stepson. She sipped her coffee as the men sat across from her.

"Good morning, Marie," Tom replied cheerfully.

The breakfast progressed with little opportunity for Marie to ask questions. The two men seemed to find a multitude of things to discuss, including Tom's departure. Nothing was said about Sheila or any possibility of Tom's return to Kansas. Anger boiled up inside Marie. Why couldn't Cortland have stayed in his room? Why, this morning of all mornings, had he chosen to come down for breakfast? She knew her time was limited. In less than an hour Thomas would be leaving for the train station. Would Cortland insist on taking him?

Marie was about to take the bull by the horns when Sheila entered, looking as though she hadn't a care in the world. Cort and Tom stood, acknowledging her arrival. When Sheila sat down, the two men returned to their seats.

"Are you all packed, Tom?" Sheila asked sweetly.

"Yes, and I believe Byron has already taken my cases to the carriage." Tom placed his napkin on the table and let out a sigh of contentment. "An excellent meal, Marie."

"Thank you, Thomas, it will probably be the last good meal you'll have. I understand the food is terrible at train stops." She turned hard eyes toward Cort. "Will you be taking Thomas to the depot?"

Cort leaned back in his chair. "I don't know. I haven't decided. Why do you ask?"

"Seeing as how you've chosen to spend very little time entertaining our guest, I think it would only be appropriate for Sheila and I to drive him."

Sheila gave her brother a pleading look.

"Oh, I wouldn't want to put you to all that trouble," Cort said nonchalantly. "I'm sure there are things around the house that need your attention. Sheila is perfectly capable of driving him if I decide not to go."

"How can you say such a thing?" Marie asked, her voice quivering with anger. "Sheila should not be allowed to go unchaperoned. I would hate to think what could happen to her in such an unruly town with rough men everywhere. As usual, Cortland, you have no concern for your sister's well-being!" she snapped. "I'm sure Thomas would never let such a thing happen to a lady of good breeding."

Sheila saw Cort's eyes narrow, and she shuddered. She glanced over at Tom, feeling sorry for him for having to witness this clash of wills.

"Very well, dear stepmother, I'll go with them. Does that please you?" Cort asked, his voice low and cutting.

Marie, sure she had the situation well in hand now, decided to take matters into her own hands. "I think I should be the one to go. Besides, I have some shopping to do and I want to talk to Thomas."

"There is nothing you have to say that can't be said now. If you have shopping to do, we'll all go."

Marie's black eyes sparkled with hatred. She wasn't about to let Cort prevent her from asking the question that needed answering. "Very well. I had hoped to handle this in a more appropriate manner—"

"Mother!" Sheila groaned.

"Sheila, you go ahead and take Tom to the depot." Cort looked relaxed, but his cold brown eyes glared at Marie, silently warning her not to say another word. "I'll meet you there."

As Tom and Sheila left the room, Marie rose, ready to follow.

"Sit down!" Cort's words whipped out at her.

Marie fell back in her chair, shocked. "I will not—"

"Don't push me, Marie, or you'll regret it." The muscles in Cort's jaw flexed as he worked to keep his temper under control. He stood, then placed his hand on the back of his chair, his piercing eyes still on Marie. "Why don't you just put Sheila out on an auction block? Did you ever stop to think she might have been married a long time ago if you hadn't run off every suitor who came calling? What man would want you for a mother-in-law? You'd drive the poor fellow to his grave, just as you did my father and the husband before him. And don't think you're passing anything by me. I know what's on your mind. When Sheila marries, you plan on moving in with her." Cort saw the surprised look on Marie's face as the words were spoken.

"And be rid of you once and for all!" Marie spit out.

"Well, think again." Cort's voice was as smooth as satin. "You will stay with me, beloved Mother, and you know you have no other choice unless I deem otherwise. You have already been to see two lawyers, and they all concurred that Father's will is incontestable. I told you once before what your choices are. Either live with me, or I'll set you up in a home of your own with an allowance. I'll not have you ruin Sheila's life. From now on, you will *never* say anything to *any* man about marriage. Do I make myself clear? I don't think you'd be too happy if I bought you a house out in the middle of nowhere and left you there. Don't think it isn't tempting."

"Oh! Those are fine words for a man who has never cared for or supervised Sheila's upbringing! You set yourself up as some kind of god in the girl's eyes, always letting her have or do whatever she wants. You put grand ideas in her head about marriage, and look at you." She laughed bitterly. "You sent for a mail-order bride who didn't even show up, then turned around and married a woman just so you can have a child!" She laughed bitterly.

Cort gave her a wicked smile. "But it was my choice, wasn't it? And so is your future!" He turned and left.

Chapter Nine

Cort had trouble controlling his anger as he headed the dappled gray south. With everything else going on, he certainly didn't need Marie running Sheila's life into the ground. Fortunately, one cocklebur was fixing to be removed from his side. Tom was leaving.

Cort's foul mood lightened somewhat when he arrived at the depot and saw his sister's gleaming face. He had just enough time to dismount, make his way through the various people standing around and shake Tom's hand.

Tom stepped onto the metal platform of the passenger car, then turned. "See you in a few months," he called just as the conductor gave the final call.

Cort quizzically raised a dark eyebrow at his sister as Tom disappeared inside.

"He's going to stop here on his way back," Sheila explained happily.

The whistle blew, and black smoke gushed out of the engine's stack as the large train wheels started turning. Emperor snorted nervously, then backed away.

"Easy, boy," Cort crooned while taking up the slack in the reins. Again the whistle pealed out a long, mournful cry as the train started to gain momentum. Emperor rolled his

eyes and tried to rear. It took all of Cort's attention to settle the horse before the animal could kick someone.

With the horse under control, Cort glanced at Sheila, who
had headed toward her buggy. She hadn't gone far. The fury
that had smoldered beneath a thin veneer of friendliness returned. Two bushy-haired trappers were blocking his sister's path.

As Cort neared the scene he heard the broadest of the pair
say, "Oh, come on, baby. It ain't gonna hurt you to have
just one little drink with us."

"Get out of my way!" Sheila demanded.

"Now that ain't no way to act," the skinny, weasely man
said. "We's just tryin' to be friendly."

"I suggest you let the lady pass," Cort stated, stepping
between the men and his sister. Both trappers reeked of
whiskey and sweat.

"Hey!" yelled the big man with the long beard. "You
mind your own business. We seen her first, prissy britches."
He gave Cort a shove.

Cort's reply was a fist to the man's jaw. Sheila backed
away as the second man jumped Cort from behind, hoping
his partner would get up off the ground. In the next instant, the two men were lying beside each other, with Cort
standing over them.

Several of the locals had gathered and were laughing
among themselves. Everyone enjoyed a good fight, but this
was no contest. They knew King Lancaster could take care
of himself, and the two strangers really hadn't stood a
chance.

The thin man looked at his pal, still out cold, and his desire for a fight quickly vanished. "We didn't mean no harm,
mister," he proclaimed, "we was just tryin' to be friendly."

"Next time a lady tells you to get out of her way, maybe
you'll listen," Cort growled.

Cort grabbed Emperor's reins from one of the locals, and he and Sheila continued on their way.

Once Sheila was settled on the buggy seat and had unwrapped the reins from around the whip, she gave her brother a wicked grin. "Do you feel better?"

Cort laughed and swung atop the stallion. "As a matter of fact, yes. Where to now?"

"I certainly don't want to return home." Sheila glanced down the railroad track, but the train was out of view. "I think I'll ride over to Mrs. Blakely's and see if she can make me a few new dresses. I was quite impressed with the gowns she made Jessy, and I want to look especially nice when Tom returns." Realizing what she had said, Sheila quickly added, "You can never rely on a seamstress having clothes done on time. Especially this one. From what Mother said, the lady has far too many customers. Well, I guess I'll be on my way."

"Oh, no." Cort moved Emperor around to block her departure. "I've earned an explanation, young lady. I don't expect you to tell me everything the two of you discussed, but as Marie would say, just what are my friend's intentions?"

"Oh, Cort, he said he was quite taken with me," Sheila exclaimed, her excitement rushing to the forefront, "but that he wouldn't return if I didn't feel something toward him."

Cort grinned. "And what did you say?"

"You and I are blood, Mr. King, and I'm no fool, either. I know a good thing when I see it. I told him I'd be looking forward to his return."

Cort moved his horse out of the way. "Smart girl. Do you want me to accompany you to the dressmaker's?"

"No, I'll be fine."

"Then I'll see you later at the house."

From the window of her bedroom, Jessy had seen Tom and Sheila leave. At first she'd felt guilty at having overslept and not saying goodbye. But after a second thought, she decided it was probably for the best. She was growing too fond of Tom. She had enjoyed his visit, but just like the wonderful time she'd had at the ball, it couldn't go on forever.

A little later, Jessy watched Cort ride off. Without waiting for Prudence to return and finish her toilet, Jessy quickly threw on a blue muslin skirt and blouse. Today she'd work in the garden no matter what Cort said. Before coming down sick, she had discovered that working in the soil took her mind off her troubles.

Snatching up her gloves, Jessy was about to leave her room when she saw the door leading to Cort's bedroom. A sudden, overwhelming desire to snoop enveloped her. Would Byron be there? Well, if he was, she could always say she didn't know Cort had left.

Not wanting to look suspicious, Jessy opened the door with a firm hand. The room was empty, and everything meticulously in place. Byron had already seen to his duties. Cort's quarters were hardly larger than her own, but there was no doubt they belonged to a man. They were completely unadorned except for the heavy, green velvet drapes hanging to the side of the open windows, the bedcover of the same fabric, and two large Oriental rugs covering a good deal of the hardwood floor. Curiosity getting the better of her, Jessy sauntered over and slowly opened the drawer of the chiffonier. She saw a woman's chemise folded neatly on top, and slammed it shut and moved to the clothespress. Her husband certainly didn't lack for clothes. However, the three sheer nightdresses hanging to the side certainly didn't belong to him!

Jessy sat on the edge of the bed, staring at the wisps of material. Well, what did you expect? she asked herself. You knew there were other women in his life. Still, being confronted with this . . .

Jessy was shocked to realize she was jealous. Downright, infuriatingly jealous! It didn't seem possible, but it was true. How could she feel moony-eyed over Tom one minute, then turn around and feel this way about Cort? But she should have known. It had been staring her in the face for days. Hadn't she been upset over the Rothchild woman as well as the women who had gone out of their way to talk to him at the ball? And what about the ones he'd danced with? She certainly hadn't liked seeing them in his arms.

Jessy placed her face in her hands and groaned. What had happened to the woman who never wanted another man in her life? Jessy sat up straight and dropped her hands to her lap. She had no trouble answering her own questions. Cort's looks, carriage, expressions, all projected a masculinity that was difficult for any female to ignore. She was probably the only woman foolish enough to deny him his right to her bed. To make matters worse, he was building a web, and she was becoming very tangled up in it. She couldn't, and wouldn't, let herself get any more deeply involved! To hell with him.

Jessy rushed to her room. It was time for her to leave. Throwing open the doors to the armoire, she reached for the carpetbag on the top shelf. It wasn't there.

Prudence stepped into the room and was shocked to see a mess. Jessy was pulling out drawers, and clothes were flying everywhere. "May I be of help?" Prudence asked, frightened by the woman's frenzy. Her mistress had a wild look in her eyes.

"Have you seen my carpetbag?"

"No, ma'am."

"Are you sure?"

"Yes, ma'am." Prudence backed toward the door.

"I'll bet *he* has it," Jessy snarled.

When Jessy headed toward Cort's room, Prudence took the opportunity to leave.

Furious to the point of not caring, Jessy attacked her husband's room like a woman possessed. But the carpetbag was not to be found.

"Are you finished?"

Jessy turned around and saw Marie standing in the doorway. "I'm searching for something," she proclaimed.

"So I've heard. Prudence came downstairs looking like she'd seen a ghost and muttering something about a carpetbag."

"Have you seen it?"

"No, but if you feel such a desperate need to find it, I'll question the servants."

Seeing the prim and proper woman with her arms folded across her chest and her expression of displeasure, Jessy began to feel guilty about what she'd done. "I would appreciate that."

"Now," Marie said, distaste showing in her voice, "if you're finished, I'll have everything put back in its proper place."

Though still panicked at the thought of having lost her money and necklace, Jessy wasn't happy about the extra work she'd caused Byron and Prudence.

"When was the last time you saw the bag?" Marie asked, refusing to let Jessy know how much her curiosity was piqued. What could have been inside that was so important? she silently wondered.

But Jessy wasn't in such a state that she couldn't read the expressions on Marie's face. Forcing herself to appear hurt and dejected, she said, "Actually, I am making a big to-do over nothing. You see, that carpetbag belonged to my father, and it's the only thing I have left of his. Perhaps it's silly, but it meant a great deal to me.'' She watched a look of disinterest enter Marie's dark eyes. ''I'm going to work in the garden. If you find out anything, will you let me know?''

''Of course.''

Most of the weeding had already been done, so Jessy set herself to clipping the dead flowers. Marie had brought up a very good question. When did she last see the carpetbag? After much thought, Jessy decided it was the day she had gone to the dressmaker's. The day she became sick. With all that had happened since, she hadn't thought to see if the leather bag was still in its proper place.

It was hard for Jessy to believe Cort had taken the bag. He would have done so only if he thought there was something in it, and had he thought that and taken it, he wouldn't have missed the opportunity to taunt her with his discovery. On the other hand, hadn't he done just that when he gave her the earrings?

Still leaning over, Jessy clipped off several good rose buds before she realized what she'd done. Who else could have taken it, if not a servant? Yana? Prudence had told Jessy how furious Cort had been and how the worthless girl had been fired.

It hurt Jessy deeply to know she might never see her mother's beautiful necklace again, but in all truthfulness, the jewelry did seem to carry a curse with it. Her whole streak of bad luck had centered on the rubies and diamonds. In some ways, she could accept the loss. But the one thing that had kept her going through thick and thin was the knowledge that she had the financial means to escape if the situation became intolerable. Unless the carpetbag was discovered, she belonged to Cort until her dying day. Should she have put everything in a bank? No, Cort would probably have found out. Besides, she didn't trust banks, especially after what had happened to her father during the war.

Jessy continued cutting, her depression growing by leaps and bounds.

"She did what?" Cort roared after Marie had told him about Jessy tearing up the rooms.

"I know you were desperate to wed, Cortland. However, you might have warned us that Jessy was unstable." Marie leaned over the kitchen table and dusted the cake crumbs from the front of her black dress. "Considering her behavior, you might give a second thought to having a child by her. What if the child suffered from the same malady? I've never heard of anyone getting so upset over an old carpetbag, even if it did belong to her father." Marie stood.

Grabbing Marie by the arm, Cort marched her into the study. "I don't like private matters discussed where the servants might hear," he said angrily as he closed the door behind them. "Now, tell me what this is all about."

Marie jerked her arm away. "Your wife should have thought of the servants before throwing her tantrum and causing all that work for Byron and Prudence. Prudence was scared out of her wits when she saw what Jessica was doing. It's a bit late to keep anything a secret."

"If you don't mind, Marie, would you be so kind as to tell me just what went on?" Cort asked as he sat behind the desk.

"I did. Jessica tore up both your bedrooms looking for a carpetbag and went into a rage when she couldn't find it."

"Has it been found?"

"I questioned all the servants, and no one has seen it."

Cort leaned back, deep in thought. Ever since he'd me[t] Jessy, she'd been tugging that damn carpetbag around wit[h] her. Why? He suddenly remembered when he'd found he[r] in the Gordon House. She had bought new clothes as wel[l] as some traveling bags, and upon seeing her stuff some[-] thing in the leather carpetbag, he had scathingly asked wh[y] she hadn't bought a new one. Her reply had been, "Be[-] cause it belonged to...*Jonathan*." Had Marie misquoted hi[s] wife? If not, why did Jessy lie? And exactly what ha[d] thrown her into a tizzy? Unless...

"If we're through talking, I have work to do," Mari[e] stated flatly.

"Where is Jessy now?"

"Working in the garden, and without a bonnet."

"Sit down, Marie, I have a few things to say."

"I would think chastising your wife would be more im[-] portant."

Cort's eyes narrowed. "I'll take care of Jessy in my ow[n] way. Now sit down."

Even though she was aggravated at being detained, Mari[e] sat on the brown leather sofa.

"The reason Jessy became so sick was that she was poi[-] soned." Cort watched Marie carefully for any telltale sign[s] of guilt.

"That's impossible!" Marie gasped. "Who would tell yo[u] such a thing?"

"Dr. Mattson."

"Well, he doesn't know what he's talking about."

"I think Yana slipped the poison into Jessy's food. Th[e] question arises as to who put her up to it. Let's consider [a] couple of things." Cort leaned forward and placed his el[-] bows on the desk. "For example. It was you who hired th[e] girl behind my back, and it's you who would do anything t[o] keep me from having a son."

Marie's cold, unwavering eyes met his. "I do not have to defend myself to the likes of you, Cortland. If you have questions, ask Yana."

Cort stood and, after rounding the corner, sat on the edge of the desk. "But isn't it interesting. She has disappeared. I know. I've tried to find her."

Marie couldn't hide the shudder that ran through her body. Though she'd had a lot of bouts with her stepson, she had never seen him look quite as deadly as he did at this moment. She actually felt as if her life was in danger.

"Now I don't have any proof that you were behind this, but I'm going to personally hold you responsible for Jessy's well-being. And if anything else happens to her, you will regret having been born."

"But... but you can't hold me responsible! How am I supposed to keep an eye on her all the time?" she asked, panic beginning to take over.

"That's something you'll have to work out while we're gone."

"You're leaving?"

"Yes. I'm taking Jessy to the ranch. It will be a while before we return."

"But that's my house!"

"No, Marie. It's my house, and Jessy will become its mistress."

Marie slowly rose to her feet. "You can't do this to me, Cortland."

"You brought it upon yourself, Marie. When we return, I hope you remember that I have made you personally responsible for Jessy. If you can't share a house with the woman who is my wife, then you had better move to a place of your own."

"Are you finished?"

"Yes."

Now for my dear wife, Cort thought as he followed Marie out of the room.

Hearing the metal gate creak, Jessy's first thought was that it still hadn't been oiled. But upon realizing it could be Marie with good news, she stood up, waiting hopefully for the woman to round the small group of trees. When she saw Cort and the thunderous look on his sun-darkened face, she groaned. After what had already happened this morning, she was in no mood to have a confrontation with him. She leaned over and started working again.

"I understand you've lost something," Cort said as he came to a halt behind her.

"Do you have it?" Jessy asked, trying to hide any telltale signs of concern.

"No, but what difference does it make? The carpetbag was old, so I told the servants not to bother looking for it."

"How dare you!" Jessy threw the shears to the ground, squared her shoulders and faced him. "It's mine, and I want it!"

Cort looked down at the ball of fire in front of him. Jessy's lavender eyes flashed with anger, and short strands of silver hair clung to her cheeks and damp temples. Though she wasn't aware of it, Jessy presented quite a tempting picture. "Why is it so important?" he asked innocently.

"Because it belonged to my father, that's why. I demand you to have the whole house searched!"

"You once told me it belonged to Jonathan."

"You must have misunderstood me."

"I didn't misunderstand you, my dear. The necklace was hidden in it, wasn't it?"

"You bastard! You do have it!" Completely out of control, she started pounding his chest with her fists. "I want it back, do you hear me? I want it back . . . and the money. It's mine!"

Cort was taken off guard by her assault, and it took a few moments to grab her flaying hands. But he hadn't missed a word she'd said. Next came her knee, trying to catch him in the groin. Missing, she resorted to kicking. With no other recourse, Cort put his foot behind her and shoved. Jessy landed hard on her rear. She jumped up and charged him with her head, but he easily stepped aside.

Next thing he knew she was pounding him on the back with all her might. Cort swung around and, grabbing a firm hand of hair, he held her at arm's length and watched her strike out at the air.

"Let me go, you coward...womanizer...thief...scum...blackmailer..." Exhausted, Jessy quit struggling, her breath coming in hard gasps.

Cort waited a moment to see if she had given up before turning her loose. She might be little, but she sure as hell was strong. "Now are you ready to finally tell me the truth?" he demanded. "Or am I going to have to turn you over my knee and give you a good spanking."

"You wouldn't dare!" Jessy spit out while trying to straighten her disheveled clothes.

"Don't bet on it. At this moment, I can't think of anything that would give me more pleasure. So you've had the necklace all along. And did I hear you say money?"

"You should know. You've got it!"

"You're wrong. I don't have it. You put your own neck in the noose this time, lady. How the hell did you hide it from me at the river? I went through everything." Seeing Jessy wasn't ready to supply him with the information, he started rubbing the small scar on his jawbone and thinking.

Jessy would have liked to climb in some hole and bury herself. How could she have been stupid enough to assume he had her belongings? She stood there, refusing to say another word.

"A secret compartment?" Cort asked.

Jessy turned her back to him.

"Of course. It had to be that. Considering your *beloved's* underhandedness, it would make sense. Who else knew about it?"

"No one."

"Not even BJ?" Jessy slowly turned, and Cort could see the uncertainty in her eyes.

"I don't know," she said, trying to think. "He and Jonathan did a lot of things together. I guess he could have known about the compartment. Do you think he did this? Are you telling me he was in the house?"

"Where did the money come from?"

Seeing no reason to continue with her lies, Jessy answered with the truth. "Gambling. While BJ was off grabbing up land, Jonathan would go to Kansas City. He always came back with a good sum of money. And of course there was the money he and BJ swindled together." Jessy relaxed. It felt good to finally tell the truth.

"If he had so much money, why did you live in a sod house?"

"He didn't want anyone to suspect just how much he had. I didn't even know until the night he was shot. He did talk about moving to Kansas City some day and buying a house."

"Is that why you wanted to go to Kansas City? To buy a house or to gamble?"

Jessy looked up at the man who always seemed to tower above her. Seeing a smirk on his face, Jessy stiffened. "No, I wanted to get away and start a life of my own. If you choose not to believe that, I'm not going to stand here and try and convince you."

Cort couldn't decide if she was telling the truth or not. That she had had the necklace from the start, plus the money to pay him off, didn't set well with him. "When I found you in Topeka, you offered to give me a down payment on the debt Jonathan owed. Did you plan to pay it with Jonathan's money?"

"Yes, but you had it in your head I'd been gambling or sharing my bed."

"Why didn't you give the money to me when I first came to your house?"

"I wish I had. But you were trying to take away the only money I had."

"Tomorrow we'll be leaving for the ranch, so you'd better see to your packing."

Jessy watched him walk away. "Cort," she called. "Who took the carpetbag?"

"I don't know," he said, stopping. "My guess is Yana, but BJ probably put her up to it."

Jessy went to the gazebo, feeling terribly alone. When would she be through with BJ once and for all? And was Cort taking her to the ranch for safety, or did he want to get rid of her so he could spend more time with his lady friends? She heard the gate screech again, but this time it was Marie.

"I brought you a bonnet, dear," Marie said in a friendly manner, a rare smile stretched across her face. "You really should wear one if you're going to be out here much longer."

"I'm coming in shortly. I have to start packing."

"Though Sheila and I shall miss you, I think going to the ranch will be good for you. And don't forget to take some of those herbs I showed you."

"Aren't you and Sheila going?" Jessy was already starting to worry. Would she be left at the ranch all alone?

"No, no, we couldn't possibly leave at this time. Sheila and I have too many social commitments."

"I see."

"I have to return to the house and tell Mrs. O'Grady what to fix for supper. Cortland said he won't be joining us, so we can have a nice little farewell party. Try not to stay out here too long, dear. Your face will turn red, and we certainly wouldn't want that to happen, would we?"

Marie hurried away, reminding Jessy of a black bumblebee.

All desire to work in the garden had fled. It was beginning to look so pretty, an absolute bed of colors and sweet odors. But when and if she returned, the weeds would have already grown back, so why should she waste her time?

That evening, Sheila, Marie and Jessy tried to act cheerful, though no one pulled it off successfully. However, Jessy did think it strange that Marie smiled a lot and was overly attentive toward her.

Chapter Ten

Though Jessy was itching to let the black gelding run, she held the prancing horse to a trot as the spring buggy covered the distance to the ranch. Cort had offered to take the reins, but Jessy refused, saying this was her first opportunity to drive any distance. Looking like a gunman in his black clothes, his gun belt riding low on his hips, Cort rode Emperor beside the buggy. Prudence, Byron, Mrs. O'Grady and the luggage would be following later, with one of Jessy's guards driving the carriage and the other one on horseback.

Absorbed in their own thoughts, Jessy and Cort exchanged few words as the miles passed. But when Cort pointed out the house in the distance, Jessy could no longer contain herself. Grasping the reins firmly in her gloved hands, she allowed the gelding to stretch out. Cort nudged Emperor, and the race was on.

Cort won easily, and had already dismounted when Jessy brought the buggy to a halt in front of the huge two-story house. He noticed how pink her cheeks were, and how her lavender eyes sparkled with excitement.

"I've been dying to do that ever since you gave me my wedding gift," she said, a bit out of breath.

Cort laughed. "Why didn't you tell me? We would have done it sooner. If you like, tomorrow I'll get you a horse and we can take a ride out on the range."

"No, thanks." Jessy giggled as she straightened out her skirts. "Sitting astride that mule, then riding your gray all the way to Topeka was enough for me."

"Then ride sidesaddle," Cort suggested, taking her hand and leading her up the three steps to the porch.

"And fall off? Not on your life."

"You mean you don't know how to ride sidesaddle?"

Jessy saw the challenge leap into his dark brown eyes. "No, and I don't intend to learn." As she untied the bonnet from beneath her chin and glanced at the large windowed front door, her humor quickly subsided. After a few days, Cort would probably leave her here alone.

Suddenly, Cort swept her up in his arms, and Jessy looked questioningly at his handsome face.

"A bride should always be carried over the threshold," he said with a broad grin. "Or at least that's what I've heard." He leaned down and opened the door. "I want to be sure I do everything right."

As always, Cort's lightheartedness was infectious, and Jessy found herself laughing. What a difference this was compared to her arrival at his house in town.

Again Jessy was introduced to all the servants, but this time by Cort, who made it quite clear that henceforth, Jessy would be their mistress, and they were to answer to no one else, not even Marie. Could it have been her imagination, Jessy wondered, or did the servants actually let out a sigh of relief upon hearing Cort's words?

The morning turned out to be quite an enjoyable one. After coffee and biscuits smothered with butter and jam, Cort took her through the first floor of the house, giving a detailed description of how long ago the place was built and how the house had been added to over the years. He also showed her the atrium, which was almost completed. The house and furnishings were beautiful, and the kitchen had a huge coal stove.

Upstairs, Cort pointed to the doors that led to Sheila and Marie's rooms, mumbling something about respecting their privacy. Then he showed Jessy her living quarters. If she had thought her room large in his other house, it was nothing compared to this. It was actually an apartment of two light and airy rooms. The furniture was white, gilded in gold, with touches of green and blue.

"My heavens!" Jessy exclaimed as she wandered about. "This looks like it was designed for a queen."

Jessy looked toward Cort, who was still standing in the doorway, his shoulder resting against the frame. He wasn't smiling. "You had this fixed up for me, didn't you?"

"Yes."

His dark eyes were studying her, and a lump formed in Jessy's throat. "Where are your rooms," she asked reluctantly.

"Through that door over there."

Jessy glanced to where he pointed.

"The room suits you, Jessy, dear. I thought it would. Didn't I say you'd want for nothing?"

Jessy knew that in essence, Cort was informing her he had kept his end of the bargain. Though she didn't want to, Jessy felt guilty. She had done nothing to hold up her end of the agreement. Yet he continued to bestow gifts and privileges on her, one after another. "I'll make you a good wife, Cort," she whispered.

"Oh? I didn't know it was a wife that I was actually looking for. You have, however, piqued my interest. Tell me. As far as you're concerned, just what does being a good wife entail?"

Jessy refused to blush. Instead, she raised her chin. "I'll see that your house is properly cared for, your meals are always ready and..."

"And?"

He remained where he was, and Jessy was reminded of the first time they had met. He had been dressed in black then also, and had leaned against the door. "I'll be a good companion, a friend you can discuss things with—"

"I want a woman, Jessy, not a friend. But you're afraid to let yourself be a woman, aren't you?" he asked vehemently. "You know you enjoyed every moment we spent together on our wedding night."

Jessy lowered her head. She could feel her face turning red, remembering.

"You know I want a son, I've never lied to you about that. But that doesn't mean in the process of creating one, two people can't enjoy the natural pleasures to be shared. I'll have you in my bed, Jessy," he stated in a low, determined voice, "I guarantee it. Fight it if you need excuses, but soon you'll come willingly and gladly."

"Cort..." Jessy looked up. Cort was gone.

Why can't he understand? she asked herself as she strolled to the window and looked out. But what was Cort supposed to understand when she no longer understood herself. Her arguments seemed to have lost their validity. She couldn't honestly deny the growing need that Cort had created in her on their wedding night.

Something caught Jessy's attention, and her eyes focused on the carriage arriving at the front door with Prudence and the others.

What with unpacking and being sure everything was properly put away, the day passed in a flurry of activity. It pleased Jessy when a servant came to her and asked if the laundry would still be done on Mondays. Even Mrs.

O'Grady consulted her about the evening meal. She discovered Cort had even made sure that clippings had been brought from the garden in town. Now she could have flowers year round. Jessy concluded that being wealthy wasn't bad at all. But again, Cort was doing all the giving.

It didn't occur to Jessy until she went downstairs for supper that this would be the first time she and Cort had eaten alone. She realized how much she had depended on Sheila and Marie to help keep a distance between her and her husband.

"You look lovely tonight," Cort said as he pulled her chair out at the long, mahogany dining table. "Is that one of your new dresses?"

"No," she lied, not wanting Cort to think she had put it on for him.

"I haven't seen it before. You wear white very well." He took his own seat.

Though his skin was dark from spending time out in the sun, it looked even darker against his doe-colored jacket and white shirt. Jessy couldn't help but notice how his thick, dark hair curled up at the ends as it met the collar of his coat. Immediately she turned her eyes away, paying attention to the bowl of snap beans being held in front of her by the maid. Jessy was grateful that Cort seemed disinclined to continue the conversation they'd had earlier in her room.

"I must compliment you on your selection of food," Cort said, taking a thick piece of succulent ham from the offered platter.

"Thank you, but Mrs. O'Grady really deserves the credit."

"Are you unpacked and settled in?" Cort asked, trying to make small talk. So far, all Jessy had done was toy with her fork.

"Yes, everything has been put away."

Seeing he wasn't going to get much conversation out of
Jessy, Cort decided to enjoy his food. In town she had been
quite talkative with Sheila and Marie during meals. It
pleased him to know she was finding it uncomfortable to be
alone with him. He had brought her here because he thought
it would be safer, but also to keep his presence constantly on
her mind. Now she had no one but him to turn to, or talk to.
One way or another, they were going to come to an understanding.

Jessy had trouble keeping her eyes on her food. For some
reason, she became fascinated with Cort's hands. They were
much larger and stronger than hers. He had amazingly long
tapered fingers. She noted how he cut his ham with the
agility of a doctor. Perhaps, she thought, it was his long
fingers that made him a quick draw with his gun. Though
she had never actually seen him draw, she knew he was fast.
And it was those same fingers that . . . Jessy took a quick
bite. Not particularly hungry, she ended up picking at her
food.

After the completion of their meal, Cort escorted Jessy to
the parlor.

"May I pour you some sherry?" he inquired as they entered the large, comfortable room.

"No, thank you, but feel free to fix yourself one. I'm
really much too full." Still feeling nervous and not sure what
to do or say, Jessy moved over to the piano.

Full? Cort found the comment amusing. She'd hardly
eaten a thing. "Do you play?" he asked, watching Jessy run
her finger across the ivory keys.

"No, but I wish I did." Jessy left the beautiful instrument and took a seat on the sofa. Again she became caught
up in watching Cort's actions as he moved to the sideboard
to pour his drink. It was feral . . . No, that wasn't right. There
was more of a supple quality to his walk. No wasted mo-

tion, and only the right muscles used when necessary. Very much like a cat, ready to pounce at any moment.

"Do you mind if I smoke?"

"Not at all. My father always enjoyed a good cigar after his evening meal."

Cort removed a long, slender cigar from the humidor, made a hole in the end with a pick, then lit it. Jessy had always enjoyed the smell of rich tobacco, and as a child had sat on the floor by her father's knee, wondering what it would be like to smoke. Now that she thought about it, and considering her insatiable curiosity, it was surprising she hadn't tried it at one time or another.

"Since I won't always be here to keep you company," Cort said, sitting across from her, "I hope taking care of the house and the atrium will be enough to keep you busy."

"Oh, I'm sure it will, and I love to read. You have so many books in the library, I doubt I could read them all in a lifetime." Realizing she was rattling on, Jessy made a mental note to slow her speech and talk intelligently. Of course if Cort would stop watching her with those knowing eyes, it would certainly help her peace of mind. "Do you plan on being gone a great deal?" she asked, tilting her chin just a fraction.

"No, I'll just be working around the ranch or going to Topeka to take care of business. I'm sure most of the time you can go to town with me."

"I see. Will Marie be upset with me running the house?"

Cort sat with his elbows resting on the arms of the chair, both hands holding the round glass in front of him. He looked over the rim at the silver-haired woman sitting so rigid and looking so damn pious. Jessy, he thought, needs to learn how to relax and stop taking everything so seriously. She's beginning to look and act like Marie. "It's my house, not hers, and now that you're my wife, you're free to do anything you like with it.''

''It's a beautiful home, and I certainly wouldn't want to change a thing. I'll try to save you money on food and household supplies.''

Cort released a throaty chuckle. ''Money is the least of my problems. Once every two weeks a buckboard is driven to town for supplies. Whatever you need, just tell one of the boys and they'll bring it back.'' If he was reading her face correctly, dear Jessy actually wanted to smoke. He found the idea interesting. The one thing he didn't want to do was curb the lady's curiosity.

Cort rolled the glass between his hands. ''How would you like a cigar, Jessy?''

''I...what?'' Jessy sputtered. He couldn't have possibly read her mind!

''Would you like a cigar?''

''No...I couldn't.''

''Have you ever tried one?''

''No, but—''

''Then how do you know you wouldn't like it?''

''I don't, but that doesn't mean... Cort, you know ladies don't smoke.''

''Nonsense. You never know what you'll like unless you try it. Besides, there are just the two of us, no one need ever know.''

''Well...'' Jessy was dying to try it, and surely one puff wouldn't hurt.

''Believe me,'' Cort said, returning to the sideboard, ''a cigar always tastes best with a good drink.''

A few moments later he handed her a glass filled with amber liquor and a cigar and proceeded to sit beside her.

''Now,'' he said, leaning forward, ''what you *don't* want to do is suck in your breath.''

Jessy listened intently, nodding.

Cort had never taught anyone to smoke before, and he was rather enjoying himself. "You simply want to draw in the smoke slowly, then blow it out. Now try it, that is unless you've changed your mind." Cort was hard put to keep from laughing as he watched Jessy's eyes become as big as saucers.

Jessy lifted the cigar to her lips and quickly inhaled. Immediately she broke into a fit of coughing.

Cort started hitting her on the back. "I told you not to swallow the smoke. Here," he said raising her hand with the glass, "take a drink."

The strong liquor only seemed to compound her problem, but after a minute, she was finally able to breathe normally. A thought suddenly entered Jessy's foggy brain. If she handled this right, she could probably get Cort drunk, thereby ensuring herself a good night's sleep.

She looked at Cort and, lifting her glass in the air, said, "Aren't you going to join me?"

He gave her a crooked grin. "Are you going to smoke with me?"

As Jessy raised the cigar to her lips, he took a long drink from his glass. This time Jessy did it right and, more than a little proud of herself, broke out laughing. She took another puff, enjoying the sensation of being able to do something men did, then followed it with a small sip of her drink.

This time Cort lifted his glass. "Bottoms up," he said lightheartedly.

Jessy compared the two glasses, and seeing his contained more than hers, she tipped hers up and drained the contents. Cort would soon find out she could hold her own.

*   *   *

Jessy's mouth tasted like foul wool. It was all she could do to drag herself out of bed and close the drapes across the windows. The sun shining in was like daggers to her eyes. Falling back on the bed, she let out a long groan. Every movement seemed to make her head ache that much more. She couldn't even remember what had happened last night, or when Prudence had put her nightdress on. She did remember finishing the cigar.

"Good morning," Cort said cheerfully as he bounded into the room. He went directly to the window and opened the drapes.

Jessy immediately jerked the sheet over her head. So much for getting him drunk, she told herself angrily. That he felt so good disgusted her.

"Breakfast is ready along with a large pot of coffee. I shall expect you downstairs in no more than thirty minutes. I've decided today is perfect for teaching you to ride side-saddle."

Jessy gritted her teeth. Why did he have to talk so loud? "I am not going downstairs, I do not want any breakfast and I am definitely not going to climb on a horse!"

"The fresh air will do you good."

"I repeat. I am not going downstairs, I do not—" The sheet was suddenly yanked away.

"Shall I dress you?"

Jessy glared at the man standing by her bed. His eyes told her he did indeed intend to dress her if necessary. "No!" she snapped at him.

"If you're not down in a half hour, I shall return and take care of whatever needs to be done."

"I can't possibly be ready in that short a time!"

"But I think you can. Prudence is already on her way to help you. The girl is going to be quite embarrassed if I have to return."

As Cort proceeded to leave the room, Jessy had an overwhelming desire to throw something at him. The man was absolutely devoid of pity!

Jessy sat stewing as Cort drove the black buggy over the range. A lead rope had been tied to the rear of the conveyance, and on the other end of the rope a roan horse followed with a sidesaddle on his back. Though Jessy was feeling considerably better after drinking some concoction Cort had literally forced upon her, plus several cups of black coffee, she wasn't about to admit it.

Jessy adjusted the frilly parasol she was holding over her head. Cort was comfortably dressed in boots, tight black pants and a white shirt with the neck open and the sleeves rolled up to his elbows exposing his strong forearms. His black hat was pulled low on his forehead. She had deliberately chosen to wear five petticoats, a dress with yards of material and covered with lace, bows and ribbons, a hat with flowers, white gloves and her parasol. Any man with half a wit would have known she couldn't possibly mount a horse in such an outfit and would have dismissed the entire project. Not her husband. He had made no comment whatsoever as to her attire, and they were now headed toward some unknown place for the ungodly purpose of teaching her to ride sidesaddle!

When Cort finally brought the buggy to a halt, Jessy didn't know what to think. On one side was lush grazing land, on the other a plowed field. The musty smell of freshly tilled dirt still hung in the air.

"Why are you stopping?" Jessy asked after Cort had stepped down from the buggy. "There aren't any roads here."

"The soft dirt will bog the horse down and make it easier for you to ride him," he explained, moving to the front of the buggy to hobble the horse.

"Wait just a minute! Are you telling me you chose a horse that I'm going to have to fight, plus learn to ride?"

Cort gave her a slow grin. "It will keep you on your toes, and you won't take things for granted. Besides, I'm not sure how he'll react to a sidesaddle."

Jessy could hardly believe she was hearing this! She could get killed! "I'm not going to do it!" she said, looking away.

Jessy's fury continued to build when Cort lifted her out of the buggy and stood her on her feet. Snatching the parasol, he gave it a toss and grabbed her firmly by the hand. She was marched around the buggy, and Cort released the slip knot of the lead rope. Jessy balked. "I am not going to do this!" she repeated. "Can't you see I'm not dressed properly?"

"What you're wearing was your choice, Jessy, dear. You knew what we were going to do, so obviously you thought your attire proper for the occasion."

Jessy didn't like the glint in his eyes. With her hand still firmly clasped in his, and leading the horse with the other hand, Cort headed toward the field. He half dragged and half pulled her along, the big clots of freshly plowed dirt bruising her feet through the soft soles of her shoes. She could hear material rip when her toe got caught in the hem of the long skirts.

To Cort, what had begun as something amusing was now out-and-out war. It had started the moment he saw the ridiculous dress Jessy had chosen to wear. He wasn't about to let her think she could pull such a stunt. Had she asked nicely, he would probably have backed away from the whole idea. Not now. He was going to stop her temper tantrums and bullheadedness one way or another, and this was a good place to start. The plowed field would serve two purposes. It would bog down the horse, and it would also take some of the fight out of his dear wife.

They continued on for what seemed like an eternity to Jessy. When Cort finally stopped, she looked back. The buggy seemed miles away.

Cort finally released her hand. Jessy knew that to try to flee was useless, so she straightened her hat, shoved back the hair that had fallen in her face and squared her shoulders. All right! She'd show him and ride the damn animal, dress and all. Her eyes shifted to the small saddle. How in the world did he expect her to sit on that little piece of leather with the pommel crooked on the side and only one stirrup?

"Come on," Cort said, motioning her forward.

Jessy suddenly had second thoughts. "You try it first, and I can see how it's done."

Cort smiled. "Now you know I'd do just about anything you asked of me, my sweet, but I'm afraid I wouldn't fit on that little saddle." He cupped his hands together. "Put your foot in here, and I'll give you a boost up."

Knowing she had no recourse, Jessy placed her left foot in his hands. As he raised her up, she lost her balance and threw her arms around his head while at the same time extending her other leg in an effort to make it to the horse's back.

The unexpected action knocked Cort off balance, causing them to tumble to the ground, which in turn spooked the horse. The gelding reared up and tried to pull away, but fortunately Cort maintained a firm hold on the lead rope.

Untangling himself from Jessy's skirts, Cort jumped to his feet. In a matter of moments he had the horse calmed down. Aggravated, he looked at Jessy, ready to give her a piece of his mind, but his anger was replaced with hoots of laughter upon seeing his beloved wife. Her skirts were hiked up around her neck, she was covered from head to toe with dirt, her hat rested on her ear and her hair hung in her dirty face.

Jessy grabbed a handful of dirt and flung it at him. The action only served to make Cort laugh all the harder. Furious, Jessy scrambled to her feet and kicked him on the shin.

Cort looked down at the small woman standing in front of him, hands on hips, her lavender eyes flashing with fury. Her full lips had taken on the quality of a most appealing pout.

"If you're through laughing," Jessy growled, "you can take me back to the house!" She continued to stare at him, ready to do battle.

"Would you like me to dust you off?"

Seeing the corners of his lips twitch, Jessy was tempted to kick him again. Instead, she turned to walk away. Suddenly two hands circled her waist, and the next thing she knew she was plopped sideways on the horse's back. Her hands groped for the curved pommel to keep from falling.

Cort picked his hat up off the ground and hit it against his leg, knocking off the dirt. "Do you want to learn?" he asked, putting the hat on.

"Do I have a choice?" she countered.

"Let's put it this way. Living on a ranch, you never know what might happen, and it takes a hell of a lot less time to saddle a horse than to hitch up a buggy."

Jessy nodded her head in agreement.

"All right. To begin, that thing you're holding on to for dear life is a cushioned horn to wrap your right knee around. Your left foot goes here," he said, placing her foot in the stirrup. "Now balance yourself so you can swing your leg around the horn."

Jessy managed to follow his instructions, even though she was wobbly and could feel the horse's nervousness beneath her. It frightened her to know she had absolutely nothing to grab onto.

For almost an hour, Cort led the horse around in a wide circle. Jessy felt quite proud of herself when Cort said, "Good girl. Now that wasn't so hard, was it?"

As they neared the edge of the plowed field, a breeze suddenly kicked up, causing Jessy's skirts to flutter. The movement spooked the horse, and without warning, he began kicking. Jessy felt herself flying in midair. She would never know how Cort managed to catch her, but the force of her fall threw them both to the ground, and she landed hard on top of him.

"Are you all right?" Jessy asked, scrambling off him. She couldn't stand hearing his gasps for air, and she didn't know what to do. Her first thought was to get help, but the horse had taken off, leaving a trail of dust behind him. Jessy brushed the dirt from Cort's face, tears starting to form in her eyes. Suddenly his arm came up and circled her neck. She fought against the pressure, and her head was slowly pulled toward his. "You no-account bastard!" she accused. "You were only acting!" Her head was so close she could feel his breath on her face.

"Something I learned from you," Cort said before placing his lips on hers.

Jessy struggled angrily. But her mind started saying something else. Why was she fighting? Hadn't she longed for, even dreamed of this happening? Why should she deny the hunger that ached within her? He was only kissing her, and already she could feel desire creeping into her blood.

When Jessy started kissing him back, Cort pulled her down beside him. Wrapping her in his arms, he rolled out of the dirt into the soft, knee-high grass. It had been too long since he had touched her, and it took every bit of self-control he possessed to keep from tearing her clothes off and satisfying his lust. As he kissed each closed eyelid, he reached up and removed the silly, battered hat hanging from her neck. He felt her arm curve around him, and she stroked his back while her body began making sensual movements. It pleased him to know that by making love to her so many nights ago, he'd released a tiger from its cage.

"Jessy," he said, his voice husky with desire, "I want to take your clothes off." He felt her body stiffen.

It suddenly occurred to Jessy where they were and that it was broad daylight. No man had ever seen her completely unclothed in the light. "What if someone rides by?" she exclaimed, her ardor starting to fade.

Cort chuckled. "What would anyone be doing out here? And if someone should happen by, they'd best keep riding if they know what's good for them."

Jessy sat up and looked around. The land stretched for miles in every direction, and she could see neither man or beast. She looked at Cort stretched out in the grass, a smile flickering at the corner of his chiseled lips.

"You want me to actually undress?" she asked, with a great deal of uncertainty.

"Uh-huh."

"I can't... I mean, no man has ever seen me without... and there's no roof over our head..."

Cort reached over and started undoing the buttons on the bodice of her dress. "And what about a man? Have you never seen one naked?"

"No," Jessy groaned. His arm was brushing across her breast as he slowly undid each button, and the fires within her were starting to build again.

Cort sat up and removed his boots. "Then I would say it's time you had an education," he whispered before placing his lips on the curve of her long neck. He trailed his tongue up to her jaw and across to her wanting lips, which were already partially open. Slowly he withdrew, Jessy's lips clinging to his until the last moment.

As he had done their first night together, Cort removed his shirt, but this time the rest of his clothes followed. Jessy couldn't take her eyes off him. The hard, corded muscles that she had only felt before seemed so much larger, and she suddenly wanted to run her fingers across the dark mat of curly hair on his chest. Jessy's eyes traveled up and met his warm brown ones.

"A body is a beautiful thing to behold," he said, "and certainly not something to be ashamed of, Jessy."

Undoing the last button, Cort tugged at the shirt, releasing it from beneath her, and slipped the garment over her head. It pleased him to discover she wasn't wearing a corset. Grasping the bottom of her chemise, he pulled it off, freeing her full breasts. The pantalets followed. He leaned back and blatantly admired the woman lying next to him in the sun.

"You're beautiful," he said. His desire was such that he had difficulty getting out the words.

"So are you," she whispered.

Bending closer, he sucked her firm, hardened nipple.

Jessy's pulse beat double time as Cort's mouth tugged gently at the brown area. The sun's warmth caressed her skin, and she felt more alive than she'd ever been in her entire life. Her body was screaming for satisfaction. "Please," she whispered, "I need you."

Jessy's arms circled his neck and she moaned with abandoned joy as Cort gently penetrated deep within her. Without being told, she wrapped her legs around his hips, enjoying the musky scent that was his alone.

After only a few hard thrusts, Jessy felt wave after wave of pleasure sweep over her, and still Cort continued. To her surprise, her need began to build again, until she thought she would die if she didn't receive satisfaction. She knew she was muttering and begging, but she wasn't even sure what she was saying, and she didn't care. Then everything exploded, throwing her into exquisite ecstasy and making her body a prisoner to Cort forever.

Chapter Eleven

Cort stood in the garden of his house in Topeka, inhaling the sweet smell of flowers and enjoying a good cigar. Winter would soon be showing its face, he reflected, already feeling a nip in the night air. Though Jessy had wanted to come with him, he still felt it was safer for her to remain at the ranch, at least until he heard something about BJ.

Cort's lips curved into a smile. Since three weeks ago, when they had made love in the field, Jessy had willingly become his bed partner. On more than one occasion she had sought him out.

It felt good to know that so far, his plans for Jessy continued to go well. She was becoming quite adept at riding sidesaddle. He'd also been quite pleased that she didn't bother him when he discussed business with his foreman, Russ Green, and she never complained when he went out to the pasture with Russ to discuss new breeding stock. More than once he'd arrived home late at night and found her curled up in a chair with a book. Still, Cort refused to be drawn in by the lady's charm. He just didn't trust her. Jessy never discussed the past, and his suspicions were a yoke around his neck, reminding him to beware.

Things just didn't fit. If she had loved Jonathan so much, how could she turn around and seem so fond of him? From

her actions, Jessy would have him believe she cared noth
ing for the dead man. But Cort knew better. The lady had
clearly expressed her love when she'd been poisoned and
wasn't aware of what she was saying. No lies or acting, just
the plain truth. And what about the money and the neck
lace she had lied to him about? And just what were her ne
farious dealings with BJ and Jonathan? He still couldn'
ignore the times she'd threatened to shoot him for turning
her body into a quivering mass of desire, albeit jokingly
Still, dear Jessy had to know that if anything happened to
him, she'd get everything. For the present, however, she
seemed content to remain with him. But why shouldn't she?
She was getting everything she could possibly need.

Cort had told Jessy he was coming to town to take care of
business, but part of that business was a will that would give
Marie and Jessy a sizable income for the rest of their lives.
If there was no son, Sheila would inherit everything when
she reached twenty-two.

Ashes fell from Cort's cigar onto his clothes. As he leaned
over to brush them off, a shot rang out, and a searing pain
ran through his left arm. He was momentarily stunned,
wondering if he'd conjured up the whole thing in his mind.
Then he heard the front gate bang shut. Shaking his head to
clear it, he took off running, hoping to catch the perpetra-
tor.

Cort circled the house several times, but found no one.
Blood had already started dripping off his hand by the time
he headed for the carriage house.

"Howdy, Mr. Lancaster," Tod greeted him cheerfully,
tossing aside the rag he was using to clean the carriages.
"Mighty nice night . . ." The younger man paused, noticing
the blood on Cort's shirt. "Mr. Lancaster, what happened?"

"Bridle and saddle Emperor and make it quick," Cort ordered as he collapsed onto the wooden chair by the door, his arm throbbing with pain. "And make damn sure nothing has been tampered with," he added as Tod rushed toward the tack room.

Cort was already weak by the time he reached the doctor's. Fortunately, Sidney Mattson was home.

"You were lucky, King," Sidney commented as he wrapped the injured arm. He studied the man sitting on the edge of the table. King's face was taut, and lined with pain. Sidney proceeded to place the arm in a sling, thinking how some men were just too damn hard. The bullet had taken a sizable chunk of flesh with it, but had not lodged in the arm. Even so, most men would have passed out by now. Not this one. He'd clenched his teeth, and nary a sound had left his lips. "You're going to have to be real careful so as not to pull the stitches out and start the bleeding again. Do you know who did it?"

"No, my back was turned."

Sidney shook his bald head. "Topeka's getting to be a mighty rough town. Before long, it'll be another Dodge City. It's not even safe to walk at night any more." He helped Cort off the table. "I'm going to drive you back in my buggy. And don't go giving me any back talk, boy. You've lost a lot of blood. I want you to stay in bed for at least two weeks."

When they arrived at the house, Sheila was waiting in the entry hall. Tod had told her about the blood. With his sister acting as though he was dying and Sidney telling him he'd be back in the morning to check the dressing, Cort headed for his room, his legs threatening to buckle beneath him. Fortunately Marie was out visiting. Having her there would have been the last straw.

The next morning, Sheila brought Cort's breakfast on a tray, and Marie was right behind her. Cort groaned. He'd had little sleep and wasn't up to listening to the woman's sharp tongue. He raised himself to a sitting position, not allowing the pain to show on his face. Sheila stuffed a pillow behind him then placed the tray on his lap.

"Shall I feed you?" she asked, her voice soft with worry.

"He looks well enough to feed himself," Marie remarked.

Cort glanced at the older woman before shaking his head. Seeing him disabled, Marie's claws were beginning to show. "I'm sure you're quite disappointed I only got a small nick in the arm, dear stepmother," he said smoothly, not wanting her to know how bad the wound was.

"As a matter of fact, yes."

"Mother! How can you say such a thing?" Sheila chastised.

"I've never made my feelings a secret, nor am I surprised. He was probably shot by someone holding a grudge, and it's too bad they didn't hit him in the heart."

Marie turned and left with Sheila following right behind. As they went down the hall, Cort could hear their angry arguing.

Marie doesn't know just how close she came to the truth, Cort reflected. Had he not leaned over, the bullet would have been in his heart. It infuriated him to know that BJ had caught him off guard again, and strangely enough, both times he'd been thinking about Jessy.

After a week, Cort had had all the coddling he could stand. Though his arm was stiff and still sore, he decided to put on his clothes and pay the sheriff a visit. Dressing proved to be more difficult than he'd anticipated, and he cussed himself for leaving Byron at the ranch.

"Cort!" Sheila gasped upon seeing her brother come down the stairs. "What are you doing up? I was just going to the kitchen to get you something to eat."

"I have business to take care of, and I certainly can't do it lying in bed."

"But you can't—"

"Don't tell me what I can't do," he bit out. At his sister's crushed look, he softened his voice. "I won't be gone long, and I'm not going to do anything I shouldn't."

Sheila gave him a weak smile.

When Cort returned home, the thunderous look on his face spoke volumes, and neither Sheila nor Marie was willing to buck the impending storm. They even kept their mouths shut when Cort announced they were all going to the ranch.

The next day, the small entourage headed southwest. Marie and Sheila rode in the spring buggy with their fringed parasols opened to protect them from the sun. Their large trunks were firmly strapped on the back. In front, Tod held the reins to a pair of prancing matched bays, while Cort rode Emperor alongside. The top of the buggy had been folded down at Sheila's insistence, and the vehicle moved at a steady but leisurely pace so as not to churn up dust from the road.

Sheila enjoyed the ride, knowing that before long snow would cover the ground. The blue sky had only a few white, puffy clouds decorating it, and the fresh air was exhilarating. For some time she watched a hawk lazily circling above. Marie's nose was still red from all the sneezing she'd done when they drove down the road with tall golden fields of wheat on either side, ready for reaping. But now they were traveling through open grazing land, and her stepmother appeared to be comfortable.

Because of their late departure and slow pace, they wouldn't arrive at the ranch until dark. But Sheila didn't mind. She needed to sort out her thoughts. The night before Cort had been shot, she had attended a dinner party given by the governor and his lovely wife. Her dinner partner had turned out to be divinely handsome and quite charming. She hadn't wanted to leave Topeka because Jordon Thomas had promised to pay her a call. It bothered Sheila to know Tom had been gone such a short time and she was already attracted to someone else. Perhaps she had more of her brother in her than she realized.

"I hope we brought everything," Marie complained, interrupting Sheila's daydreams.

"I'm sure we did, Mother."

"As usual, Cortland has given us absolutely no consideration. No one should be expected to leave with only a day's notice."

A sigh escaped Sheila's lips. She knew her mother was about to expound on Cort's bad traits. She lowered her parasol, her wrist tired from holding it.

"You put that right back up, young lady," Marie barked out. "You wanted the top down, so you can just accept the consequences. You certainly do not want a red face."

Slowly Sheila raised her arm. When they stopped for lunch, she'd have the top raised. She simply could not go all day holding the thing up. Parasols were so silly. What was wrong with letting the sun shine on her face? Why did women think their complexions had to look like china? The sun certainly didn't affect Jessy's looks.

"I suppose Jessica has completely rearranged my house."

"I don't know. Cort's said nothing about it to me." Sheila glanced over at her brother riding so straight and tall in the saddle. It hurt her to see the small lines of pain around his mouth.

"Jessica is too good for Cortland. She should have married someone who could make her happy."

Her mother's words of praise shocked Sheila, but she
made no comment. She preferred to return to her thoughts
of the handsome men pursuing her.

Cort was also deep in thought. His visit to the sheriff had
produced news he certainly hadn't expected. BJ was dead.
There was no question about it, the description matched
perfectly. A farmer had found BJ's twisted body on top of
a tree, left there by the tornado that had missed Kathleen.
The farmer, not knowing who the man was, had buried BJ.
Once the crops were harvested, the farmer had finally ridden into town to inform the sheriff of what had happened.

So who had cut his cinch and taken a shot at him? Cort
doubted very seriously an irate husband would have gone
that far, and all his enemies from when he was building an
empire had gone on to other things. Besides, had any of
them wanted revenge, why would they have waited so long?
That narrowed the number to two. Jessy and Marie.

Either one could have gotten the poison from Yana, and
who was to say Jessy hadn't given it to herself? Of course
not enough to kill her. It would be the perfect way to throw
off any suspicion. And hadn't Yana been sitting in the
room, completely unconcerned? On the other hand, Marie
had hired the girl. Both women had access to the carriage
house, but neither was around when he was shot. Now that
Jessy could ride, she could have easily come into town, then
returned to the ranch. He knew, even though it had been
years, that Marie knew how to handle a gun. Did Jessy? It
suddenly dawned on him how strange it was that Jessy and
Marie got along so well. Were the two women in cahoots?
And now that he thought about it, how did he know Jessy
had money and the necklace in the carpetbag? He certainly
hadn't seen them. Another lie?

Since no other attempts had been made on Jessy's life, Cort no longer felt concern for the lady's well-being. No, he was the target, and one way or another, he'd damn well find out who was behind all this. That's why he wanted the two women together. So he could keep an eye on them.

Shortly after noon, Cort motioned Tod to bring the buggy to a halt. Though he said nothing, he needed to rest his arm. While the women stretched their legs, Tod spread a rug on the ground for the ladies to sit on and eat the food that had been carefully packed in a woven basket. When the trip resumed, the top of the carriage had been raised.

Jessy had tried to remain busy and push thoughts of Cort to the back of her mind, but as the days passed, she had sunk into a deep depression. Prudence and Mrs. O'Grady constantly scolded her, saying she was eating less than a bird, but Jessy had no appetite. She couldn't tell the well-meaning pair how much it hurt to know Cort had not returned. He had told her he'd be gone no more than four days, and a week had already passed. No wonder he hadn't taken her with him. She couldn't help but believe he was enjoying another woman's pleasures. She thought of Amy Rothchild. Though the woman was admittedly attractive, Jessy couldn't understand why he would seek out the favors of a woman so much older.

By the second week, Jessy's lethargy had passed and was replaced with pure rage. She'd be damned if she'd let another man drag her down. Two people could play the same game, and if she found one of the cowhands particularly interesting, she'd have no qualms about taking him to her bed. She'd been a fool not to encourage Tom. Even though nothing had ever been said, Jessy knew he would have welcomed the opportunity. And hadn't Cort talked about leading separate lives when he was trying to get her to marry him?

With the same energy she had used to tackle the flower garden in town, Jessy attacked the house. She insisted the structure go through a complete cleaning. The servants tried to remind her it wasn't spring, but Jessy turned a deaf ear. Everyone fell into bed at night as the woman, who never seemed to tire, worked their tails off. Jessy also spent time in the completed atrium. She drew a certain peace from the plants and large fountain in the center, and it helped to calm her frayed nerves.

If she wasn't planting flowers or cleaning, Jessy was out riding the range, familiarizing herself with the area. The cowhands waved their hats in recognition as she rode by. She even developed the beginning of a friendship with the foreman, Russ Green, and his wife. Jessy enjoyed being around the happy couple, and spent several nights at their small house playing cards. Russ was hard muscled where Eula was plump, and both were in their early fifties, tall and jovial, with brown graying hair. In her own way, Jessy was beginning a life that had no need for Cort.

When Jessy heard a carriage drive up to the front of the house, she went out on the long porch to greet her visitors. A smirk formed on her lips at the sight of Sheila and Marie. She didn't even look at Cort. Had he brought the women as a buffer, or better yet as a peace offering? Jessy was happy to see the two of them. In all truthfulness, she'd been quite lonely.

Marie and Sheila deposited their bonnets and parasols on the hall tree. Continuing on, they entered the parlor. Marie was quite pleased to see how clean everything looked, and that Jessica hadn't changed a thing.

"Would you care for tea?" Jessy offered.

"Have it sent to our rooms," Marie commanded. "Come along, Sheila. One should always make sure the servants put things away properly."

Jessy watched the women head up the wide stairs. "Supper will be ready soon," Jessy said before hurrying off to the kitchen.

Cort was the last to enter the house. Pleased to see no one around, he headed directly for the study, in need of something to relieve the pain in his arm.

After pouring a stiff drink, he sank down in his father's favorite chair and tried to relax.

Taking a sip, Cort allowed the liquid fire to trickle slowly down his throat. His eyelids felt heavy, and in a few minutes he dozed off, the glass falling to the floor, the whiskey being soaked up by the carpet.

Once Jessy had informed Mrs. O'Brian that the family had returned and sent the maids scurrying up to help Sheila and Marie, Jessy retired to the atrium. She knew she was deliberately avoiding Cort, but she didn't care. He certainly wasn't going out of his way to find her. In his absence she had had the door between their rooms and leading to the hall strongly reinforced, and outfitted with sturdy wooden bars that fit into a slot and locked with a key. No amount of kicking would knock them down now.

Jessy had no intention of joining the threesome for supper. Instead she took some food to her rooms and locked the door. She'd spend the rest of the evening curled up in her bed, reading. She hadn't seen Cort since he arrived with the carriage, which was all for the better. There was no doubt in Jessy's mind that she and Cort were eventually going to have a fight, but it could wait until tomorrow.

Jessy awoke just as the sun peeked over the horizon. Still disinclined to see Cort, she decided a long ride would clear her head. Quickly she pulled out the blue riding habit Prudence had made. Jessy had been overjoyed to discover the girl was so handy with a needle.

Jessy rode for some time through buffalo grass, enjoying the stillness broken only by the swishing grass and the birds singing to one another. Occasionally a magpie would fly by, seeking a prize tidbit, its black and white feathering easily recognizable.

When Jessy heard a horse coming up rapidly from behind her, she turned, but wasn't surprised to see Cort atop his gray stallion. Resigned to her fate, Jessy pulled back on the reins and waited.

"How nice that you finally decided to return home."

Cort chuckled. "Tell me, my dear sweet wife, did you miss me?"

"Should I have?" Jessy nudged her horse, and Cort followed alongside. "There are too many men on this ranch for me to worry about your comings and goings."

Cort reached down and grabbed the reins close to the bit, bringing her horse to an abrupt halt. "What the hell are you saying?" he demanded. Ignoring the pain that shot up his arm, he held firm.

"I'm saying, if you can spend your time in Topeka bedding your lady friends, I can certainly have male friends!" Jessy tried to act unconcerned, but knew she wasn't doing a good job of pulling it off.

"Like hell you can!"

"Please try to remember, you are the one who showed me the pleasures of being with a man, and you're the one who said we could live separate lives. Now are you telling me that it only applies to you?"

"That's exactly what I'm saying. I'll be damned if I'm going to raise a child when I don't even know who the hell it belongs to! I could care less what you do after that!"

Jessy was just as furious as Cort, and she had a desperate need to hurt him as he'd hurt her. "And who's to know?" she said flippantly. "You can't keep an eye on me all the time, Mr. Lancaster." Her horse began moving its rump around nervously, but Jessy had no trouble keeping her seat. "Now turn my horse loose and leave."

Cort jumped off Emperor, grabbed Jessy around the waist with his right arm and jerked her off the saddle. "Now you listen to me, Jessy," he said, stepping away, "if I catch you with another man, or even so much as hear rumors, the man is dead, and you will be shipped off to Timbuktu! Do I make myself clear?"

As always when he was angry, his voice had become low and very quiet. The small scar that ran along his jawbone had turned almost white from the effort it took to contain his temper, and his eyes were black with anger.

In a burst of rage, Jessy raised her quirt and began striking him across the arm. Suddenly she stopped the quirt in midair. Several spots of blood had appeared on his shirt. "Oh, my God," she whispered, "what have I done?"

Seeing her face turn pale with worry, Cort's anger began to subside. There was no woman he knew who could make him want to strangle her and make love to her at the same time. If she chose to act as though she cared, why shouldn't he take advantage of it? He pulled her to him, kissing her deeply and feeling her resistance fade. She was more woman than any female he'd ever met.

Jessy slowly pulled her mouth away, "We can't," she whispered as his hand cupped her already swollen breast. "Your arm."

"To hell with my arm, I have a greater need."

After they made love, Cort and Jessy remained on the soft bed of grass, their naked bodies still entwined. Though she knew loving Cort left her vulnerable and that he didn't return her love, she couldn't stop her feelings. Cort was her life. When he told her about getting shot and having spent most of his time recovering in bed, Jessy guiltily accepted that her jealous rage had been over nothing.

"Do you think it was BJ who shot you?" Jessy asked, running her hand over the dark mat of hair on his chest.

"No, I think whoever did it mistook me for someone else," he lied smoothly, "and I think BJ has probably returned home and given up."

Jessy rolled over on her back, staring at the blue sky. "I hope so," she whispered, but not convinced. Plucking a piece of grass, she stuck it between her teeth.

"Just to be on the safe side, you should carry that derringer when you go riding by yourself," Cort cautioned.

"I do."

"Can you shoot accurately with it?"

"I don't know. I've never fired it."

What did you expect? Cort asked himself. Naturally Jessy wouldn't admit to knowing how to fire a gun, especially if she was guilty. Stupidity was certainly not one of her faults.

Taking the grass from her mouth, Jessy playfully ran it back and forth across his chest.

The sun to her back formed a halo around Jessy's hair, making the silver sparkle and dance when she moved her head. Her lavender eyes were doelike and deep in color. She had high, firm breasts, a waist so small he could easily put his hands around it, nicely rounded hips and long, well-shaped legs. A truly beautiful woman. It occurred to him that he wished to God he could believe Jessy's innocence, but he couldn't afford the luxury. More than one man in history had fallen because of a beautiful woman.

"I think we should be heading back." Cort reached for his clothes. "I don't know about you, but I'm hungry as a bear."

"And I can rebandage your arm," Jessy said, getting to her feet. "I'm pretty good at doctoring."

"Oh?"

"Mammy Mae taught me a lot. She pretty much raised my mother and me, and when we came West, she came with us." Jessy started putting her clothes on. "Of course a lot of her remedies could only be found in the South."

"Like what?" Cort encouraged. Like poisons? he wondered.

"Well, if someone had an earache, she'd peel back rotted wood and catch snapping bugs. She'd pop the neck of the shoulders of the bug and take the one drop of oil and place it in the ear."

"Did it work?"

"Every time."

Cort gave Jessy a hand up on her horse, then mounted Emperor. "Tell me some other things," he said as they headed the horses toward the house.

"Oh, you're really not interested in that sort of stuff."

"But I am."

"Well, let me think," Jessy said, not realizing she was digging a deep hole for herself. "She would boil sheep sorrel then mix it with goose grease. It was a salve for cuts and abrasions, and smelled a lot better than the buffalo grease they used on the wagon train. And did you know that if you boil vinegar and hold your head over the fumes it will get rid of headaches?"

"Is that a fact?"

Jessy continued on about various cures, but Cort paid little attention. He'd heard enough.

"Let's go to the kitchen and I'll take a look at your arm," Jessy stated as they rode up to the big house.

"No," Cort replied, his tone gruff. "I'll take the horses to Tod and he can cool them down. If my arm needs rebandaging, Byron can take care of it."

"But—"

Jessy watched her husband gather the reins and head toward the corral. Is he mad about something? she wondered. He certainly has no reason to be. It must be my imagination.

Her step jaunty, Jessy entered the house and headed for her room. She wanted to make sure the bars were removed from her doors before Cort saw them.

Chapter Twelve

It was starting to become light outside when Jessy felt Cort climb out of her bed. She'd been awake for some time, bu chose to keep her back turned and feign sleep. For a mont now, their coupling had changed from pleasurable giving t raw need. They no longer talked and laughed, yet Cort sti made sure their lovemaking was a satisfying experience fo both of them. She enjoyed...wanted...needed his love, bu felt used.

Jessy waited until she heard the adjoining door close be fore rolling over. She stared at the imprint where her hu band had been lying only moments ago. This was the fir time he'd spent the entire night with her since his return month ago. She had no idea why they now made love in he bed instead of his. Slowly she ran her hand along the in dentation.

"How touching."

Lifting her head, Jessy saw Cort standing near the doo His lean, sculptured face looked set in stone, and she kne he was angry about something. Not wanting an argumen she chose to ignore the taunt and smiled. "Good mor ing," she said in a pleasant voice. "You were so quiet, didn't even hear you slip into your robe."

"I didn't think you were asleep, my sweet," Cort said scathingly. "Tell me, is there ever a time when you're not acting?"

Holding the cover to her chin, Jessy sat up. "What do you mean by that?"

"I thought it was a simple question. Since my return, you've gone out of your way to be the perfect wife. Why, I ask myself."

"What in the world are you talking about? When you first brought me to this house I told you I would do everything I could to be a good wife. Now you sound like you're damning me for it!"

"And I told you I wasn't looking for a wife, I wanted a mother for my son. But that hasn't happened, has it? Can you explain why?"

"No...I can't," Jessy replied nervously. She couldn't look him in the eye, so she began tucking the cover around her. "We probably haven't given it enough time."

"Now this is an interesting twist. Am I to believe my dear wife has become docile and now wants to have my child? Or has she been deceiving me all along?"

Fear started to creep into Jessy's veins. Had he found out about the herbs? "I don't know what you're talking about," she said defensively.

Cort studied his wife. Even after their night together and little sleep, she was still beautiful. Her silver mane cascaded around her face, and her eyes seemed to beckon him into their lavender depths. The devil's temptation, he reminded himself. "Perhaps you've known all along that you can't have children but didn't bother to inform me. I find it rather strange that after being married to Jonathan for five years, plus your romps with BJ—and let's not forget our time together—there are still no children." He cocked an eyebrow.

"Why are you making these accusations now, Cort?" Fear was quickly being exchanged for anger. "If you had your doubts, why didn't you confront me with them before we married? I told you I never had anything to do with BJ, but you persist in believing differently. And as for Jonathan, he never touched me after our wedding night."

Cort snickered viciously and leaned against the door. "Do you honestly expect me to believe that?"

"No, because you don't want to. You'd rather think the worst of me. If you didn't, you might learn to like me, or possibly fall in love with me. That's what you're afraid of, isn't it?"

"You're deluding yourself, my dear. But now I understand what you've been up to. If you could get me under your thumb, you'd have everything, including my forgiveness for not producing an heir. Well, think again. It won't happen. I'm going to have my lawyer draw up a will that stipulates that without a son, you get nothing. And while I'm at it, I'll also make sure my dear stepmother receives nothing. Everything will go to Sheila when she reaches twenty-five."

"You can't be that cruel!" Jessy proclaimed, knotting her fists in the cover. "Marie's an old woman! How do you expect her to live?"

"Very well done, darling! Another brilliant performance, I must say. Your concern for Marie instead of yourself is most touching. But to answer your question, if the cards were turned, Marie wouldn't bat an eye at kicking me out without so much as a penny. Even the smartest of people can become victims of their own traps, you included. Be careful you're not the one who falls in love, my dear." He left the room, shutting the door silently behind him.

Jessy shivered. Not from the cold room, but from Cort's words and expression. "He really doesn't love me!" she whispered. She'd thought, hoped, even prayed, but it wasn't going to happen.

Jessy forced herself to climb off the bed, the same bed that they'd made love on such a short time ago. Dragging the cover with her, she moved to one of the two high-backed chairs adorning her room.

As she'd done on other occasions, Jessy wondered what had happened in Topeka. Sheila's story about the shooting had certainly not produced any clues.

Jessy rubbed her throbbing head, remembering how, prior to Cort's trip to town, they had spent most of their time together. He'd been everything she could ever want in a lover or a husband. She had truly thought . . . but now he was cold and throwing out vicious accusations, the way he'd done when they'd first met.

Has he fallen in love with someone else and does he regret our marriage? she wondered. The thought of another woman in Cort's arms threw Jessy into a fit of jealousy. Bounding off the chair, she marched to the adjoining door. "If you want a divorce, that's fine with me!" she yelled as she jerked the door open. The room was empty.

The air was crisp, the sky dreary, and Cort could hear the cracking of thin ice beneath Emperor's hooves as they moved across grazing land. "Snow'll be here soon," he grumbled as he buttoned his sheepskin-lined coat. He leaned down and patted Emperor's strong neck. "We'll be at the line shack soon, boy, and you can have some fresh hay."

It had been a week since he'd left the house after his words with Jessy; a week of riding from one herd to another, seeing that all was in readiness for winter and checking to be sure Russ was still doing a capable job. His being gone would also allow Jessy and Marie to stew over his proposed will. For over a month he'd stayed around the house, waiting for another attempt on his life. When nothing had happened, he knew it was time to force the issue. Telling Jessy about the will was his way of bringing the culprit out in the open. She would in turn tell Marie, and one of them would be forced to make a move. Tomorrow morning he'd head home and wait for the ax to fall.

Cort frowned, thinking about the hurt look on Jessy's face when he'd left her. Damn! he thought. The minx almost had me right where she wanted me. I was beginning to let her get under my skin. Thank heavens I found out about BJ when I did. Even if she isn't the one behind these attempts, how can I honestly believe anything she says? A woman of quality would never have loved, married or stayed with a man like Jonathan, let alone condone the man's actions. No, people tended to want to be with their own kind, and BJ and Jonathan were far from saints.

Cort was near the bottom of a small hill when a shot suddenly rang out, the bullet hitting the ground in front of him. Cort sank his heels into the stallion's sides and reached for his rifle. But before he could pull it from the scabbard, there was a second shot, and Emperor stumbled. Kicking free of the stirrups, Cort jumped. The next shot brought the horse to the ground a short distance away.

Out in the open and defenseless, Cort started running in a zigzag manner toward the animal. Several shots peppered the ground around his feet, but none hit home. He knew it was useless to draw his revolver. The person shooting was using a rifle and was out of range.

When he got close enough, Cort made a dive for the horse's heaving underbelly. The shooting had stopped. Knowing the gunman was reloading, Cort pulled his rifle free and waited. When the person fired again, he'd know where to aim. But instead of a shot, he heard the sound of a horse galloping away out of sight behind the hill.

Cort reached out and gently patted Emperor's bulging stomach. The stallion's breathing was labored and raspy. Cort stood and slowly raised his rifle.

"Don't you get tired of spending so much time out here?"

Jessy looked up at the woman in black. "Not really," she replied as she placed the spade in the dirt and removed her work gloves. Jessy knew that after their conversation several days ago, Marie had been waiting to catch her alone in the atrium.

"Dear, just how long do you think Cortland intends to be gone?"

"I have no idea, Marie. He didn't even bother to tell me he was leaving."

"Certainly you don't think he was serious, do you?"

"If you're referring to the will, my answer is yes."

"Did you try talking him out of it?"

"Marie, we've already gone over this." Picking up the spade, Jessy started thinning out the canna bulbs again. "More discussion isn't going to change a thing."

"Unless I can convince you that getting pregnant would be advantageous to all of us."

"Pregnant?" Jessy gasped as she spun around. "How can you even suggest such a thing? I don't want to have a child by a man who doesn't love me."

"Now you sound like Sheila. A child would secure your future, and you would have someone to love."

Jessy stared at the woman. As always, Marie stood straight with her hands clasped in front of her. "I don't think you understand, Marie. My first marriage was to a man I didn't like, and now I'm married to someone who doesn't like me." She removed her gloves and brushed off the front of her once white apron. "Strangely enough, the two marriages have a lot of similarities. I've already been through this once, and I'm not sure I can continue to live in a house that harbors so much bitterness and mistrust again. Having a child isn't going to change that. From what I've heard and what you've told me, your marriage certainly was not a love match. Has the fighting and loneliness really been worth it, Marie?''

"A woman hasn't much choice. She does what she has to do to survive."

Jessy was surprised at the hurt that momentarily flashed across the older woman's face. "I'm sorry," Jessy quickly added. "I had no right to say that. I'm upset."

Marie walked over and took Jessy's hands in hers. "You love Cortland, don't you?"

"Of course not!"

"You poor girl. I honestly believe Cortland is incapable of loving anyone. Does he know?"

Jessy shook her head, fighting to hold back the tears that were suddenly threatening.

"My dear, you are a good woman, far better than Cortland deserves. I have some money saved, and a good deal of jewelry. Should you decide to move on, let me know, and I'll help you. Now, enough said. Did you know Sheila received a letter from Thomas Sterling a little while ago?"

"No," Jessy answered, relieved at the change of subject. "What did he say?"

The two women started walking toward the doorway.

"I have no idea," Marie replied. "She went straight to her room and hasn't made an appearance since. You look like you haven't eaten in days, dear," she said, looking at Jessy's thinning body. "What do you think of the two of us going to the kitchen and getting Mrs. O'Grady to fix us something to eat?"

"Do you think I should go up and see Sheila?"

"Heavens, no. The girl never could keep a secret, and before long she'll be down telling us everything. I do hope something develops from this relationship. Thomas appears to be just the man to control that girl. Cortland has put too many grand ideas in her head."

Carrying his sleeping roll, saddle bags and rifle, Cort had taken off on foot, stopping only when it became too dark to see. As soon as the sky began to lighten he continued, cussing the blisters on his feet from the heeled boots, which were not designed for walking.

Not until the afternoon of the third day did he finally meet up with a cowhand riding line.

"What the hell happened, boss?" the hand asked as he slipped his foot from the left stirrup so Cort could climb up behind the saddle. "You look like you've been through hell. Where's your horse?"

"Broke a leg, and I had to shoot him," Cort lied.

Sam nodded his head knowingly and nudged his horse forward. He knew what it was like to lose a good cow pony. A cowhand's life could be pretty lonely, and his horse was not only a means of making a living, but many a time someone to talk to.

When they reached the line camp, Cort slid off the horse's rump and thanked Sam for the lift. Riding double wasn't the most comfortable way to travel, Cort thought, but it sure as hell beat walking.

By the time Cort was through grabbing a quick meal at the chuck wagon, one of the men had caught a mustang from the herd and had him saddled. With a nod of thanks, Cort leapt into the saddle and headed the horse toward home.

Most of the men were out working when Cort rode up to the corral. He was tired, furious and frustrated that he wasn't any closer to discovering who wanted him dead than when he'd left.

Cort dismounted, opened the gate and led the mustang inside.

"Howdy, Mr. Lancaster. Where did you leave Emperor?"

Cort turned and saw Tod standing outside the tall split rail fence. What caught Cort's attention was the rifle tucked under the young man's arm. "Emperor's dead," he informed Tod as he removed the bridle and saddle from the horse. Free, the mustang headed toward the other horses enjoying the fresh hay piled in one corner.

"I'm sure sorry to hear that, Mr. Lancaster. He was a fine animal. Not another one like him in these parts."

"That's a good-looking iron, Tod. Where did you get it?" Cort asked as he closed the gate and looped the leather thong around the post.

"Found it right near here a few days ago. No one seems to know who it belongs to, so I thought I'd just hold on to it. Is it yours?" He handed the rifle over to Cort.

"Nope." Cort cocked it open and looked down the inside of the barrel. "Doesn't look like it's been fired lately."

"It was pretty dirty, but I cleaned it. A nice piece like that should be taken care of. Can't imagine why anyone would just leave it."

"Well, Tod, looks like you've got yourself a rifle," Cort said, handing it back to the young man.

"Thanks, Mr. Lancaster," the boy said excitedly. "I've never had a gun before."

"Well, make sure you learn how to fire it properly."

As Cort entered the front door he was greeted with the sound of busy voices and laughter coming from the salon

It grated on him to know his family was having such a pleasant day.

Standing in the doorway, Cort watched the seven or so women attending one of Marie's teas. Everyone was talking at once, even Sheila and Jessy, who were sitting sedately on the sofa. It reminded Cort of hens clucking around a chicken pen. He glanced at Marie, who was regally positioned on her favorite chair looking like the queen bee.

One of Marie's friends looked up and saw Cort. "Oh," she uttered, placing her hand on her breast in an overly dramatic manner.

All eyes turned toward the doorway.

"Ladies," Cort said, tipping his hat. He strolled over to the sideboard, poured a stiff drink of whiskey, downed it, then lit a cigar. He deliberately allowed the smoke to drift toward the women.

"Cortland!" Marie snapped.

"Excuse my bad manners, ladies." Cort held up his empty glass and cigar. "Would anyone care to join me?" He grinned as one woman, then another stood and made a weak excuse about having to return home.

"I hope you're satisfied, Cortland," Marie stated after the women had departed. "How can you run off my friends by coming in looking like that? It only goes to prove what I've said for years. You're no good." She leaned over and removed her embroidery from the basket.

"Marie is right. Why would you act like that?" Jessy demanded.

"Now that I've heard from my beloved wife and stepmother, do you have anything to add, Sheila?"

"No," Sheila answered, her head lowered.

"Very well, now I'll have my say. Someone tried to kill me a few days ago, and it's not the first attempt that's been made on my life.'' Cort watched the surprised look on the three faces, almost as if on cue.

"Oh, Cort, who would want you dead?'' Sheila asked worriedly.

Marie let out a snort. "Probably half the state.''

"Funny, I can only think of two, and they're sitting in this room.'' Taking his time, Cort refilled the glass then sat on a soft light-rose chair. Tossing his dusty hat on the floor, he stretched his legs, defying anyone to say a word about his filthy clothes.

"I think you have gone too far this time, Cort!'' Jessy said, rising to her feet.

Cort's brown eyes turned hard. "Sit down, Jessy.''

She remained standing.

"Sheila, I want a word alone with these two women.''

"But Cort, Jessy or Mother would never do—''

"Go to your room.''

Sheila rushed out crying.

"Now, ladies, it's time we call a spade a spade. I've come to the conclusion that one or both of you want me dead. But think again. After I left here, I went directly to Topeka and signed a will. I'm sure you both know what's in it by now.'' He took a drink then gave the two women a hard look. "Killing me will get you nothing. I suggest you both start walking a very narrow path, because if I ever discover who's been trying to take my life, I'll personally escort her to the sheriff. Do I make myself clear?''

"I've had enough of this!'' Jessy hissed. "I don't know what's come over you, Cort, but I for one refuse to be a part of it. I'm leaving, and if you want a divorce, that's fine. Go find someone else to have your children!''

Cort grinned. "As a matter of fact, we're all leaving.''

"What do you mean we're leaving?" Marie demanded. "You can't expect us to keep moving back and forth from one house to the other because of your whims."

"Now that we have an understanding, I think it is a good idea to spend the winter in town. I've neglected my friends for too long." He stood and walked over to Jessy. "As for a divorce, my sweet, you can forget it. I've decided being married can be most beneficial." He leaned over and placed a kiss on her cheek.

"Not for me," Jessy stated as she wiped the spot with the back of her hand. "I'm sick of this conversation. I'll be in my bedroom until supper is ready."

"We'll be leaving in two days," Cort called after her.

Jessy banged her door shut, fell on the bed and began pounding the white spread with her fists. "The nerve! How can he stand there and accuse me of trying to kill him! The idea is tempting, though. At this moment I'd like nothing more than to wring his stubborn neck!"

Rolling onto her back, Jessy stared at the ceiling as she kicked one slipper, then the other onto the floor. "How could I possibly have felt sorry for him standing there in the doorway?" But she had. Jessy thought about how haggard his handsome face had looked, how his shirt, pants and coat had been covered with dried dirt. He had the appearance of a man who had been on the trail for weeks. Even the beard indicated it. Had someone really tried to kill him? If so, why would he accuse her and Marie? Surely it had to be BJ raising his ugly face again.

Jessy heard muffled voices coming from Cort's room. He's probably having Byron attend to his every need, she thought bitterly. "Oh, Cort," she whispered, a tear falling from the corner of her eye, "why can't things return to the way they were when we first came here? We were so happy."

Rising from the bed, Jessy unbuttoned her yellow day dress and let it fall to the floor. "I'm not going to let you do this to me, Cort," she uttered as she wiped the tears from her cheek. "I won't let you drag me down the way Jonathan did."

Little was said during the evening meal. Jessy had hoped Cort wouldn't make an appearance, but she should have known better. She'd thought about eating in her room, but considering Cort's mood, it would have been just like him to come after her.

Glancing across the table, Jessy suddenly wondered if her face was as white as Sheila's and Marie's. Cort, clean shaven and dressed in a brown suit, seemed to be the only comfortable person at the table.

"I received a letter from Tom," Sheila announced uncertainly when dessert had been served.

"Oh?" Cort responded before taking a bite of the chocolate cake.

"He's going to stop here on his way back from Colorado."

"Did he say when he'd arrive?"

"Next week."

Cort shoved his chair back, his appetite suddenly gone. Though he was loath to admit it, he didn't want Tom around Jessy. "Is he planning to stay awhile?" he finally asked.

Because he truly sounded interested, Sheila gave her brother a brilliant smile. "I guess that depends on how we feel after not seeing each other for some time."

"I guess it does." He looked at Marie, then Jessy. "It's been a long day. If you ladies will excuse me, I think I'll retire for the night."

As soon as Cort had left the dining room, Marie spoke up. "I do believe Cortland is going mad."

"Mother, I won't have you saying that about him."

"Well, what would you call it?" Marie asked after finishing her dessert. "He has accused Jessy and me of trying to kill him!"

"Jessy, surely you don't believe he's going mad?"

Jessy could see the pleading look in Sheila's black eyes. "I don't know what to think. His moods have been a puzzle ever since I've known him. He doesn't confide in me, and I can't even begin to guess what's on his mind."

"Well, I for one do not believe he's going mad," Sheila persisted. "Something is bothering him deeply, and I think we should give him all the support we can until he works it out. I know Cort, and I'm sure that, given time, he'll return to his old self."

"That doesn't excuse his accusations, Sheila!" Marie snapped. "How would you feel if he'd included you? Even his old self isn't much better. Cortland sets his own rules and expects everyone to follow them. It frightens me to think of the example he's set for you. Why do you think I've wanted you to marry? To be rid of his influence, that's why!"

Sheila and Marie were still bickering when Jessy went to her rooms. Both women had valid arguments, and she didn't know what to think.

Jessy remained awake late into the night, wanting and not wanting Cort to join her. When she decided she would be spending the night alone, she rolled onto her side and fluffed the pillow beneath her head. Before falling asleep, she wondered how it was possible to love and hate at the same time.

Chapter Thirteen

As she sat in the carriage with Sheila awaiting the arriving train, Jessy couldn't help wondering about Tom. Would there still be that unspoken attraction between them? She really hadn't wanted to come with Sheila, but she'd finally given in to Marie's insistence. Marie had wanted to remain at the house and be sure all was in readiness for the arrival of their guest. Jessy knew Marie had no intention of allowing Tom to leave again without a commitment of marriage to her daughter.

Jessy pulled back the heavy covering over the carriage window and looked at the snow-covered ground. She watched some men enter the Harvey House. It seemed like ages since she'd worked there. She'd visited there several times lately, but only to see Miss Cragshaw. Kathleen and Lora had married and left while she'd been living at the ranch.

"I hope Tom's train is on schedule," Sheila mused, interrupting her thoughts. "It seems as though we've been waiting for ages."

"I must say, you don't seem excited," Jessy commented.

"Jessy, I need someone to talk to. I can't talk to Cort," Sheila moaned. "Since we arrived in Topeka he's never home."

Seeing her sister-in-law's pale face, Jessy felt guilty at having been so wrapped up in her own problems that she had paid little attention to the girl. "I'm always willing to listen," she said softly.

"This is a terrible thing to say, but I'm beginning to believe I'll turn out like my brother."

"In what way?"

Sheila fidgeted with the wool rug across her lap. "All of a sudden I'm meeting men I find most attractive."

"So I've noticed," Jessy commented, a smile forming on her lips. "You're keeping your mother quite busy with all the men that have come calling."

"But what about Tom? I thought he was the right one for me. But he was only gone a short time when I began looking at others. Mother thinks I'm being terribly wicked."

"I don't believe that for a moment. You're growing up, that's all. There is nothing wrong with looking and comparing as long as you don't carry it too far. Don't be in a hurry to get married, Sheila," Jessy cautioned, her smile fading. "You're a lovely woman, and you'll never suffer from not having a beaux. As for Tom, you'll know how you feel after he's been here a few days."

Sheila thought for a moment about what Jessy had said, then slowly nodded in agreement. "You've been a good friend, Jessy. For the life of me, I can't understand why Cort doesn't see what a wonderful woman you are."

Jessy was saved from having to reply by the sound of the train whistle screeching through the chilled air. Tod opened the door, and the two women climbed down from the carriage. There was a breeze blowing, and Jessy hurriedly pulled the hood of the heavy wool coat over her head, the ermine lining keeping her body snug from the biting cold. As they stepped onto the platform to await Tom's arrival,

Jessy shoved her hands deep into the large fur muff and decided that Sheila wasn't the only one with misgivings.

As Tom stepped from the train, Sheila hurried forward. Jessy held back, allowing the pair a moment to themselves. Amazingly, Jessy's heart didn't skip a single beat. Tom was still handsome in a rugged way, but she realized that he couldn't hold a candle to her husband. She moved forward. "Welcome back," she said, shaking Tom's hand.

"You've changed." Tom's eyes momentarily bored into hers, a wide grin on his face.

"Is it that obvious?" Jessy asked, trying to keep the conversation light. "But then we all continue to change, don't we? I hope for the better." Jessy glanced at Sheila and saw a confused look on the girl's face. "Shouldn't we be heading back to the house? I'm sure Tom's getting cold standing out here."

"Oh...of course," Sheila replied.

When they returned to the carriage, Jessy was pleased that Tom sat next to Sheila. Tod moved the horses forward, and after a few polite words of inquiry about Tom's trip, Jessy pulled back the curtain and looked out the window at the passing stores. She closed her ears to Tom's and Sheila's rapid conversation, and thought about Cort.

After his wild accusations at the ranch, she'd had every intention of leaving. But that hadn't happened. Since moving back to town, she'd become more and more involved in Marie's social affairs, always playing the part of a happily married woman. She listened intently to all the gossip and had learned a great deal about the people who inhabited the Topeka social circle.

Cort had escorted her to several balls, but they spent little time together otherwise. Even though she was continually surrounded by men—and Cort certainly had his share of women—none of the occasions proved to be as enjoyable as her first ball. It came as a surprise that prior to each outing, Cort continued to present her with a piece of fine jewelry. In fact, she was wearing his latest gift, a large emerald-cut ruby ring surrounded with diamonds. But other than those few outings, Cort was never home, nor had he shared her bed since his accusations at the ranch. Jessy tried to tell herself she should be glad, but jealousy continued to tear her apart. The questions of where Cort was staying, and with whom, constantly hounded her.

Why have I become so weak that I live day to day in hopes of seeing him, deluding myself that he'll come to my room? It's not going to happen, she chastised herself.

Marie was waiting in the entry when the threesome entered the house. Though she maintained a certain aloofness, her joy at seeing Tom was obvious.

They were in the process of removing their coats when a deep voice said, "It's good to have you back, my friend."

Seeing Cort headed toward them, Jessy's mouth dropped open. He was never home this time of day! She began fumbling with her coat in an effort to hide her shock.

"Good to be back," Tom replied as the two men shook hands.

"Let's go into the parlor where it's warm. I may very well be interested in buying some land now that Colorado has become a state, and I'm anxious to know what you found out."

"Cort, you owe it to yourself to see the place," Tom said excitedly. "It's absolutely spectacular. When I first arrived..."

The two men disappeared into the parlor, and Jessy could no longer hear what they were saying. Cort looked so handsome in his black pants, white shirt and green brocade vest. It hurt to know he hadn't even so much as glanced at her.

"Tom is looking well," Marie commented. "Being in the wilds seems to have agreed with him."

"He's not nearly as good-looking as I had remembered." Sheila glanced at Jessy with a smile playing at the corner of her lips and winked.

"Oh!" Marie exclaimed. "You wouldn't see a tree if it was standing in front of you. Supper will be ready in two hours." She left in a huff.

"If I don't watch out, Mother's going to steal Tom right out from under my nose."

The two women were laughing as they climbed the stairs and headed for their rooms.

The evening meal was monopolized by Cort's questions and Tom's answers. Jessy was fascinated with Tom's detailed descriptions, and could almost picture the huge, majestic mountains in her mind.

"The place abounds with every kind of wildlife imaginable," Tom continued. "I tell you, King, a man could live his entire life away from all civilization and never miss a meal."

"Sounds to me like you've given some serious consideration to moving there," Cort commented as he placed his napkin by his plate. "Shall we retire to the study for a smoke and a drink, Tom?"

When the men departed, Jessy, Sheila and Marie went to the parlor to await the gentlemen's return. A warm fire crackled in the stone fireplace, making the room quite cozy.

"Surely Cortland was jesting about Thomas moving to Colorado!" Marie said, her voice amplified with horror. She sat in the burgundy chair, her back straight and head held high. "Sheila, has Thomas said anything about taking you to that horrible wilderness?"

"No, Mother."

The maid brought in the highly polished silver tea set and placed it on the oval table set off to the side. Jessy began pouring.

"Thank heavens. No man should expect a woman of proper breeding to live around Indians and Lord knows what else."

"I'm sure you have nothing to worry about, Mother." Sheila took the china cup and saucer Jessy handed to her. "It was Cort who brought up the subject, not Tom. Besides, even though Tom referred to Denver as a cow town, it's probably quite respectable."

"Speaking of Cortland, it seems strange he decided to be home when Thomas arrived." Marie accepted her cup. "We've hardly seen him since our return, and now he is giving every indication of remaining constantly under foot."

"This is his house, Mother."

"That may be, Sheila, but you'll have to admit everything runs smoothly until he makes an appearance. I was so foolish not to put my foot down when I married Arthur. I would have been rid of Cortland once and for all."

Sheila rolled her eyes at Jessy, who had taken the seat across from her. She needed to change the subject, quickly. "That is such a pretty dress, Jessy," she said truthfully. "I don't believe I've seen you wear it before. Is it new?"

"No, I had it made just after Cort and I married. I guess you weren't around when I wore it before."

Marie set her cup down with a clink. "Why would you want to wear a summer dress in winter? And white at that. At least you wore a shawl."

Already upset about the dress, Jessy felt the anger rise in her throat and had to clench her jaw to keep from telling Marie that what she wore was none of her business. She'd deliberately chosen the dress because she had hoped to stir some fond memories within Cort. It was the dress she had worn on their first night at the ranch, and he'd commented on how lovely she looked. She had even had Prudence fix her hair the same way, a loose knot on top of her head, with small spit curls falling to the side of her face. A lot of good it had done. Cort had acted as though she wasn't even at the dining table.

"Jessy looks beautiful no matter what she has on," Sheila remarked. Since she'd brought up the subject, she felt she should defend her sister-in-law.

Cort and Tom entered, and the conversation quickly changed to small talk. Cards were eventually brought out, and Jessy was forced to play rummy with Cort as her partner. Shortly after the game began, Marie made the proper apologies and retired to her room.

Though Jessy had not wanted to play, as the game progressed she became relaxed and actually began enjoying herself. Cort acted the perfect, attentive husband, and the evening passed quickly.

After several games, the hour grew late and the small group agreed to call it a night.

"Next time, we'll win," Tom declared as he helped Sheila from her chair.

"Don't be so sure of that." Cort pulled a long, narrow box from his vest pocket and handed it to Jessy. "My wife is very good at cards."

From the shape, Jessy knew the box contained another piece of jewelry, but was perplexed as to why Cort had given it to her. She glanced at Cort, and though a smile was on his chiseled lips, his eyes were dark and cold.

"Don't just stare at it," Sheila said excitely, "open it."

Jessy removed the lid, and lying inside was the most beautiful ruby and diamond necklace she'd ever seen. A feeling of foreboding gripped her in the throat. Her mother's necklace had brought bad luck. Would the same thing happen with this one? She handed the box to Sheila.

"It's magnificent!" Sheila exclaimed, showing it to Tom. "Is this to celebrate something?"

"Does there have to be an occasion to give my beautiful wife a gift?" Cort chuckled. "Diamonds and rubies are Jessy's favorite stones. In fact, it was because of a similar necklace that we met."

"I've never heard how you met," Sheila said.

"How did you meet?" Tom inquired.

Jessy felt sick to her stomach. The necklace was already starting to weave its spell. Cort was about to tell his version of what happened.

"It's a long story, and too late to go into it tonight," Cort replied smoothly. "Perhaps another time."

Jessy expelled an inner sigh of relief.

"Actually, I've had the necklace for some time, and seeing Jessy in the same dress she wore our first night alone, it seemed the proper occasion to present it to her."

Sheila blushed, Tom smiled knowingly, and Jessy's heart overflowed with sudden happiness. Cort really had noticed! Without a moment's hesitation, she leaned over the small table and placed her arms around his neck. "Thank you," she whispered before kissing him thoroughly on the lips.

The kiss caught Cort completely off guard. Knowing that to push Jessy away would create questions in Sheila's and Tom's minds, he had to sit and bear it. It wasn't until Jessy leaned back that he discovered Tom and Sheila had left the room. Reaching out, he pulled Jessy back into his arms. She was his wife, and why should he continue to deprive himself of her pleasures?

"You're the most tempting witch I've ever known," he muttered before returning his lips to hers.

Jessy was sleeping peacefully when Cort climbed out of bed and went to his room. After stoking the fire and lighting a cigar, he began pacing the floor. He'd been a happy man until he met Jessy. Since then, nothing had gone right, including the move back to town. He'd planned on reestablishing his place with his various lady friends, only to discover they no longer appealed to him. Parties with old cronies were now of little interest, and even his vow to never return to Jessy's bed had been shattered by a simple kiss.

Cort tossed his cigar butt into the spittoon and collapsed on the bed, a smile creasing his lips as he looked at his situation from the brighter side. Just maybe the cards were finally starting to turn in his favor. While they were making love earlier, Jessy had said she loved him. If she had spoken the truth, or was even beginning to have feelings toward him, he'd have her just where he wanted her. It could also cause her to drop her guard. She'd pay for not telling him she couldn't have children, and if she was the one who had tried to kill him, she'd eventually make a slip. He'd finally have his answer.

Realizing his remaining away from the house had served to make Jessy more pliable, Cort chuckled. It was time to give up his hotel room and remain at home. He would do everything within his power to make her love blossom.

Content with how things were going, Cort climbed under the covers and immediately fell asleep.

Several mornings later, Jessy left her room feeling as happy as a lark. Cort had spent the entire night again, and though he hadn't said so, she was convinced he loved her. Paying little attention to where she was going, she almost ran into Tom walking down the hall.

"Good morning," he said cheerfully. "You look awfully pleased with yourself."

"I am. Did you have a good night's rest?"

"Slept like a log. Jessy, I need to talk to you in private."

Caught off guard, Jessy wasn't sure what to say.

"Could we meet somewhere?"

"I suppose we could meet in the study shortly before noon if it's important."

"That would be fine." He gave her an ingratiating smile. "May I escort you downstairs?"

For some strange reason, Jessy suddenly wondered who picked Tom's clothes. His attire was never fashionable, and the brown corduroy jacket he had on was well worn. Though a wealthy man, he obviously paid little attention to his dress.

Jessy was the first to enter the study, and though she had no reason to feel guilty, she was relieved that Cort wasn't there. Their relationship was still on shaky ground, and she didn't want anything to happen that might upset the apple cart again. A few minutes later, Tom joined her.

"You are a truly beautiful woman, Jessy Lancaster," Tom said before lifting her hand and kissing her knuckles.

Jessy jerked away and moved behind the desk. *Did I make a mistake by meeting him here?* she wondered.

"It was meant as a compliment, Jessy, nothing more." He gave her a wide grin and sat on the leather sofa. "Do you feel safer now?"

Jessy wasn't sure she felt safer, but she certainly felt foolish. Still, she remained where she was. "What did you want to talk about?"

"Sheila, you and me." He leaned back, making himself comfortable. "When I went to Colorado, I had a lot of time to think. I'm sure you were aware just how attracted I was to you, and I believe for a short while my feelings were returned."

"Tom, you shouldn't be saying such things." Jessy sat in the large chair and began toying with a letter opener. "You are a fine man, but . . ."

"Please, let me finish. I think we should get this out in the open, at least between the two of us. If we don't we'll never be comfortable around each other. And since I have every intention of becoming a part of this family, I think it's important.

"Your beauty and Cort's apparent lack of appreciation would have touched any man's heart, including mine. But it's obvious you've fallen in love with your husband, and I think Cort loves you."

"That's a laugh," Jessy grumbled.

"I'm not sure he realizes it yet, but I feel sure time will prove me right. And even though it's quite difficult for my male ego to admit, Jessy dear, I fear you are more woman than I could ever handle. What I'm trying to say is, I know you're married to the right man. You'll always hold a special place in my heart, and should you ever need me, I'll be there. But Sheila is the right woman for me."

Never having had a man talk to her so openly about his feelings, Jessy was touched. It took a moment for her to compose herself. "Tom," she finally said, "has Sheila agreed to be your wife?"

"I haven't proposed. I wanted to talk to you first. Sheila thinks very highly of you, and I don't want that to change from misunderstandings."

Jessy sat the letter opener down quietly and looked directly into Tom's eyes. "I'm sure you'd make Sheila a wonderful husband, but you can't marry her if there's no love, Tom. She'd be miserable."

"But I do love her. Admittedly I wasn't sure until I saw her at the depot." He stood and smiled. "Now that you know you're quite safe and I'm not out to make trouble or change anything, are you going to come over here and give your soon to be brother-in-law a hug?''

"I hope Sheila doesn't turn you down." Jessy was laughing as she rushed into his open arms.

At that moment, the door opened and Cort walked in with Sheila right behind him. Sheila's face mirrored shock, then anger before she rushed out of the room with Tom right behind her.

Cort was an entirely different matter. His expression was one of evil amusement.

Knowing the best way to get out of a bad situation was to attack, Jessy did just that. "Why are you looking like that?" she demanded. "You look like I'm guilty of something."

"Now why would I think that?"

His low, calm voice caused Jessy's apprehension to grow. She always felt at a disadvantage when he towered over her like this. With a determined tilt of her chin, she looked into his dark brown eyes. "Well . . . I imagine it did look rather strange being in each other's arms."

"But you've told me you love me, and if that's the truth, I'm sure there is a reasonable explanation."

Jessy reached up and touched his arm. She felt the hard, tensed muscle beneath his shirt. "Of course there is." She laughed nervously and moved away. "I was congratulating Tom. He'd just informed me that he planned on asking Sheila for her hand."

"Strange, Sheila knew nothing about it. Are you telling me Tom came to you first?"

"Yes, he did."

"Why?"

"Why?" Jessy turned and faced her husband. How could she possibly tell him the truth? Again she chose to attack. "I should be the one to ask why! Why are you questioning me about an innocent hug? Why do I have to keep defending myself to you? Why is it you never believe me? I am so sick and tired of always having to walk carefully, trying not to upset you!'' She banged her fist on the desk effectively.

"Who you choose to take in your arms is your business, and certainly none of my concern, since I can no longer anticipate a child who would some day inherit everything I've worked so hard for,'' Cort snapped. "But I'll not have you taking the man Sheila loves away from her.''

Jessy felt as though her blood had been drained. "I'm such a gullible fool,'' she whispered. "I honestly thought things were starting to go right between us, and that you loved me. But that isn't true, is it?''

Jessy waited for an answer, but Cort only stood there, a nasty smirk spread across his handsome face. She had a strong desire to slap him, but what would that accomplish? Instead she slumped down on one of the chairs and watched him casually go to the sideboard and pour a drink.

"You owe me an explanation, Cort,'' she stated flatly. "I've done everything I can think of to make this marriage work, short of bearing your child. Why do you hate me so? Does it have anything to do with those silly accusations you made about Marie or me trying to kill you? Or were you just making that up?'' Jessy impatiently shoved back the silver strands of hair that had escaped from the bun at her neck.

"Emperor didn't die from a broken leg, Jessy. He was shot out from under me.''

Jessy wasn't sure whether to believe him or not. "If that's true, did it ever occur to you that BJ could be the guilty party? You knew what he was like when you married me.''

Cort propped himself on the edge of the desk and looked at his wife. He took a sip of brandy before saying, "Oh it occurred to me; that is, until I found out he's dead.''

Jessy's eyes widened, and she sank back in the chair. "Dead?" she gasped. "How?"

"How is of no importance, my dear."

"Did you kill him?"

"No, but had I had the opportunity, I certainly would have, without a moment's hesitation."

Suspicion began to prick at the corner of Jessy's mind. "Did you find this out when you went to Topeka alone?"

"As a matter of fact, yes."

"So you assumed Marie or I tried to shoot you! Marie was right. You have lost your mind!"

"You'll have to admit it's rather strange that nothing has happened since I changed my will."

Jessy rose from her chair and went to the sideboard. She hadn't had a drink since the night she'd gotten drunk, but at this moment she could certainly use one. Somehow she knew, without a shadow of a doubt, that Cort was telling the truth. She picked up the decanter, then set it down and turned. "Cort," she whispered, tears forming in her eyes, "I have never done anything to hurt you. I believe you, so why in God's name can't you believe me?" She rushed out of the study.

Cort released a tired sigh then finished his drink. Is the truth staring me right in the face and I'm too blind to see it? he wondered.

He stood and went to the bookcase. It still amazed him to know his father had read every one of the hundreds of volumes. He pulled one of the books out, flipped through the pages, then replaced it.

"You're on your own, King Lancaster," he muttered. "You're going to have to make a decision about Jessy, and you're going to have to do it soon."

After leaving Cort, Jessy went straight to her room. Brushing away the tears with the back of her hand, she yanked the blue velvet riding outfit from the clothespress. At least the sun was out today, and she hoped a ride in the cold air would clear her foggy brain.

Chapter Fourteen

"Are you sure this is what you want?" Cort asked his sister.

"Yes, it's what I want. I'm so happy, Cort, I think I'm going to burst. Mother has even agreed to go with me to meet Tom's parents."

Cort looked at Marie, who was dressed in black and sitting in her usual chair. Her smug look reminded him of a cat. The woman was all but licking her chops. "How very kind of her." He turned his eyes to the happy couple. "Where do you plan on getting married?"

"If you're not averse to the idea," Tom said, "and Sheila finds Boston to her liking, I'd like us to be married there. As you know, my parents aren't getting any younger, and I doubt they would be able to make the trip to Kansas."

The women held their breath as Cort moved to the parlor window and looked out, pondering the situation.

"Naturally Sheila will need a complete new wardrobe," Marie spoke up, "and the material for her wedding dress will have to be ordered and sewn. If we start right away, Sheila and I should be able to leave in two months. And we'll have to give an engagement party before Tom leaves so everyone can meet him."

230 Fire and Ice

So it's finally happened, Cort thought. Even sooner than I'd expected. He was loath to let Marie out from under his grasp, but Sheila did need a chaperon, and he knew Marie would watch over the girl like a tiger. Though she seldom showed her affection, Cort knew Marie loved Sheila deeply. Marie had no quarrel with his sister, only with him.

Cort turned and looked at the small group. "I see nothing wrong with those arrangements." He walked over to Tom and extended his hand. "You've chosen a fine lady, my friend. Sheila will make you a good wife."

After the men had shaken hands, Sheila rushed over and threw her arms around her brother's waist. "I love you so much," she said happily. "No woman ever had a greater brother than I do."

Cort heard Marie say "Ha!" as he reluctantly turned his sister loose and allowed her to go to Tom. Cort had mixed feelings. He was happy for Sheila, but he would have liked nothing better than to sock Tom in the jaw for taking Sheila so far away.

"You'll be leaving in two weeks, Tom?" Cort asked, maintaining an outward composure.

"Yes, I have business I need to attend to." Tom considered saying something to Cort about what had happened in the study, but changed his mind. He'd had a hard enough time explaining it to Sheila and had no desire to bring the subject up again. Besides, since Cort was agreeable to the marriage, Jessy must have made some acceptable explanation.

"Where is Jessy?" Sheila asked. "I can't wait to tell her the good news."

"I have no idea," Cort replied dryly.

"I'll go see if she's in her room. She's going to be as excited as I am when I tell her the news."

"Why don't you let Jessy go with us," Marie suggested after Sheila had left.

"No. Jessy stays here."

"Why?" Marie snapped at him. "So you can continue to make her life miserable? Thank heavens Sheila isn't marrying the likes of you."

Neither Cort nor Marie heard Tom excuse himself and leave the room.

"At least Sheila will be getting away from a house filled with nothing but hate," Marie persisted.

"And just who initiated that hate, Marie?" Cort asked dryly. "From the time you married my father, you've been full of nothing but venom. And don't think you're going to escape me. When Jessy and I come to the wedding, you'd best be ready to return. I don't think you would like the Sterlings to discover just what kind of family their son married into. Think of the scandal that could cause. I'm sure it will be a huge wedding, attended by every stitch of society, including many from Topeka."

"Cort," Sheila said as she reentered the room. "I can't find Jessy." Her face mirrored her disappointment.

"Did you search the house?" Cort asked.

"Well . . . no."

"I'll find her."

"Maybe she's left," Marie said, a faint smile on her thin lips. "You've certainly tried hard enough to drive her away."

It wasn't until Cort entered the kitchen that one of the servants said she'd seen Jessy leave by the back door an hour or so ago.

As soon as Cort stepped outside, he saw the small boot prints embedded in the snow. They led directly to the carriage house.

"Tod?" Cort called, closing the door behind him.

"Up here, Mr. Lancaster." Tod dropped the pitchfork and moved to the edge of the loft. "What can I do for you, sir?"

"Have you seen Mrs. Lancaster?"

"Yes, sir. She went for a ride some time ago. As cold as it is, I figured she'd be back by now. I tried to get her to take a buggy, but she wouldn't listen."

"You mean she rode sidesaddle?"

"Yes, sir."

"Damn that woman! She's going to be the death of me." Realizing what he'd said, Cort had to laugh. The next thing he knew, he was laughing uproariously. Sometime between their argument and now, he'd made his mind up about his wife. He believed what she'd said in the study. After everything was ready, and Sheila and Marie had left for Boston, he was going to sit Jessy down and they were going to have one hell of a talk.

"Are you all right, Mr. Lancaster?" Tod called.

"Yes, as a matter of fact, I'm just fine."

Bitter, hurt, depressed, were just a few of the words Jessy thought of to describe her feelings as she dismounted in front of the Shawnee County Abstract Office. She simply couldn't take any more of Cort's up and down moods and unfounded accusations. I'm going to Kansas City, she vowed angrily, if I have to sell everything I own. It wasn't until she was headed toward town that she'd thought about her parents' land. Opening the office door, Jessy walked in.

Though still miserable, Jessy felt somewhat better when she left the abstract office. The gentleman inside had been most helpful, and had promised to get her the brief of title for the land. He'd also assured her there were always people looking to purchase good, fertile land. At last she would have money in her pocket again.

Jessy glanced down the boardwalk at the various shops and decided to spend some of Cort's money. More than once he'd told her to buy anything she wanted, so why shouldn't she? I've earned it, she thought bitterly. She'd been a fool not to have done it sooner. She stood for a moment and watched the carriages and horses trudge through the deep, thick mud. Trying to cross the road was definitely out. She'd have to ride.

Jessy's first stop was at a furrier, where she purchased an expensive cape she'd had her eye on for some time. That was followed with a visit to a millinery shop and an hour of trying on hats. She chose several, and the woman promised her they would be delivered tomorrow. Jessy received a considerable amount of satisfaction at charging everything to Cort, and would have continued her shopping spree, but it was getting late.

Still disinclined to return home, she decided to make a quick stop at the Topeka Academy of Music. Though she didn't plan on being in Topeka much longer, she was curious about how much piano lessons would cost. She always enjoyed listening to Sheila play, and perhaps when she reached Kansas City she'd have enough money to learn to play the beautiful instrument.

After getting the information, Jessy left the academy and decided to head home. She wasn't looking forward to having words with Cort again, but the sun had already started going down and the air had turned bitterly cold. Dark clouds were forming overhead, and she knew that the snow would be falling by morning.

Jessy was about to untie her horse from the hitching rail when she felt a tap on her shoulder. Sure it was someone she knew, and irritated about having to stand in the cold and talk, she turned, ready to get rid of the intruder. Her eyes suddenly became huge pools of lavender, and she staggered backward. "It can't be!" she whispered. "You're dead!"

"Do I look dead? You don't seem too happy to see me, Jess."

Jessy crumpled to the ground.

When Jessy came to, she was still a bit groggy, and she was being carried inside the academy by a stranger.

"My, my," groaned Mr. Rosenstein, the elderly music teacher. "What happened to Mrs. Lancaster?"

"The lady fainted," the stranger replied. "She's shaking, probably from the cold."

"Here, take her to my office."

Jessy knew her shaking wasn't caused by the weather. She glanced around the room to make sure there were only the two men. Of course there is no one else, she told herself. I must have been hallucinating. Jonathan is dead!

"Thank you, sir," Jessy said when the kindly-faced stranger had placed her on a chair. "I'm sorry to have caused you so much trouble."

"My pleasure, ma'am."

"Mr. Rosenstein, I know it's a terrible day, but could you send someone to fetch my husband? I'm feeling too weak to ride back alone."

"I'll see to it right away," the old man answered, nodding.

As the men left the office, Jessy straightened out her skirts and wrapped the fur cape tightly around her. But the shaking didn't cease, and her back ached from the strain. Even her teeth were chattering. It had to have been a dream, Jessy told herself. Jonathan is dead! Either that, or I'm losing my mind.

It seemed to take forever for Cort to arrive. When she saw his tall, muscled frame enter the room, she rose from the chair and hurried toward him, needing to feel his strength and protection. Not until he placed his arms around her did she finally feel safe.

In one quick swoop, Cort lifted her into his arms and carried her out to the buggy. It took only a moment to collect the horse she'd ridden into town and tie him to the back of the buggy.

Cort didn't know what to think when he climbed into the buggy and Jessy slid next to him and snuggled close. They hadn't seen each other since their quarrel, and it wasn't like Jessy to forgive and forget so quickly. If he didn't know better, he'd think she was frightened.

He slapped the reins across the horse's back, and in no time the buggy was moving at a fast clip. Not until they were away from the main traffic was Cort finally able to transfer the reins to one hand and place his arm around her shoulder. "We'll be home soon, Jessy," he tried reassuring her. "When we get there I'll send for Dr. Mattson."

"No!" Realizing how harsh she sounded, Jessy softened her voice. "That won't be necessary." She sat up straight, but remained close to her husband. She felt considerably better now that the shaking had subsided and her teeth were no longer chattering.

"But you fainted."

"I blame Prudence for that," Jessy replied, trying to make light of the situation. "The girl pulled my corset strings too tight. Of course being out in the cold too long probably didn't help either. I'll have Prudence prepare a hot bath, and after some chicken soup, I'll go right to bed. You'll see, by tomorrow I'll be just fine."

Cort knew something was amiss, but since Jessy seemed unwilling to say anything, he remained silent.

By the time Jessy climbed into bed, she knew her glimpse of Jonathan had been nothing more than a hallucination.

Cort came in several times to make sure she was all right, and Marie even paid her a visit, suggesting different herbs she should take for her malady. But it was Sheila who brightened Jessy's spirits with news of the engagement.

"Jessy," Sheila continued as she pulled a chair to the side of the bed and sat, "I want you to know I'm not angry about what happened in the study."

"I'm so glad to hear that." Jessy reached down and patted the girl's hand.

"I have to admit I was seeing red when I left, but Tom caught up with me and forced me to listen to what had happened. He told me how the hug was to wish him luck. Jessy, didn't you feel strange when he asked for advice as to how to propose to me? The man is old enough to have figured that out for himself."

So that's how he got out of it, Jessy thought. "No, I considered it a compliment. But what difference does it make? He obviously did quite well on his own."

Sheila giggled but managed to say, "He certainly did."

The girl's gaiety was infectious, and Jessy found herself laughing.

"Actually," Sheila continued after calming down somewhat, "I should be thankful it happened. It wasn't until I saw you in each other's arms that I realized just how much I loved Tom."

Sheila chattered on about Tom, the trip to Boston, the style of wedding dress she wanted, how she'd miss her family and anything else that popped into her mind.

By the time she left, it was quite dark outside, and Jessy was exhausted. Reaching over, she turned out the oil lamp and settled down in bed.

Jessy awoke with a start. She knew she'd had a bad dream, but couldn't remember what it was about. Nor could she rid herself of the lingering fear.

This is ridiculous, she thought as she sat up and swung her legs over the side of the bed. Suddenly she smelled the faint odor of Lavender Water, the kind Jonathan had always used. "My God," Jessy whispered, desperately trying to remain calm. "I really am losing my mind!"

Scrambling off the bed, Jessy attempted to light the oil lamp, but her shaking hands wouldn't cooperate. Groping around in the dark, she accidently knocked over the glass chimney, and it crashed to the floor. At almost the same moment, the door to Cort's room flew open. She almost expected Jonathan to walk in, and Jessy's fear became so strong she didn't even breathe. Light filled the doorway, then she saw Cort standing there with a candle in his hand. Jessy was so relieved she started to take a step forward.

"Don't move," he ordered, "you'll cut your feet." He leaned forward and lifted her away from the shards of glass.

"Please, Cort, let me sleep with you," Jessy murmured as she wrapped her arms tightly around his neck.

Cort took Jessy to his room and climbed into bed with her. "Jessy, what's wrong?" He drew her into his arms and held her shaking body next to his.

"I had a bad dream." With her face pressed against his bare chest, the words came out muffled. What was she supposed to say? Cort, I've become addle-brained?

The next day Jessy felt considerably better, but still edgy. When Cort suggested she take it easy for a day or so, she flatly refused. She needed to stay busy and not think about what happened yesterday or last night. But nothing worked. As she busied herself around the house giving the servants orders and checking on things, her mind kept drifting to what had happened. For the life of her, she couldn't figure out why her mind had conjured up Jonathan. She'd heard the Gypsies were capable of such things, but this was the first time such a thing had happened to her, and she hoped it was the last.

Cort, on the other hand, was looking at things from an entirely different angle. When they were together he watched Jessy's every move, trying to decide if she was pregnant. It was the only thing he could think of that explained her fainting and the fact that she now suffered from no apparent miseries. It seemed a good rationalization, but some warning kept pricking at the back of his neck. If she wasn't pregnant, there was something going on he didn't know about. Something bad enough to make Jessy very uneasy.

With the plans for an engagement party, Jessy finally became quite busy and managed to push any thoughts of Jonathan to the back of her mind. There were invitations to be written and sent out, food preparations, musicians to hire, furniture moved for dancing, ball gowns to be made, and all in a very short period of time.

Jessy and Marie handled everything regarding the house, while Tom and Sheila took care of the invitations. Cort took care of the rest of the chores. He even hired a seamstress and helpers to stay at the house until the gowns were completed.

Jessy saw little of Cort during the mad whirl of activity, but she did notice a definite change in his attitude. He was attentive and considerate, and Jessy was leery. Every time she decided to leave the man, he always managed to do or say something that rejuvenated her hopes of a happy marriage. He was doing it again. But this time she remained cautious. Instead of telling herself his attitude had permanently changed, she simply waited for his mood to swing. In the meantime, she enjoyed spending her nights in his bed and having him make wonderful love to her.

Jessy sat in front of the diamond glass mirror wringing her hands as Prudence tried in vain to dress her mistress's thick hair.

"Mrs. Lancaster," Prudence said, watching the hair she'd just pinned, "you're going to have to stop moving around or you'll never be ready on time."

"I'm sorry," Jessy apologized, placing her hands in her lap and trying to sit still. This was the first social gathering she'd helped prepare, and she just knew everything was going to go wrong.

Prudence pulled her hair to the side and twisted it into a knot, allowing curls to cascade out the center. Satisfied the hair would remain firmly secured, Prudence finally allowed her mistress to rise.

Looking in the mirror as Prudence fastened the tiny hooks in the back of the gown, Jessy was quite pleased. The material was almost the same color as her hair. The seamstress had explained that because of Jessy's dark complexion, the look would be stunning. Jessy had to agree. The large puffed sleeves stood high off her shoulders, and the low-necked bodice crisscrossed in the front where soft pleats of material hugged her breasts and waist before billowing out into a full skirt with a multitude of small rosettes. Jessy's normally tiny waist was even smaller after Prudence had finished pulling the corset strings unbearably tight. At first Jessy had thought she wouldn't be able to breathe.

"How do I look?" she asked as she gave Prudence her first smile of the evening.

Pleased with her handiwork, Prudence giggled. "There's not another woman in all of Topeka that can match your beauty. You are going to have such a wonderful time."

Seeing a look of innocent envy in the girl's eyes, Jessy suddenly felt sorry for her maid. "Do you have a beau,

Prudence?" Jessy asked kindly, as she slipped on her lace gloves. The girl was quite attractive.

Prudence lowered her head and blushed. "No, ma'am. I'm too tall for most men."

"I'm sure some man will come along and sweep you off your feet."

"I wouldn't mind that one bit."

Jessy gave the girl an encouraging pat on the arm and left the room.

The party was an enormous success. So far, nothing had gone wrong, and if it did Jessy knew the guests wouldn't even notice.

Between dances, Jessy made a point of spending time with Marie's snobbish lady friends. She had long since learned that being on their good side was definitely advantageous. They were the matriarchs of Topeka, and their tongues could quickly destroy a woman socially.

After a particularly long, fast dance with Cort, Jessy unobtrusively collected her new fur shawl and stepped out onto the front porch for a breath of fresh air. The cold night felt good against her hot cheeks, but she knew she couldn't remain outside long. She smiled, wondering what Marie's friends would think if she returned to the house with blue skin.

Suddenly an arm circled her waist and at the same time a gloved hand covered her mouth. Consumed with fear, Jessy struggled desperately, but it did no good. Slowly she was pulled into the black shadows at the end of the porch.

"It's not nice to fight your husband, Jess," the man whispered in her ear.

Jessy became very still, her breathing shallow.

"That's more like it. I'm going to turn you loose, and I would advise you not to scream or make any kind of disturbance. If you do, I'll simply explain to your other husband how we planned on getting him to marry you. Or better yet, maybe I'll just kill him. Do we have an understanding?''

Jessy nodded, then felt Jonathan slowly turn her loose. He had no sooner taken his hands away when he spun her around to face him.

"We need to talk," Jonathan demanded. "In a few days I'll have a note delivered telling you where to meet me."

"No!" Jessy whispered.

"Yes! If you care anything about the great King Lancaster, you'll do as you're told. You can tell him about this, but remember one thing. You are a bigamist, sweet Jessy, and that can put you in jail. And do you really think he'll believe you didn't know I was alive?"

"But I didn't," Jessy gasped.

"Try to convince him of that."

Jessy knew Cort would never believe her. "How did you . . ."

"No questions until I see you next time."

Jessy heard him move away, and a moment later saw him pass a snowbank. The moonlight shone on his blond head before he disappeared from view. Jessy fell against the wall for support. Jonathan was alive! The horror of her situation was overwhelming. She wanted to pick her feet up and run and keep running. But where to?

"Jessy? Are you out here?"

Hearing Cort's voice, Jessy knew she was going to have to give the performance of her life. She couldn't allow Cort to become suspicious. Pulling together every ounce of strength she possessed, she stood straight and walked toward him. "I'm right here," she said sweetly. "I needed a breath of air."

Cort took her in his arms and kissed her passionately. Pulling his lips away only inches, he asked, "Have I told you how beautiful you look tonight?"

"No. I'm glad I please you."

"Please me? Lady, do you have any idea how much I'd like to pick you up and carry you to my room this very moment?"

Jessy knew that if Cort found out about Jonathan, this could very well be their last night together. She had an overwhelming desire to be in the arms of the man she loved. "I'd like that, too," she replied as she ran a finger lovingly along the small scar on his jawbone. "But what about the guests?"

"To hell with the guests. I want you all to myself. I've already seen too many men with their arms around you." Taking her by the hand, he led her around to the back entrance and up the stairs.

Chapter Fifteen

Jessy lay alone in her room, watching the sun come up and fighting the sick, giddy insanity that threatened to consume her. Of late, her life was a living hell of waiting. Over two weeks had gone by since she had seen Jonathan, and the promised message still hadn't arrived. Every time she heard someone at the door, her stomach knotted with fear and apprehension. She'd lost a considerable amount of weight and because her sleep consisted of short naps, there were ugly dark circles beneath her eyes. Marie certainly wasn't helping matters. Since Tom's departure, the woman had made several bitter remarks about how embarrassed she'd been the night of the party when Jessy and Cort had left early and failed to return.

Ignoring the chilled room, Jessy tossed off the covers and rolled onto her stomach. Again she silently cursed herself for not looking in the coffin to make sure Jonathan was dead. If she had, she wouldn't be experiencing the worst misery she'd ever known. She flopped over on her back, remembering all the times she'd started to leave Cort and now wished she had. So much could have been avoided if she hadn't let her love dictate her actions.

Cort already knew something was wrong. How could he help but know? Even though she kept a smile glued to her face and acted excited about the forthcoming marriage, all Cort had to do was look at her. On several occasions he'd even tried to get her to confide in him, but she couldn't stand to see the hate that would return to his brown eyes when he found out about Jonathan. She could talk until her jaw fell off, but Cort would never believe the truth. Jessy pulled a pillow from beneath her head and threw it across the room. Because she wouldn't confide in him, he was now withdrawn again, and they no longer slept together. Oh, well, Jessy thought sadly, maybe it's for the best. With Jonathan alive, Cort and I have no future.

Jessy rose from the bed, knowing that to remain would only bring on more thoughts and worry. The floor felt cold against her bare feet, and by the time she finished splashing her face with water from the washbowl, she was shivering.

Sheila's trip to Boston has really proved to be a blessing, Jessy thought as she slipped into a gray wool day dress, appreciating its warmth. The shopping, fittings and packing for the girl's trousseau had kept everyone busy. And being busy was the only thing that was keeping Jessy from falling apart.

Later that afternoon, Jessy sat in Sheila's bedroom, trying to relax after another day of shopping. Sheila talked nonstop about the trip to Boston while the seamstress carefully took in the waist of another dress.

"Jessy, I wouldn't admit this to another soul," Sheila said, trying to stand still, "but I'm so afraid Tom's parents won't approve of me."

"Are you sure in your mind that marrying Tom is what you really want?"

"Cannonballs, Jessy, of course it's what I want."

"Then if it's what you want, and what Tom wants, what difference does it make what his parents think? Tom isn't the type of man whose choice can be predicated on what his parents say. Sheila, I can't picture anyone not liking you, but should that happen, you and Tom have each other and you'll get along just fine." Jessy smiled at the girl, who looked so serious. "Besides, with you being the sister of the great King Lancaster I don't see that they would have a choice."

"Or he'll punch them in the nose?" Sheila giggled, picturing the scene in her mind.

"Has the material arrived for the wedding dress yet?" Marie demanded as she came into the room.

"No, ma'am," the seamstress replied after removing the pins from her lips. "I'm sure it will take another week at least."

"Jessy," Sheila said, plucking at the blue wool sleeve, "don't you think this should stand higher at the shoulder?"

Jessy couldn't speak. Her eyes were glued to the small envelope Marie was twisting back and forth in her hand.

"It looks fine, Sheila!" Marie snapped. "Are you going to have the wedding dress completed in time, Mrs. Fletcher?"

The plump seamstress again removed the pins, with obvious agitation. "Yes, Mrs. Lancaster. I will have five helpers sewing full time."

"I'm aware of that. Don't go getting snippety with me or I'll hire someone else to do the work."

"Mother, stop worrying. I'm sure we'll leave on time."

"Ah, Marie," Jessy finally spoke up, amazed at how calm she sounded, "is that note in your hand by chance for me?"

"Oh, yes. I forgot all about it. I found it sitting in the hallway. Lord knows when it arrived. I need to have another talk with the servants. They're getting too lackadaisical for my liking."

Jessy wanted to jump up and snatch the missive from the older woman, but she forced herself to rise slowly. "I agree, Sheila," she said as she accepted the note, "I think the sleeve should stand higher on the shoulder." Seeing the stern look of disapproval on Marie's face, Jessy smiled wickedly and left the room.

The moment she closed the door to her bedroom, Jessy tore the envelope open, easily recognizing Jonathan's swirly handwriting.

Jessy
Now that I've given you time enough to think, I expect you to meet me in front of the Cock-eyed Bull saloon promptly at four this afternoon. We have a lot to discuss.

Jessy crumpled the paper and let it fall to the floor. The moment she'd dreaded had finally arrived. Originally she'd thought to tell Jonathan she was happy and plead or even beg him to stay out of her life. Of course as the days passed, she'd realized it wasn't worth the misery of wondering when he would reappear. As Jonathan would put it, the cards had been dealt, and she'd lost the pot.

Jessy glanced around the bedroom. In years to come, she would remember it with fondness. She wanted to tell Sheila and Marie goodbye and thank them for everything, but of course that was impossible. And then there was Cort. She longed to share his bed just one more time and pretend he really loved her as much as she loved him.

Slipping off her rings, Jessy set them on the dressing table. She started to pull out her fur cape from the clothespress, but changed her mind. She would take nothing except the dress she wore and a wool coat.

Rushing down the stairs, Jessy suddenly sucked in her breath at the sight of Cort entering the front door. It was impossible to go back to her room and hide. Cort had already seen her.

"Where are you going in such a hurry?" Cort asked as Jessy neared him. He gave her a lazy smile, reached out and pulled her into his arms. "I've missed having you in my bed," he whispered in her ear.

The unexpected action and words caused tears to form in Jessy's lavender eyes. This was where she wanted to be for the rest of her life, but that was impossible. Hardening herself, Jessy pushed Cort away and followed her actions with a hard slap across his face. "You miss me in your bed?" Jessy purposely raged at him. "That's a laugh! I am sick and tired of being used when *you* feel the need. In fact, I'm tired of a lot of things. I'm tired of living with a man whose moods change from one day to another, who accuses me of every foul thing that comes to his mind and treats me like someone below him. I want a divorce, King Lancaster, and right away." Seeing Cort's eyes darkening with anger and his powerful body tense, Jessy had to turn away. "Since I've failed to bear a child, I'm sure the idea is not an objectionable one. And you need not worry about money or personal items, I plan to let you keep everything. In fact, I won't even be around!"

"Are you finished?"

"Yes. Now I have an appointment to go to, so please let me pass."

"With whom?" Cort asked angrily.

"Damn it, Cort, who I see is none of your business," Jessy declared as she jerked her heavy coat on. "You certainly don't like anyone questioning your whereabouts, so why should I be any different? But if you must know, I'm going to a millinery shop to cancel an order of hats I've never received.''

''Perhaps I should accompany you.''

''For what purpose?''

''To prove I'm not as insensitive as you would make me out to be.'' He stepped aside and waved his hand toward the door.

Afraid he might very well go with her, Jessy looked him straight in the eye. ''I don't want your company!''

''Whatever pleases you, my dear. But there is one thing I guarantee. Before much longer, you and I are going to sit down and have a long talk, and as the devil is my witness, you're going to come up with some truths.''

As Cort watched Jessy leave the house, he was suddenly filled with a strange, overwhelming urgency to get Sheila away from the house. Every hair on the back of his neck told him something bad was about to happen, and Jessy was very much involved. For both Sheila's and Marie's well-being, he needed to get them on the way to Boston as soon as possible.

Retiring to the study, Cort poured himself a drink and proceeded to light a cigar. As had happened on other occasions, the humidor was almost empty. Had Jessy decided to take up smoking? When this thought crossed his mind before, he'd found it amusing, but not this time. He was angry, and not just about Jessy's slap on the face.

Cort sat behind the desk and leaned back. What had happened that day in town when Jessy had fainted, and again the night of the party? Cort wondered as he unthinkingly circled the rim of the glass with a long finger. Though she tried to cover up her fear, it was always there, especially lately. When they made love, she became excessively clinging, as if possessed with desperation, and sometimes she'd move to the side of the bed and not want him to touch her.

On more than one occasion he'd woken during the night to find her crying in her sleep. When he'd finally broached the subject, she'd become defensive and decided to sleep in her own room. Now she was blaming him for not joining her! None of it made sense, but beneath it all, there was something very vicious lying in wait. Cort knew it was all going to come to an explosive head soon, and he intended to be ready. In fact, he almost welcomed it. He'd been in the dark too damn long, and by God, he wanted some answers!

Rising from the chair, Cort left the study and headed for Sheila's room. He tapped on the door and stepped inside.

"Cort," Sheila acknowledged, her face glowing with pleasure. "Mrs. Fletcher has just completed the final fitting for this dress. Do you like it?" Sheila turned a slow circle, allowing him a complete view.

"What does he know of women's clothes?" Marie grumbled from where she sat.

"I find the dress to be most becoming, sister dear. However I feel sorry for Tom."

"For heaven's sake, why?"

Cort cocked a dark eyebrow and gave her a clean smile. "Because he's the one who's going to have to chase all the other men away."

"You're prejudiced," Sheila accused, trying to stifle a giggle.

"You're doing a fine job, Mrs. Fletcher," Cort said to the seamstress, who was standing beside Sheila with a proud smile on her face. "How long do you think it will take to complete my sister's trousseau, without the wedding dress?"

"Without the wedding dress?" Marie gasped.

"I believe that is what I said, but I don't believe I was asking you, Marie. Mrs. Fletcher, can you have everything else completed by the time the wedding dress material arrives?"

"Well . . . I guess I could."

"Fine. If you need help, let me know. I'm not averse t
hiring more women to get the clothes sewn and ready."

"What are you getting at, Cortland?" Marie snapped a
him. "Sheila has to have a wedding dress!"

"Does she? Don't you think you're being a little prema
ture in your assumptions, Marie? As soon as you chang
clothes, Sheila, I'd like you and Marie to meet me in th
parlor." He turned and left.

Cort was standing by the large window when the tw
women joined him. Cort noted that Marie's face expresse
anger, while Sheila's showed shock. "Have a seat, ladies,"
Cort said graciously, "I can assure you there is nothing t
be upset about. In fact, I'm doing you a favor.

"It was my understanding that Sheila is going to Bosto
to meet Tom's family and to determine whether she woul
be happy living there," Cort continued when the two wome
were seated. "And if everything is to Sheila's liking, a mar
riage would take place. Am I right?"

Both women nodded their heads, and for some reason
Cort thought of puppets.

"Then I propose you leave as soon as possible and ge
everything settled as to what you want to do." Cort claspe
his hands behind his back and smiled at his sister. "Don'
get me wrong, Sheila, take as much time as you like. I don'
want you rushing into something without a lot of thought
Should you decide to marry, the dress can be made in Bos
ton. Believe me, they have many fine seamstresses."

"Oh, Cort," Sheila said excitedly, "that's a wonderfu
idea."

Even Marie showed pleasure at leaving sooner.

"Now it's up to you ladies to let me know just how soo
you can be ready, and I'll send a wire to Tom."

The women nodded and stood.

"It will probably take a couple of days before we can give you an answer," Marie said, suddenly all business again.

"That will be fine."

"Cort, have you seen Jessy?" Sheila asked. "She left my room after Mother gave her that message and didn't return."

"She went to town to see about some hats she was displeased with."

"That's strange, she seemed so happy when she showed them to me. I wonder why she would want to take them back."

"What did the note say?"

In her excitement, Sheila didn't notice how cold her brother's voice had suddenly turned. "I have no idea."

"Come along, Sheila," Marie said impatiently, "we have a lot of work to do. I'm sure Jessica will be back shortly."

Furious, Cort wasn't even aware the women had left. All he could think about was Jessy's lie about not receiving the hats. He passed Marie and Sheila busily talking in the hall, went up the stairs two at a time and entered Jessy's room, slamming the door behind him. The first thing he noticed were her rings sitting on the dressing table. Wondering where she would have hidden the note, he began scanning the room until he spotted a wadded up piece of paper by the end of the bed. Sweeping it up in his hand, he slowly unfolded the paper.

Upon reading the message, Cort was consumed with a fury so deep he would have liked nothing better than to strangle his two-timing wife. The note proved there was another man in her life, and also that she still had friends in bad circles. The Cock-eyed Bull was a notorious hangout for every thief in Kansas. It was a small compound situated several miles from town that even the marshal left alone.

It was Jessy who had been behind the attempts on his life all along. It all made sense. She hadn't actually pulled the trigger—she was too smart for that. Instead she'd used an accomplice, and when Cort told her about the will—which he foolishly hadn't attended to—she had changed her mind. From the way the letter read, a new plan was being devised.

A short time later, Cort rode away from the house, wearing his black clothes and a sheepskin-lined jacket. The pistols nestled in the holsters strapped to his hips were loaded.

It was after four when Jessy arrived at the Cock-eyed Bull. The building was surrounded by tall spiked logs, and it reminded Jessy of a fort. She started to turn away, but knew she had no choice. By the time she pulled the buggy to a halt in front of the noisy saloon, her hands were shaking. She jumped when a gunshot suddenly rang out, and a man staggered out of the place and fell. Blood dripped from his back, turning the snow-packed ground red. Jessy tried to scream, but no sound escaped her throat. Looking at the doorway, Jessy saw Jonathan standing there with a three-barreled derringer in his hand. He shoved the gun up the sleeve of his coat and moved toward the buggy. Four of the meanest, dirtiest men Jessy had ever laid eyes on walked behind him. Frightened beyond words, Jessy slapped leather across the back of the black horse, but before it could move, Jonathan grabbed the reins.

"What's your hurry?" Jonathan asked in a silky voice. "You just arrived, and we have so much to talk about."

Fear gripped Jessy as she stared at her green-eyed husband. Jonathan had changed since she'd lived with him. There was now an evilness about him, and she had the feeling he could be very dangerous. "I won't stay here," she finally managed to say.

"I didn't expect you to." Jonathan got in on the driver's side, forcing Jessy to move over.

"Where are you taking me?" Jessy demanded.

"To a friend's cabin so we can be alone."

The other men climbed on nags and followed as Jonathan drove the buggy out of the compound. Jessy was sick with worry. Dear God, she moaned, what have I gotten myself into?

After going only a short distance, Jonathan produced a piece of black cloth and held it up for Jessy to see. "Sorry, Jess, but I'm afraid I'm going to have to blindfold you."

"Why?" Jessy asked, raising her hand to prevent it.

"Because if you decided to do something foolish, you won't know where I took you. Now be a good girl or I'll be forced to mess up that pretty face of yours."

He leaned over and placed the material across her eyes, securing it in the back. Knowing a fight would accomplish nothing, Jessy didn't resist.

Lost in her own misery, Jessy paid scant attention to how long they traveled. All she could think about was Cort, her love for him, and how much she hated Jonathan. Not only for what he'd done to her in the past, but also for having the audacity to be alive. Though still frightened, she was becoming angry. Cort was a hundred percent more man than Jonathan had ever been. And how could she have ever considered Jonathan handsome? He was too pretty and had the delicacy of a woman. Even his blond hair was thinner than she remembered.

Jessy felt the buggy stop, and the next moment her blindfold was removed. In front of them was a dilapidated lean-to built of wood scraps, track railings and canvas. It looked as though, if anyone leaned against it, the whole thing would fall to the ground.

"You men wait out here," Jonathan ordered, "the lady and I have business to discuss."

Not wanting Jonathan to touch her, Jessy climbed out of the buggy by herself. She pulled back a heavy canvas flap and entered the one-room shack. She was amazed to discover how clean the place was. Then Jessy saw Yana. The girl had a large bruise on her cheek, but she wore a clean calico dress, and her thick, black hair hung free around her pretty face and down her back. But what drew Jessy's attention was the girl's protruding belly. She was with child.

Yana looked at Jessy with a satisfied sneer, then spit on the dirt floor.

"Now be nice," Jonathan said with heavy humor, "after all, we have to take good care of our investment."

"I don't want her in my house."

"And I don't give a damn what you want, Yana! Now get out of here so I can talk to the lady alone. The boys are outside, so why don't you entertain them with one of your dances? The one where you lift your skirts high in the air so they can see you have nothing on underneath."

"Maybe I will," Yana said angrily. "And maybe I'll let them feel me and spread my legs while this bitch is spreading hers for you! But she won't give you near the pleasure I can!"

"That's up to you. Now get out of here and don't return until I call."

Jessy watched Yana snatch up a heavy shawl and march out, her head held high. Though sickened by the words that had been exchanged between Jonathan and the girl, she couldn't help but feel sorry that Yana had to stand outside in the snow.

It suddenly occurred to Jessy that she'd outsmarted Jonathan before, and maybe she could do it again if she kept her composure. Acting as if she had all the time in the world, she walked around the small room looking at everything, then sat in a rough, hand-carved chair. "If you think I'm going to live with you again, Jonathan, you're wrong," she stated matter-of-factly.

"Quite the contrary. I wouldn't dream of taking you out of that lovely house you now claim as your own." He pulled a chair out from the table, sat down, and leaned back, balancing on the chair's back legs.

"Then what is the purpose of all this?"

"We'll get to that shortly. Are you mad at me for trying to poison you?"

"What are you talking about?" Jessy asked impatiently.

"I'm talking about the poison I had Yana put in your food."

Jessy's mind flashed back to the last time she'd seen Yana and how deathly sick she'd been.

"Ah, I can see from your face you do remember. I made sure Yana didn't give you enough to kill you, you know."

Jessy had a hard time controlling the shudder that wanted to streak up her spine. She couldn't allow him to see her fear, and it was imperative she keep a cool head. "How very thoughtful of you. May I ask why you went to all that trouble?"

"I was angry. I wanted to teach you a lesson. You needed to know that I can reach you no matter how safe you may think you are. Mr. Lancaster cannot protect you." He pulled a long cigar from his purple brocade vest and lit it.

Jessy recognized the odor immediately. "Where did you get that?" she gasped.

"I had Yana take several boxes from your house. King Lancaster smokes only the best, and since he shares my wife, I see no reason not to share his cigars."

It was slowly beginning to penetrate Jessy's mind just how dangerous a predicament she was in. Stay calm, she warned herself. "I have to give you credit, Jonathan," she said as she smoothed out her skirts, "you've been very clever. I always admired that in a man." Jessy saw the effect she was searching for. Jonathan's eyes lit up with pleasure.

"I planned it all, and no one suspected a thing. Don't you want to know how I pulled it off?"

"Of course," Jessy replied, trying to appear impressed with Jonathan's trickery.

Jonathan eagerly leaned forward, the front legs of the chair making a thudding sound as they hit the hard-packed ground. "Remember when you took me to that horse doctor? I thought I was dead for sure, but he assured me I was going to live. Knowing that, I started making plans. The night of the poker game, BJ killed the cowhand who shot me. No one came around to claim the body, so with a promise of lots of money, the old drunk doctor was more than willing to put the cowhand's body in my casket. He nailed it up good and tight, and no one was the wiser."

"And how did you find me?"

"That was the easy part," Jonathan replied as he watched the smoke from the cigar slowly trail to the ceiling. "When I found out you'd taken off, I figured you'd head for Kansas City and I'd have a hell of a time finding you. But the horse doctor kept going to the saloon for whiskey, and he heard BJ was tracking you down." Jonathan tossed the cigar to the floor, then placed his elbows on the table and cupped his hands together, enjoying his tale. "BJ was never very smart. When he found out you were in Topeka, he went to the saloon and told everyone how he was going to bring you back and get you pregnant. I wasn't well enough to travel yet, so I figured to kill him when he returned. But he didn't come back."

"He's dead," Jessy said almost too calmly. There was a brightness in Jonathan's eyes that wasn't normal, and she needed to be more careful. "Why did you want to find me?" she asked, making sure there was no touch of fear in her words.

"Because you had my money and the necklace! It all belonged to me, not you!"

"You stole the money and necklace from me!"

"Yana stole them for me, and I've put them to good use."

"That necklace was mine, damn you! It belonged to my mother!"

"I earned that necklace by taking you in when your folks died." He cocked his head. "Can't you see that, Jess? Everything you had, I gave you. It wasn't much, but when we moved to Kansas City we would have been on top of the world. Of course it wouldn't have been like what you have now."

My God, Jessy thought, the man is crazy. "Jonathan, did you try to kill Cort?" Jessy whispered.

"Several times, but the damn fool has the luck of the Irish! I knew that with him out of the way, you'd inherit everything. Since I'm your husband, it would all become mine."

Now everything made sense. All Cort's accusations about Marie or Jessy trying to kill him were valid. Who else would have been bitter enough to try to do him in? He would never suspect Jonathan was alive. Her weeping, exasperation, anger and frustration had been caused by the man sitting across from her. Jessy wished she'd thought to bring a gun. She'd have killed Jonathan without a moment's hesitation, and willingly suffered the consequences. The man was evil. She desperately needed to know his plans for the future. Maybe in some way she could find a means of thwarting them, thereby preventing any more anguish to the Lancaster family. "If that was your plan, why have you waited until now to contact me?"

"Because I now know there is no love between you two. I figured you married him for his money, and when Yana told me the servants' gossip about how he'd left the day after the wedding, I figured you'd pulled the same stunt on him that you pulled on me. But I still wasn't sure until on more than one occasion I saw him escorting a lady by the name of Amy Rothchild around town. After some checking around, I discovered he pays all her bills. I've also seen him go into the boardinghouse where she lives, and he stays long enough to accomplish what he went there for."

Jealousy pounded through every fiber of Jessy's body. She'd actually convinced herself the affair was over.

"As I was saying," Jonathan continued, "now that I know why you married Lancaster, I want you to help me kill him."

"Why would I want to do that?" Jessy asked, trying to keep the fear from her voice.

Jonathan gave her an evil grin. "Because I want his money."

"Killing him will not get you his money. He has made out a will, and unless I produce a son, I get nothing. All your scheming has gotten you nowhere."

"I don't believe you!" Jonathan rose so fast his chair fell over. "You want to keep it all for yourself."

Relieved and thankful that Cort had drawn up such a will, Jessy looked him straight in the eye. "I'm not lying."

"Son of a bitch," Jonathan exclaimed as he began pacing the floor. "Then you are going to give me money every week until you give him his damn son!"

"I have no money."

Jonathan grabbed her by the shoulders and shook her so hard her hair tumbled around her face. She heard a sleeve rip.

"You'd better give me money!" he yelled. As if suddenly returning to his senses, he let out a laugh.

When Jonathan released her, Jessy fell to the floor, her lips bleeding from where her teeth had cut them. She wiped her mouth with the back of her hand, then looked at Jonathan, who was standing over her. "I wouldn't give you a single penny even if I did have the money. Cort is finished with me, and he has demanded a divorce."

Grabbing her by the arm, Jonathan jerked her onto the chair. "Then you'd best be finding a way to make him change his mind. Maybe you're not fond of Lancaster, but according to Yana, you and his sister are quite close. Her life will be in your hands. And for the first payment, I'll take those emerald earrings you're wearing!"

Jessy screeched with pain when he yanked them off her ears.

"Maybe you don't have money, but you have jewelry. This time next week, I'll meet you in front of the McCollister Dry Goods store at two in the afternoon. You'd better bring something worth my time because I'm not making idle threats, Jess. If I have to kill your sister-in-law, it will cost you double, and the old woman will be next. And you'd best put a halt to the divorce and get pregnant, because when you run out of jewelry you're going to have to come up with money."

"I won't do it. I'll tell Cort and he'll take care of you!" Jessy threatened.

"Oh? I assure you, if you do that there are going to be some dead women before he finds me. Why do you persist in making things so difficult? You can have your cake and eat it, too."

"Are you finished?"

Fire and Ice

"Yes. And do try to clean yourself up before anyone sees you. You might find it difficult to explain why your hair is falling down and your cheeks are so red."

Jessy rose slowly, and Jonathan smiled and backed away, giving her room.

"One of my men will take you back to the Cock-eyed Bull, but naturally you'll have to be blindfolded."

"Naturally," Jessy said bitterly. She wanted to scream out her hate and frustrations, but wisely chose to remain silent.

Chapter Sixteen

Cort was smoldering as he waited in the parlor for Jessy to return. He'd left word in the kitchen that should his wife enter from that direction he was to be informed immediately. Two men lay dead at the Cock-eyed Bull, and he hadn't found a single trace of Jessy. He wanted to kick himself for not being suspicious when he'd found the note conveniently lying on the floor. It had all been a set-up to get him off her trail, and he'd fallen right into the trap. Well, it wouldn't happen again. From now on he'd know exactly where Jessy was from sunup to sunup!

"Mr. Lancaster?"

"Has my wife returned?" Cort asked the young servant standing nervously inside the room.

"Yes, sir. I believe she went directly to her room."

"Thank you, Molly."

Jessy was on her hands and knees looking for the note she'd foolishly left behind when she heard her door open and close. Leaning down, she looked under the bed and saw a pair of black boots. Without realizing it, a moan escaped her lips. Damn, it was Cort! She wasn't ready to face him yet. Why was it that when he should be around, he wasn't, and when she didn't want to see him he was always there? Accepting her fate, she slowly rose to her feet. She was surprised to see him dressed in black, his gun belt still strapped around his slim hips. But what bothered her the most was the hard look on his face and the way his eyes glittered. "What are you doing in my room?" she asked defensively. "Isn't Amy Rothchild available tonight?"

"What took you so long, my love?" Cort asked, ignoring the question as he moved toward her. "You look like you just had a good tossing in bed. Are you two-timing me, sweet Jessy?"

Before she could answer, Cort yanked her into his arms, grabbed the back of her head and kissed her. With all her might, Jessy pounded him on the back, desperately trying to escape. She could taste blood when the cuts on her lips reopened. Then, as quick as he'd grabbed her, he shoved her away. Jessy raised a hand to slap his face, but he caught her wrist, preventing the blow.

"What's wrong, Jessy?" he asked, his voice low and deadly. "I was only trying to please. From your disheveled appearance, it looks like you rather like rough treatment." He slowly wiped the blood off his mouth.

Still numb from her meeting with Jonathan, Jessy snatched her wrist away and backed toward the wall. Her anger was growing by leaps and bounds. "You bastard! You jump to conclusions without even waiting to find out the facts. After I came out of the hat shop, a man attacked me and stole my earrings. But do you care? No!" Jessy had expected to see his expression change to one of concern, but instead he stood there with his chiseled lips twisted in a smirk and his eyes unwavering.

If she hadn't stuck to her story about the millinery shop, Cort might have given some thought to what she was saying. Dried blood clung to her earlobe, as well as the collar of her dress. "What is the name of the hat shop?" he asked, watching a momentary spark of confusion enter her lavender eyes. Then it disappeared. It occurred to him that he'd become quite familiar with Jessy's actions and expressions as he noticed the small, telltale signs that she was lying.

"Why do you want to know? I would think you'd be more concerned over my well-being!" Jessy tried to figure a way to get out of her predicament, but she needed time to think, and Cort wasn't giving it to her.

"Because if they send me a bill, I'll make sure it isn't paid."

Jessy sat at the dressing table and started removing the few pins left in her hair after the hard shaking she'd received from Jonathan. "That won't be necessary," she snapped. "After I found out they had new help and the error had not been intentional, I decided to go ahead and accept the hats."

"What were you looking for on the floor?"

Suspicion began nibbling at Jessy. Had Cort found the note? "Why do you keep hounding me with questions?" she asked as she slapped her hand down. Rising from the stool, she started toward the window. She'd hardly taken more than a couple of steps when Cort grabbed her arm and jerked her around to face him.

"Because I want some damn answers! I have the note, Jessy, in fact I even went to the Cock-eyed Bull looking for you. Be glad you weren't there. I killed the two men who tried to do me in. I don't think you want to know what I might have done to you had I found you there."

"You killed two men?" Jessy gasped. She didn't even try to hide the fear she felt at his expression.

"That's right."

"What note are you talking about, and why did you go looking for me?" she asked, feigning innocence.

"You know what note I'm talking about, and I'm well aware you deliberately planted it for me to find."

"That's the most ridiculous statement I've ever heard! If you found a note in my room, then someone else put it there."

"Good try, Jessy, but you just keep digging a deeper hole for yourself. I know Marie gave you the note, and I know you didn't go to any millinery shop. You'll make it a lot easier on yourself if you confess all. Who is your partner, Jessy, and what are you scheming about?"

Jessy would have given anything to tell Cort the truth, but she couldn't take the chance of Sheila, Marie or even Cort getting hurt. A tear trickled down her cheek as she looked at him. "I can't tell you anything," she whispered.

"Tears didn't work when I first met you, lady, and they won't work now. Just remember, I gave you your chance. I'm sure whoever you had the rendezvous with will be expecting another meeting. I intend to dog your heels, my dear, and you will never leave this house again unless I'm by your side. One way or another, Jessy, I'm going to find out just what's going on."

When Cort left, Jessy threw herself on the bed, allowing deep, bitter sobs to burst forth.

It wasn't until late the next morning that she left the security of her rooms. Before retiring last night she'd made sure all the locks on the doors were secured. Though she didn't feel rested, sheer exhaustion had helped her sleep the night away. She'd spent a good deal of time this morning walking the floor and trying to come to grips with her situation. It hurt her deeply knowing how much Cort hated and mistrusted her, but there was nothing she could say or do to change his mind. Jonathan had planned well. At present, there was nothing she could do but abide by Jonathan's orders.

The house seemed abnormally quiet when Jessy went downstairs. Spying a servant walking toward the laundry room, Jessy called to her.

"Yes, ma'am?"

"Where is everyone?" she asked, trying to keep a light tone in her voice. She couldn't help but notice the way the girl hung her head and refused to look up.

"The women have gone to town, ma'am, and Mr. Lancaster is in his study."

Knowing she had to eat something even though she wasn't hungry, Jessy headed for the kitchen. Again no one would look at her. Even Mrs. O'Grady avoided any eye contact when she set a plate of food down in front of her. Prudence and Byron made separate entrances, but saw Jessy and quickly left.

After only a few bites of food, Jessy shoved the plate away and left. She was determined to find out why everyone was acting so strangely, and she knew exactly who to ask.

Without bothering to knock, Jessy flung open the door to the study and marched in. "Just what is going on here?" she demanded of Cort. It aggravated her that he didn't even bother to look up from the journal he was writing in. He was obviously busy, but she didn't care.

"I'm working," he stated flatly. "If you have a problem, take it up with someone else." He finally looked up. "Unless you've come to bare your soul."

Jessy placed her hands on her hips and tapped her foot. "I came here to find out why the servants are treating me so strangely. What have you said to them?"

"Simply that I'm to be informed if you try leaving the house without me." He placed the quill in the ink bottle and leaned back in the big leather chair. "Because they like you, they find the situation most uncomfortable and they aren't sure how to handle themselves. And by the way, Tod has also been given the same instructions."

"I see. So by turning the servants against me I have fewer friendly faces to look at? Is that your purpose? And just what have you said to Sheila and Marie? Surely you wouldn't miss the opportunity of turning them against me as well. In fact, I'm surprised you haven't already said something about my so-called seedy past!"

"It's not necessary. They're leaving for Boston in less than two weeks. Now if you'll excuse me, I have work to attend to."

"Two weeks?" Jessy said excitedly. "Are you sure?"

Cort was completely thrown off guard. What was she so damn happy about? "Of course I'm sure. If Sheila decides to marry, the wedding dress will be made there."

"Oh!" Jessy exclaimed as she began clapping her hands. "That's wonderful...so very wonderful. Thank you, Cort, you've made me so happy." Before leaving, she laughed softly, and a twinkle entered her lavender eyes. "You know, Cort, you should have worn the same clothes you had on yesterday. I like you much better in black, it goes with your disposition. You truly are the devil's disciple."

Cort rubbed the back of his neck as Jessy all but danced out of the room. Would he ever understand the woman? She'd entered the study madder than a hornet, and had left prouder than a peacock! He certainly didn't want her happy, he wanted her miserable!

Cort started to take quill in hand, then changed his mind. Keeping pressure on Jessy was more important.

Jessy returned to her room feeling as though the weight of the world had just been lifted from her shoulders. Now that she knew Sheila and Marie would soon be safe, she could make her plans accordingly. Jonathan's threats of harming them would no longer hold water. It hurt to know that very shortly she would never see Cort again, but a week after the women left, she would be gone, too. It was either that, or go to jail for bigamy.

Jessy sat in front of her dressing table and opened her jewelry box. With Cort threatening to follow her everywhere, the delivery wasn't going to be easy. Aggravated at having to give any of Cort's gifts to Jonathan, she replaced the lid. She considered what Cort had said about dogging her heels, and realized she could use it to her advantage. If she went with Sheila and Marie on every trip to town, Cort would supply the protection. The next instant, Jessy remembered he didn't wear his guns to town.

"You seem deep in thought. I wonder what's going through that devious mind of yours."

Cort's words startled Jessy, but she remained calm. She could handle anything now. "I thought you had work to do?" she commented as she opened a perfume bottle and dabbed perfume behind each ear.

"I find you more interesting. I must apologize for my bad manners in the study. I failed to comment on how much I like your dress, and how it matches your eyes."

Jessy glanced around and saw him leaning comfortably in the doorway. "Why the sudden compliments?" she asked suspiciously.

"I have always told you you're beautiful, and after all, you are my wife. So you think I represent the devil's disciple, do you?"

Feeling uncomfortable, Jessy looked away and began fidgeting with the perfume bottle.

"If you will leave, I'd like to be alone."

"I don't believe you. No, you're sitting there starting to think about how you almost stop breathing when I touch the sensitive spots on your body."

Cort's voice was low and soft, and Jessy could feel her body starting to react. She almost hated him for the power he had over her. "That's not so," she persisted.

"There's nothing wrong with admitting it, my love. Look in the mirror. Your cheeks are already flushed."

"That's a lie!" Jessy said, her voice husky. Glancing in the mirror, she saw he was telling the truth. Her body was reacting, even though she knew Cort was toying with her. Yes, she wanted him, and yes, there were telltale signs. But she'd be damned if she'd get off the stool only to have him spurn her, and she knew instinctively that's what he had on his mind. He wasn't the devil's disciple, he was the devil!

"Take your hair down, Jessy. I like it hanging loose."

"No."

"Why are you fighting your body's needs when I'm standing here and you know I can satisfy you? Everything is already being washed from your mind except unfulfilled desire."

Hearing humor in his voice, Jessy turned and threw the bottle of perfume at him. He dodged it easily and started toward her.

"Stay away from me," she warned as she reached for another bottle, but the words were weak.

He laughed openly. "You always were a challenge, my dear."

Jessy started to hurl her hairbrush, but he'd already anticipated the action. Catching her wrist in midair and twisting, he forced her to drop it. "Stop it! I don't want you touching me!"

"You're lying." This time, his words and voice were a velvet caress. "No matter what evil schemes you may plot, Jessy dear, you know you have one weakness, and that frightens you. I have complete power over your body, and there's not a damn thing you can do about it other than killing me."

He released her and, as if in a trance, Jessy rose, her need already pounding in her temples. He drew her into his arms, his kiss demanding. Jessy's heart soared as his hand cupped her buttocks and drew her hard against him.

"Close the door," she whispered as she began unbuttoning his shirt, wanting to feel his strong body next to hers.

Lifting her long skirt, he placed his hand between her legs, feeling the dampness of her pantelets. He moved his finger, touching the sensitive area.

Jessy was on fire. Without a moment's hesitation, she began undressing, her eyes watching Cort as he also removed his clothes.

"How bad do you want me, Jessy?"

Jessy opened her eyes, desire making the lids heavy. "You already know how much I want you," she moaned.

Cort drew her down on the bed and entered her. His thrusts were hard and fast, and Jessy could feel her entire body tightening and building as he sucked on her neck.

As Jessy felt everything start to explode, Cort asked, "Who did you meet, Jessy?"

Before she realized it, she moaned, "Jonathan."

His mouth came down hard on hers, but she didn't care. Only her beloved Cort could give her the satisfaction she craved. Then everything exploded as he took her to the heights of glorious pleasure.

Jessy kept her arms wrapped lovingly around his neck, savoring the aftermath of what they had just shared. Suddenly, she felt him stiffen.

Jessy pulled away and looked at her husband. The scar on his jawbone was white. "What's wrong?" she asked, completely confused.

"Have you always pretended I was Jonathan when we've shared our carnal lusts?" His voice was low and his words were cutting.

"I don't know what you mean."

"You said Jonathan's name."

Jessy flinched as she remembered why she'd said Jonathan's name.

"Did you honestly think I believed you when you declared your love for me? You married me for protection and money. And at this moment, I'm not even sure about the protection." He sat up straight, his lips curled in a snarl. "I should have let BJ have you. You were a perfect match— both as crooked as snakes!"

"You can't talk to me like that!" Jessy yelled as she jerked up to a sitting position. "I am so sick and tired of hearing you make accusations you know nothing about. Ever since we met, you've taken a one-sided view."

"Well, you haven't done or said anything that would change that view, my dear. When you're not telling lies or plotting to do away with me, you shut up like a clam. You've dug your own grave, and you're damn well going to lie in it. No divorce, no running away. I can't prove what you've been up to, but for the rest of your life you'll have to look at me, knowing I know the truth. And when I die of old age, you'll be a broken woman, Jessy. You could have had everything, but you became too greedy. When you look back at what you've done, I doubt that you'll think it was all worth it." An evil grin formed on his lips. "If you tell me who your accomplice is, I might be willing to bargain."

"Get out of my room," Jessy screamed as she flung the pillow at him.

"You should take me up on my offer, Jessy dear, next time I may not feel so lenient."

"I hate you!"

Cort chuckled wickedly. "Not near as much as you're going to."

When Jessy heard the door bang shut, she bounded off the bed. Just two more weeks, she kept telling herself as she poured water from the pitcher into the bowl and rinsed her face. "Men!" she mumbled as she dressed. "Why do they have to be such fools and cause me so much trouble?" At the dressing table she quickly brushed her hair and pinned it into a knot.

"Since you want to dog my heels, you might as well start right now!" she yelled at Cort through the door. Then she out a hat on, snatched her fur cape from the clothespress and left the room.

"Mrs. Lancaster," Tod said as Jessy entered the carriage house. "Is there something I can do for you?"

"You can saddle my horse." Jessy watched Tod glance behind her to see if Cort was nearby. "If the servants haven't informed Mr. Lancaster of my departure, I'm sure you will," Jessy snapped at him. "And don't dally. I have a lot of shopping to do."

Cort was relaxing in a tub of hot water when Byron entered and told him Jessy had left the house. She'd caught him off guard, and Cort had to do some fast scrambling. By the time he saw Tod, Jessy had already left.

"Why the hell didn't you wait until I arrived?" Cort demanded as the young man prepared a horse.

"I tried, Mr. Lancaster, but she got mad and saddled her own horse."

Cort left the carriage house and pushed his horse to a full gallop. He didn't have far to ride before he caught up with Jessy. She was riding at a slow pace, as if she had all the time in the world.

By the time they returned home, Cort was even angrier than when he'd left. Jessy had spent the entire day going from one shop to another, and had purchased only one thing.

Chapter Seventeen

Cort followed Jessy into the McCollister Dry Goods store, then moved off to the corner where he could keep an eye on her. There were only five customers besides himself and Jessy. Two gray-headed women were standing in the middle of the store gossiping, a young shapely woman was at the counter bickering with the clerk over a coffee grinder, a boy was looking at boots and there was a small Oriental man with a black pigtail hanging down his back and a cap on his head.

After a quick glance at Jessy, Cort sat on one of the three wooden chairs by the warm potbelly stove and made himself comfortable. He wondered how much longer this was going to last before Jessy tired of her little game. For the past week he'd followed her around town, but nothing had happened to make him the least suspicious. He'd made a point of never walking beside her, and when she traveled, he rode his horse some distance behind. There wasn't a shop in town she hadn't been in at least once, and he was damn tired of walking and waiting while she browsed. If he hadn't wanted to give her partner every opportunity to make contact, he'd have put a halt to this madness days ago.

He wore his guns at all times now, ready for any trouble. Friends he'd met on the street looked at him strangely and were out of sorts when he refused to stand and talk with them. But knowing his reputation, they never questioned the way he was dressed.

At least the weather had improved, Cort reflected. The last couple of days the sun had remained bright and warm, giving a needed relief to the bone-chilling cold they'd experienced for the past few months. Even the long icicles hanging from the buildings were starting to break off and...

Cort's thoughts immediately vanished as a mean-looking character entered the store. The man was lank and wore a filthy poncho over equally dirty buckskins. A skunk cap covered the top of his long, straggly hair. His sunken, beady eyes sat above a crooked nose, and a bushy, uncared-for beard covered most of his face. One hand remained beneath his poncho and Cort guessed it rested on a pistol or a knife. Cort rose slowly to his feet, his hands by his sides, ready.

Jessy, pretending to be checking some calico material, also saw the man enter. She immediately recognized him as one of the men who had followed her and Jonathan to Yana's lean-to. Seeing Cort had his eyes glued on the man and not her, Jessy pulled the piece of jewelry from her pocket and waited anxiously. As soon as the bushy-faced fellow glanced in her direction, Jessy dropped the cloth-covered bracelet in a bin.

Afraid Cort might have seen what she'd done, Jessy looked in his direction and discovered he was standing. Oddly enough, he looked remarkably relaxed and unaware of the danger he was in. Not wanting anything to happen, she lifted her skirts and headed for the door.

As Jessy climbed into her buggy, she expelled a sigh of relief at seeing Cort leave the place behind her. It occurred to her that besides wanting to be sure Jonathan received the bracelet, there was another reason she wanted Cort out of the McCollister store. She'd been afraid Cort might get hurt.

Jessy untied the reins and moved the horse forward through the deep mud covering the streets. Down the way she saw a freight wagon stuck, and a bull whacker was cracking his long whip across the backs of the twelve oxen, trying to get them to pull harder. How do I know Cort can even defend himself? Jessy wondered. I've never seen him do anything but sock that poor innocent man in the jaw at the Harvey House dance. Just because he wears guns doesn't necessarily mean he can use them. He's probably nothing but a lot of talk, and I bet I just saved his fool life. Killed two men, indeed! He only said that because he was angry about the note and wanted me to feel guilty or scared. The same thing Jonathan used to do when I lived with him. Jessy knew she was only searching for reasons to dislike Cort so that leaving him would be easier.

Having made herself sick at heart about Cort's inadequacies, Jessy was ready to return home. Besides, she needed to have the final fitting for her new gown. As if there wasn't enough work already for the seamstresses, Marie had accepted an invitation to a ball this Friday, stating it would be Sheila's last outing in Topeka. Jessy knew it would be her last outing, as well. With everything practically ready, Marie and Sheila would be departing next Wednesday.

There were vehicles parked everywhere, and as Jessy exited the carriage, she could hear laughter and music coming from within the large mansion.

"I certainly hope Tom takes me to a lot of balls in Boston," Sheila said, a bit breathless with excitement. "They do have dances there, don't they, Cort?"

"Yes, and you won't be disappointed."

Seeing her mother and Jessy move ahead and start up the stairs, Sheila placed a detaining hand on her brother's arm. "Cort, please, for me, won't you try putting a smile on your face? I haven't seen one in so long I'm beginning to think you've forgotten how.''

Cort gave her the broad smile she'd asked for. "I guess I'm just sad about you leaving."

"That may be true in part, but a tiny part. I know there is trouble between you and Jessy, and it breaks my heart."

"Has Jessy said something to you?" Cort asked as he took Sheila's elbow and started leading her up the stairs.

"No, she's been just as closemouthed as you, but it doesn't take a lot of brains to see how you act around each other. She did ask me something strange, however."

"What?"

"She asked if I'd ever seen you defend yourself, and did you really know how to shoot a pistol."

"And what did you say?"

"Naturally I said yes. I told her there wasn't a man with a faster draw, and that the last time I saw you in a fight was that day we saw Tom off and those two rough men tried to detain me."

So now my dear wife is trying to find out how dangerous I am, Cort thought furiously. "And how did she react to that?"

Sheila stopped and turned toward her brother. "Actually, it was rather funny. She was pleased, but said something about being worried that you couldn't defend yourself. Why do you have a frown on your face? Did I say something wrong?"

"Of course not, it just doesn't make much sense. Now let's go inside, or you'll catch your death of cold."

As soon as Sheila joined Jessy and Marie, the women moved on to deposit their wraps. Jessy had told no one about the red velvet dress she'd had the seamstress make. Red was never worn except by ladies of the night, but at this time she'd felt rebellious and thought it suited her disposition. Now she was having second thoughts. As she removed her cloak, she saw shock and horror mirrored on Marie's and Sheila's faces, as well as the faces of several other women in the room. Not willing to show her own misgivings, Jessy squared her shoulders and, with head held high, left the room.

Cort was chatting with several business associates when the men's wives began whispering to one another and looking across the large ballroom. Other whispers reached Cort's ears. Curious, he turned to see what was causing all the commotion. Jessy stood on the far side, regal and proud, allowing everyone to take a look. Cort's admiration for the lady's bravado was undeniable. His dark eyes traveled from the silver hair piled high on her head and shining in the candlelight to the diamond and ruby necklace and earrings he'd given her. The gown was sleeveless and low-cut and the fan hanging from her wrist was also red. She was the most magnificent woman he'd ever laid eyes on. Cort was furious at himself for falling into her trap, but he couldn't have looked away if he had wanted to. He suddenly knew he was inescapably in love with the woman. Henceforth, he would be living in a hell of his own making. He started walking across the wide dance floor to join his wife.

Seeing Cort headed toward her, everything and everyone faded from view. He looked tall and handsome in his black formal clothes, and Jessy had to fight back the crazy desire to run to him. God, how she loved this man, even more than life itself.

"May I have this dance?" Cort asked with a slight bow.

"You're not ashamed of the way I'm dressed?"

"Centuries ago, I told you there was nothing you could do to embarrass me that I hadn't already done myself. You are the most beautiful woman here, and if any derogatory remarks are made, it's only because of jealousy. I can guarantee you that come the next ball, there will be quite a few women dressed in red, trying to emulate you. But they'll never succeed."

The music started. Drawing Jessy into his arms, Cort waltzed her onto the floor.

Cort claimed a great deal of Jessy's dances, and when she was paired with other partners, her eyes searched for him. Most of the time she found him standing alone on the side, watching her. There was something excitingly romantic yet distant about Cort tonight, and though Jessy enjoyed it immensely, she couldn't understand why he was acting this way. He exuded charm, humor and raw masculinity.

The evening passed quickly with Jessy luxuriating in a state of glorious bliss. Cort continued to play the part of the charming gentleman and represented everything a woman could ever possibly want in a man. She had to force herself into accepting reality. He's doing it on purpose to put me off guard, she thought, and waiting for me to make one small mistake that will give him a clue as to what I'm up to. But maybe, just tonight, I can pretend he really loves me.

After a particularly long waltz with Cort guiding her gracefully in constant circles, he led her off the floor. Breathless, Jessy began fluttering her fan, trying to stir up a breeze.

"How would you like to stand near the open doors until you cool off?" Cort graciously inquired.

"That would be wonderful." Jessy managed to control the urge to run her fingers through the thick, dark brown hair that curled up at the collar of his coat.

He led her to the tall French doors with heavy green velvet drapes hanging at each end. "Shall I get you a chair?" he asked, his grin showing white, even teeth.

"No, I'm fine," she said, returning his smile.

"Then I'll fetch you a drink. I won't be but a moment."

As soon as Cort left, men began flocking around, vying for the next dance. With firm but gentle words, she finally managed to get rid of them. She wanted to be alone with her husband.

By the time Jessy's lavender eyes located Cort again, he was involved in a conversation with several couples. He looked at her, shrugged his shoulders as if to say he would be detained a few minutes and winked. Jessy smiled, letting him know she understood.

As Jessy waited patiently, she noticed more than one woman looking longingly at Cort, but this time it didn't bother her as much as before. For one thing, Amy Rothchild had not made an appearance, and Cort continued to lavish his attention on her. Glancing around at the many guests, Jessy spied Marie sitting with her usual group of friends. A moment later she saw Sheila dancing, obviously enjoying herself.

"Stay right where you are, and don't do anything to make Lancaster suspicious!"

Jessy froze upon hearing Jonathan's voice behind her. "Have you gone insane?" Jessy asked out of the corner of her mouth. Pasting a smile on her lips, she glanced at Cort. Thank heavens, he was still talking to the couples.

"Was it your idea Lancaster follow you around everywhere?" Jonathan asked angrily.

"No."

"I don't believe you, so I made this special little visit to prove that taking care of your pretty little sister-in-law will not be difficult."

Her face flushed with anger, and Jessy began fanning herself again.

"To teach you a lesson, I want that necklace you're wearing."

"You can't be serious," Jessy gasped. "Cort would notice that it's gone immediately!"

"You're a smart woman, so you figure out a way to explain it."

Jessy felt the necklace yanked from her neck, almost choking her. It was all she could do to keep from screaming out her hatred. Looking toward Cort again, she watched him leave the small group and head toward the drinks.

"Next Wednesday I'll expect you at Polley's Carriage Factory at the usual time, and don't be late. I'm already mad as hell, so you'd better be there if you don't want any trouble. And I'll expect something more worthy than that bracelet you left last time."

Jessy saw Cort holding two drinks. Sure that Jonathan had slipped away, she placed a hand on her throat.

"Here you are, my dear," Cort said as he started to hand her one of the drinks. Seeing how white she was around the mouth, his eyes narrowed suspiciously. "What's the matter, Jessy?"

"Oh, Cort," she moaned, "I don't know how to tell you."

"Tell me what?"

"My necklace! It's gone!" Jessy removed her hand and looked pleadingly at him. "Don't be mad at me, but I have no idea when it fell off. I just noticed it a moment ago. We need to search for it!"

Cort flashed back to when he'd been talking and had looked at Jessy. She was wearing it then, and she hadn't moved since he'd left her. The red welt around her neck would indicate someone had physically removed it, so why wasn't she claiming theft? "Searching won't be necessary. I'm sure if anyone sees it they'll turn it over to the host. How do you suppose it fell off?" he asked smoothly as Jessy accepted the drink.

"When I put it on, I noticed the clasp had become faulty. I should never have worn it. Oh, Cort, can you forgive me?"

"Of course, my dear. I'll just buy you another one." He took a surreptitious glance around to see if he could see anyone who might look suspicious. Somehow, some way,

Jessy had made contact with her accomplice, and he was positive the man now had the necklace.

"No!" Jessy blurted out. "I don't want another one. It held as much bad luck as my mother's did."

Cort could see Jessy was badly shaken, but he wasn't convinced her fear came entirely from the loss of the necklace. She had the same look she'd worn on the two other occasions. "How can you say bad luck, my dear? Had it not been for that necklace, we would have never met."

There was grit in his words, and an evil smile stretched across his lips. He knows I'm lying, Jessy thought, but I can do nothing but stick to my story. "Cort, I'm so upset about this, and I want to go home. I don't mind if you wish to stay. I'll have Tod bring back the carriage."

"I won't hear of your leaving. After all, the necklace is really of no importance. And besides, Marie would never forgive us if we left another party."

His words were overly sweet, and Jessy knew the ax had just fallen.

"You haven't even taken a sip of your drink, my dear," Cort reminded her, his voice cold, his words clipped. "As soon as you're finished, you can continue dancing the night away. I've accepted my own hell, lady, so you might as well learn to accept yours."

Jessy wasn't sure what he was talking about, but the look in his eyes carried a warning. She momentarily considered walking out, but she knew he'd think nothing of making a scene. It had happened too many times during their relationship for her to even consider thwarting him.

The rest of the night was a disaster. Cort didn't dance with her again, but he made a point of watching her every move. Even the men at the ball began to notice it and made comments to her about not wanting to lock horns with a man like King Lancaster. It didn't take long before Jessy had no one to dance with. Accepting her fate, she joined Marie and the other older women.

By the time they returned home, Jessy had a splitting headache and wanted nothing more than to climb into bed and go to sleep. But when Cort followed her into her room, she knew sleep wasn't what was on his mind.

The days became exhausting as everyone rushed to get Marie and Sheila packed and ready to catch their train. Marie had become like a bear, worrying and fussing about everything. Cort was in a foul mood, and on more than one occasion, Marie and Cort exchanged bitter words. Sheila continued to go from one to the other, trying to make peace. In between, she cried on Jessy's shoulder, saying that had she known this was going to happen she would never have agreed to go to Boston.

Jessy's nerves were constantly on edge. She was simply too busy to even think of a plan of escape, and Cort seemed to be always within spitting distance. Every night he joined her in her room, coldly taking her to the heights of pleasure. No matter how hard she tried to fight her desire, she couldn't seem to get enough of him. Her sleep had dwindled to practically nothing, and Jessy found herself sick a good deal of the time. She told no one, knowing that after Marie and Sheila left, her life would return to normal, and she could get on with her own plans.

"I've had enough. That's all there is to it!" Sheila declared when she located Jessy alone packing some items into one of the big trunks. The girl plopped down in an unladylike manner on the bed. "I'm going to put a chair against the door and remain right here until it's time to leave."

"Are your mother and Cort arguing again?"

"No, Cort must have said something to her, so now she acts stoic when he's around. At present, she's having words with the seamstress about two dresses."

"What's wrong with them?"

"Nothing that I can see, but Mother insists they're sew
wrong. Jessy, what has happened to everyone? I've neve
seen this house in such a dither," Sheila whimpered.

Jessy sat beside Sheila and placed her arm around th
girl's shoulders. She loved the gentle child-woman, and fo
a long time had thought of her as the sister she'd never had
"Once you're on the train," Jessy soothed, "all will return
to normal. You and I both know Marie is excited about thi
trip, and she's gone to extremes trying to be sure everythin
is perfect. After all, this will be her first trip on a train, an
the first time she's been out of Kansas since she was a girl.
know it's difficult, but try to be patient with her. As fo
Cort, well . . . he's losing the last real member of his family
That has to hurt whether he shows it or not."

"He still has you."

"But that hasn't worked out so well, has it?" Jessy asked
smoothing back Sheila's shiny black hair.

"No, and I don't understand why. From the day yo
walked into this house, I knew you were perfect for Cort.'

"You're dreaming again, dear. You know Cort and
married for convenience."

"I know for certain you didn't marry him for money. I
you had, you'd have bought more than just a few clothes.
also know you keep the household bills down to a mini
mum. Since you claim you didn't love Cort, what did yo
gain by marrying him?"

Jessy stood and started packing again. "It's a long story
and—"

"Oh, cannonballs, Jessy! If I'm old enough to get mar
ried and have children, I'm certainly old enough to be con
sidered a woman. Why does everyone keep trying to hid
things from me? I love you and Cort, and I think I deserv
to know what has been going on."

It occurred to Jessy that it really wasn't a young girl sitting on the bed, but a beautiful woman.

"Unless you say it's all right, Jessy, I promise I'll never tell a soul."

"Very well, I guess you do have the right to know who your brother married."

Cort, who had been standing in the hall listening, started to move forward and put a stop to the conversation. But he changed his mind. He would very much like to hear what Jessy was about to say.

"Before Cort, I was married to a very corrupt gambler who got shot in a poker game." Jessy moved to the window and looked out over the melting, hard-crusted snow. "It seems so long ago," she said, drifting back in time. "My husband had a partner by the name of BJ, a terrible man I couldn't even stand to be around who insisted I marry him after Jonathan got shot. I decided to leave and start a new life. But before I was able to get away, Cort..."

Jessy told Sheila her story. When Jessy came to the part where she knocked Cort out with a stone and how he'd come chasing after her, Sheila doubled up with laughter, saying Jessy was the only person she knew who had bested her brother, and that she could picture how angry he must have been.

"So," Jessy said as she finished her story, "when Cort asked me to marry him, I accepted."

"And Cort still believes all the bad rumors BJ spread?"

"Yes." Choked up from remembering, Jessy had a hard time getting the word out.

"I love my brother dearly, but someone should knock some sense in his head," Sheila said vehemently. "Even I can see you're a good woman. And who is he to cast stones? By no stretch of the imagination could Cort be considered a saint. I will admit, however, this family has always been a stubborn lot. And then he turned around and accused you and Mother of trying to kill him!"

"Don't be so hard on him, Sheila. I'm sure, had he really known BJ, he would never have believed the lies. And I did my share of lying, too, so what was he to believe? Furthermore, I didn't keep my part of the bargain. I haven't given him the one thing he wanted the most, a child."

"Did you love your first husband?" Sheila asked softly.

"I hate him," Jessy replied bitterly.

"But you love my brother, don't you?"

"Yes, God help me, I do." Pulling herself together, Jessy turned and said, "Now you know just about everything, and we've wasted a lot of time." She gave Sheila a warm smile. "Come over here and help me pack these things. We've done enough serious talking. Thank heavens your marriage is going to be a happy one."

Cort walked away, knowing he had some thinking to do. Jessy had left out a great deal about his role in her life, but she told her story honestly to Sheila, and without sparing herself. There was a lot to consider.

Chapter Eighteen

The day finally arrived for Marie's and Sheila's departure. To Jessy, they represented family and loved ones, and she was loath to see them go.

The trunks were placed on a wagon, which followed the carriage. The trip to the train depot seemed to take forever. Everyone tried to act gay, but there was an unspoken heavy sadness.

Marie was the only exception. She sat quiet and erect, impatiently tapping her fingers on the seat and looking out the window. Jessy had no idea what was running through the older woman's mind.

Jessy was glad the train had already arrived. By the time the trunks were loaded, it was almost time for it to leave. Had there been a long wait, the situation would have only become more uncomfortable.

"Goodbye, Sheila," Jessy said as she hugged her sister-in-law. She had a hard time holding back the threatening tears. "Enjoy your trip, and say hello to that man of yours for me."

Sheila giggled nervously. "You sound like I'm never going to see you again. Who knows, I may be back on the next train. And if I do stay, Cort has promised you'd both be at the wedding so he can give me away, and you can be my

maid of honor." She kissed Jessy on the cheek and went to
her brother.

Jessy couldn't hear what they were saying, but Cort must
have said something to lighten Sheila's spirits, because they
both started laughing.

"I shall miss you," Jessy said to Marie. Jessy was shocked
to see the older woman give her a warm smile.

"And I shall miss you, Jessica. Cortland and I had a long
talk this morning while you were getting Sheila ready. After all these years, we have come to an understanding, and
think we owe it all to you."

"Me?" Jessy asked, surprised at the statement. "Believe
me, I had nothing to do with it."

"Well, say what you like, but I believe differently. When
I return, things will be a lot different. Now I'm not saying
Cortland and I won't have our fights, but we're both stub-
born mules, so it's to be expected."

"All aboard!" the conductor called out loudly.

After Jessy received another quick hug from Sheila,
Marie and Sheila climbed the steel steps to the passenger car.
Smoke gushed out between the big wheels, and Jessy was
forced to move back. As the train moved forward, Sheila
leaned out the window and waved. She was smiling from ear
to ear, which seemed strange to Jessy. She would have
thought the girl would be crying, which was exactly what
Jessy did as soon as they were out of sight.

"Well, Jessy," Cort said coldly, "it looks like it's just you
and me now. As of today, you have one week to give me
some honest answers as to what the hell is going on."

"I don't know what you're talking about." Jessy dabbed
her eyes and nose with a handkerchief as she headed toward the carriage.

Cort reached out and jerked her around. "You know exactly what I'm talking about. One week, and no more.
You've seen me mad, lady, but you've never seen just how

mean a bastard I can be." He glanced at the sky. "Spring is here, and in a week the sun will be quite hot. The Indians have a way of making people talk. Shall I tell you how it's done?"

"No! You're only bluffing."

"If you don't come to me within a week, you'll find out just how serious I am. I don't take kindly to people trying to kill me. And while I'm at it, you might as well know there will be no more shopping. You will remain in the house and think about what I've said. At night, if I'm not there, you'll be locked in your room."

Fear gripped Jessy as she looked up at his expression. Fear of his threat, fear of what Jonathan might do and fear that she wasn't going to be able to leave as she'd planned. "But . . . but you can't do that," she gasped. "You're making me a prisoner, and I haven't done anything."

"Exactly. As for your innocence, I guess that will be up to me to decide. As I have stated before, I intend to get some answers. Now, shall we go home?"

Jessy paced back and forth in her room, trying to figure a way out of her mess. After his dictates, Cort hadn't spoken another word to her. She had come to the realization that Cort had also been biding his time until Marie and Sheila left, though for a different reason than Jessy's. Should she tell him about Jonathan and accept her fate? She shuddered at the thought of going to jail. But if she didn't tell him, her life and his would be put in danger. After seeing the sickening pleasure on Jonathan's face when he'd killed that unarmed man at the Cock-eyed Bull, she had no doubt he'd kill again. And though Sheila had assured her Cort could take care of himself, he wouldn't be expecting a shot in the back. The only answer was for her to escape. But how? She could have kicked herself for not returning to the land office. By now she might have found a buyer for her parent's land. Now she was stranded without money.

Jessy went to the window and opened it. Closing her eyes, she inhaled the fresh warm air as it entered the stuffy room and listened to the happy chirping of the sparrows in the tree outside. Her eyes flew open. The tree! How could she have been so stupid to forget about the big tree? Leaning out the window, Jessy saw a strong, sturdy branch not more than two feet down.

Hurrying to the dressing table, she opened the jewelry case and took out two rings. The stones in both rings were huge, and she knew she could get a considerable amount of money for them. She hadn't planned on taking any of Cort's gifts, but she was desperate. Tomorrow night she'd leave town and never return. Jessy was sick with the realization that after tomorrow, she'd never see Cort again. She would have liked to wait longer, but it would only cause more heartache, and to delay was to ask for trouble.

She went to her bed and placed the rings beneath it for safe keeping. As she stood up, it occurred to Jessy that she was extremely hungry. Though it wasn't suppertime yet, she decided to go to the kitchen and ask Prudence to deliver her meal to her room.

A few hours later, Prudence tapped on the door then entered, carrying a large tray of meat, vegetables, dessert and two large red apples.

"My heavens, you're not feeding an army," Jessy exclaimed as the girl placed the food on the table.

Prudence looked at her and smiled. It was the first smile Jessy had received from a servant since Cort decreed he was to be informed if she left the house.

"I hope you're not angry with me, ma'am."

"Of course I'm not," Jessy said, sitting at the table. "Why should I be angry?"

Prudence lowered her head. "Because, some days back, I'm the one who told Mr. Lancaster you'd left without him."

"You did the right thing, Prudence," Jessy said as she cut a thick piece of meat. "Mr. Lancaster hired you, and you should always obey his orders." She stuck the meat in her mouth, savoring the delicious flavor.

"Thank you, ma'am, but I'll never do it again, even if I get fired. I'm your maid, and from now on, I'll only take instructions from you."

"I don't believe I've ever had anyone say anything nicer to me, Prudence. But don't worry, you won't be faced with the situation again."

Happy, Prudence started straightening up the room. "Before you go to bed, I'll bring up some cookies and milk. Mamma says that when a woman's with child, she likes to eat a lot."

Jessy dropped her fork. "Child? What are you talking about? I can't be with child!"

Prudence looked as shocked as Jessy. "But you fainted, you haven't had your womanly time for at least two months, and you've been sick almost every morning."

"Oh, well, the sickness has stopped, and I feel wonderful," Jessy said, expelling a sigh of relief. "I'm sure that missing my time was due to all the worry and rushing to get Sheila off."

"Yes, ma'am," Prudence replied, obviously not convinced, "but how come you're so hungry now?"

"Prudence, I really do not care to discuss this any further. I am not with child, and I don't want rumors spread among the servants to the contrary. If I were, I'd be the first to know."

"Yes, ma'am."

Prudence helped Jessy undress and put on her nightclothes, then placed the dishes on the tray and left. Jessy tried reading for a while, but even though the book was good, it didn't hold her concentration. She spied the two apples Prudence had left, and without thinking, rose and grabbed one. Returning to her chair, she picked the book up, determined to read. It would be too easy to break down in tears. She munched on the apple, delighted with the crisp, tart flavor, and forced her eyes to look at the pages. As she started to take another bite, her hand froze in midair. "I am with child," she muttered as she looked at her flat stomach. "Never in my entire life have I liked apples, and I've already eaten half of this one!"

In shock, Jessy hopped up and lifted her gown. Stomach exposed, she looked in the mirror. She turned sideways, but could see no change in her body. "It can't be! I took Marie's herbs faithfully." But she knew Prudence had guessed right. It made her angry to think of all the wasted guilt she had suffered for not bearing Cort's child, and now she discovered it had nothing to do with the herbs after all! Jessy dropped her skirt, still not sure how she felt about her condition. It was all too new. One minute she wanted to laugh with joy, and the next minute she wanted to cry.

Some time later, Jessy discovered the doors to her room were locked and she knew Cort wouldn't be joining her. No, he was waiting for her to come to him with her confession. Well, he's going to have a long wait, Jessy thought as she blew out the candles and climbed into bed. She had come to terms with herself about having a baby, and the knowledge gave her the final inner strength she needed to leave Cort. Because of Jonathan, she had to leave anyway, but now she would be taking a part of Cort with her. She desperately wanted to share her good news with him, but of course she couldn't. He would never let her go. With her arms hugging her stomach, Jessy drifted off to sleep.

She awoke suddenly and couldn't understand what had brought her out of such a sound sleep. Her room was still bathed in darkness, except for the small shaft of moonlight streaming through the window. Just as she started to shut her eyes again, the smell of whiskey reached her nostrils, and she could hear someone breathing. The person was quite near.

"Cort?" The word came out almost as a whisper.

"Cort? And I thought you might awake with my name on your lips."

"Jonathan! How did you get in my room?" Jessy asked, pulling the blanket up to her chin. The moonlight glistened on something silver, and she knew it was a knife or a gun.

"By the window you left so conveniently open. I suggest you don't scream, because if you do, King Lancaster will get a bullet in the face the minute he opens the door. Why weren't you at the carriage factory today with my jewelry, Jess?"

His words sounded like a raspy growl to Jessy's ears. Now that her eyes were becoming adjusted to the dark, she could make out his image at the foot of her bed. "I'm not giving you any more jewelry, Jonathan," she declared bravely. "In fact, you will never receive another thing. Now go away, or so help me God, I'll turn myself in and report you to the marshal."

"My, my. Such brave words. Have you forgotten what I threatened to do to the rest of the family before I take care of you?"

Jessy's thoughts flashed to her baby, but she couldn't let Jonathan get the upper hand. She took a couple of deep, silent breaths to make sure there was no quiver of fear in her voice. "If you do anything to me, Cort will track you down and you'll regret the day you were born. If you don't believe me, ask anyone in town. He also knows Indian tortures. As for Cort, I could care less what happens to him. Today he said he wanted me out of his house. Sheila and

Marie are out of your reach. They left on a train and will not be returning.''

''What makes you think I don't have a man on the train with them? All I have to do is wire ahead to have them killed.''

Jessy sucked in her breath, frightened beyond words at what he'd just told her. She couldn't take the chance that he might be lying.

''You know what happens when you don't do as you're told. Where is your jewelry case?'' he barked at her.

Jessy felt weak and defeated.

''Never mind,'' Jonathan said gleefully. ''I've found it. Next week you'll be at the factory as planned, but I want you to bring money.''

''I told you, I have no money and Cort's kicking me out.''

''And I told you to pretend you're carrying his baby. And don't think I'm forgetting your...relatives. When they get off the train, my man can follow the ladies, and I'll know where to get my hands on them if you decide not to cooperate. Until next Wednesday, Jess.''

Jessy held her breath as Jonathan climbed outside. As soon as she thought it safe, she scrambled out of bed and rushed to the window. She didn't see him ride away, but she heard horses leaving, and there was more than one.

Jessy ran to the door leading to Cort's room and tried the handle. It was locked. Frantically, she began pounding her fist and calling Cort's name. No matter what happened to her, she had to let Cort know Sheila and Marie were in serious danger. But there was no answer. Running to the other door, she called and pounded again. She continued pounding until her bruised fists could take no more, and her voice was a mere squeak from yelling. It was hopeless. Cort was gone, and the servants had their own quarters on the other side of the house and would never hear her. The window! Jessy hurried over and looked down. She couldn't do it.

Near the bottom, she would have to drop a good ways to the ground, and it might mean losing Cort's child. She slowly moved to the door dividing her room from Cort's and sat down. All she could do was wait. She might hear him enter his room. It was all over now, the running away, everything. When she confronted Cort with what was happening, he'd hate her till his dying day. She would go to jail for bigamy, and when she had the baby, Cort would take it. She'd never see the child again. Hard, heavy sobs racked Jessy's small frame.

After locking Jessy in her rooms, Cort had gone to town to have a few drinks with Tim Riley, his partner in the Belly Up Saloon. When a man left the poker table, Cort gladly took his place, needing the distraction. His frame of mind was such that he didn't care whether he won or lost. As it turned out, he'd won a tidy sum of money by the time he left, several hours before dawn.

When Cort returned home, he knew that even though he'd been up practically all night, he couldn't sleep. So he went to the study to smoke, drink and stew over his problems.

Cort lifted his glass and took another drink. He'd done a lot of thinking since he'd overheard Jessy and Sheila talking. He had come to accept a lot of truths. He knew Jessy had never slept with BJ, he'd known it since their wedding night. On that same night, he also discovered she wasn't the type to share her favors. Deliberately, or maybe without even realizing it, he'd used what the bartender and townspeople of Binge had said to keep himself from falling in love with the minx. And as for her being a fast dealer, that theory had fallen by the wayside the night they played cards with Sheila and Tom. Jessy could shuffle, but certainly not with any great ability.

Cort tossed the butt of the cigar in the spittoon and poured another drink from the nearly empty bottle.

He didn't want to physically hurt Jessy, in fact he wasn't even sure he could. She'd been right, he was only bluffing when he talked about using Indian tactics on her. He would, however, like to give her a damn good shaking! After listening to Jessy tell her story to Sheila, he knew she truly loved him. It was in her voice when she talked about him. She'd also said something that had triggered something in his head. It was a slight clue as to what was going on, but for the life of him he couldn't remember just what she'd said. He knew for certain Jessy hadn't tried to kill him, it was someone else. Someone she was terrified of, the person who had taken her necklace that night at the dance. BJ? Was he really dead? No. BJ had wanted Jessy for himself. He would have charged like a bull seeking a heifer. It galled Cort to know he was so close to the answer but couldn't find the last piece to the puzzle. Only Jessy could give him that. *Why the hell can't she see that the only way I can help her is if she lets me know what is going on?* Cort thought angrily.

He downed the rest of the whiskey in the glass and moved to the leather sofa, suddenly feeling tired.

Jessy had fallen into an exhausted sleep, and it took a moment before it registered that a key had been turned. The sun shone brightly through her window, and Jessy felt sick at heart as she realized it was already midmorning. Her body was stiff, and she had to stretch her legs before standing. Reaching down, she turned the handle, almost falling over as the door easily swung open. The first person she noticed was Byron, busily brushing an article of Cort's clothing.

Cort stood off to the side of the room removing his wrinkled shirt when Jessy entered. Seeing her hollowed cheeks, swollen eyes, tousled hair and the white around her mouth, he was tempted to go to her. But he didn't, because he knew Jessy had finally come to tell all.

"Cort," Jessy said anxiously, "you have to help them. He could kill them!"

Something had happened again last night, and whatever it was had brought her to his room. Dismissing Byron and acting unconcerned, he pulled off last night's shirt and sat on the edge of the bed, looking at her and waiting.

Now that she finally had Cort's attention, Jessy suddenly didn't know how to tell him the truth. He looked so damn big and intimidating! She collapsed onto a chair, refusing to look at him. "Cort," she said, trying not to become hysterical, "Sheila and Marie are in danger."

"What do you mean they're in danger?"

He spoke slowly, and Jessy easily recognized the dangerous tone of his voice. "Please, Cort, send the marshal, Tom, or anyone a wire saying that someone may be following them."

"Am I to understand you don't know who the man is or even if he's on the train?"

"Damn it! Would you listen to me? Send the wire! When you get back I promise to explain everything!"

"How do I know you're not doing this to get me away from the house so you can leave?"

"Lock me in my room! If you had stayed home last night you would have known about this sooner. I pounded on the door until my fists could take no more, and yelled until I lost my voice."

Cort went to her and picked up her arms. The outer part of her hands were indeed black and blue.

It wasn't just the bruises, but the desperation in Jessy's voice that spurred him into action. "All right," he said, pulling out a clean shirt, "but I warn you, Jessy, you'd damn well better be here when I return. Do you have any kind of description as to what the man would look like?"

"Only that he's dirty, and looks as crooked as a snake."

"Very well, I'll send a couple of wires," Cort said as he put on the shirt. He grabbed his black, wide-brimmed hat and stuck it on his head. "I'll send Prudence up."

Jessy looked in the mirror as Prudence finished dressing her hair. She had had cool, damp cloths placed on her eyes. After breakfast, fresh clothes, a touch of pink rubbed across the top of her cheekbones and having her hair combed, no one would have believed what she'd gone through last night. Now she was ready to face Cort. But not in the bedroom, she decided. There were too many memories.

When Cort returned, Prudence met him at the door to inform him Jessy was in the study. Tossing his hat on a peg, he headed in that direction.

Cort was considerably relieved to see Jessy sitting in one of the deep leather chairs looking healthy and normal. He sat behind the desk where he could watch her expressions. After lighting a cigar, he leaned back and made himself comfortable. Jessy placed her hands in her lap and tilted her chin up.

"You sent the wire?" she asked.

"Yes. Now what's this all about, Jessy?"

"I guess the first thing I should tell you is that Jonathan is not dead." The irises of Cort's eyes turned to an almost glassy black, and Jessy could see his strong jaw tighten, but he said nothing.

Now the puzzle fits, Cort thought. That's why she said Jonathan's name when we were making love and I asked who she'd seen. He also remembered that when Sheila asked if she had loved Jonathan, Jessy had replied, "I hate him," not "I hated him."

"Jonathan has four henchmen," Jessy continued, "and it would be my guess that if he has someone on the train, it will be one of them. Since you've never believed anything I've told you, I don't expect you to believe I thought he was dead. But I did. You wanted the truth, and that's what I'm giving you. I first found out that Jonathan was alive the day I went to the music academy, but I thought I was seeing things."

Jessy told Cort in detail everything that had happened and had been said. Occasionally Cort asked a question, but it was always brief. By the time she repeated what had taken place last night, Jessy was almost whispering. Though Cort looked outwardly relaxed, there was an underlying fury in him that she had never seen before, and it frightened her. She suddenly remembered he had looked the same way in the dry goods store, only then she'd thought him oblivious of the danger. Jessy realized that now, as then, she was seeing Cort at his most deadly.

"You said there are four men besides Jonathan?"

"Yes. Cort, I expect you to take me to the marshal. I'm willing to tell him everything, including that I am a bigamist. I realize this can bring down a hoard of gossip," Jessy said bitterly, "but with your money and power, you can probably keep the Topeka society from finding out your wife is in jail."

"I'm taking you nowhere," Cort said, rising to his feet. "I'm going to pay Jonathan a little visit. I'm sure I'll find him at the Cock-eyed Bull."

"Cort!" Jessy gasped, also standing. "You can't! They'll kill you."

Cort gave her a sardonic smile as he headed for the door. "Then you won't be a bigamist any more, will you?"

Jessy ran and threw her arms around his waist. "Please, Cort," she begged, "don't go. I couldn't stand having you dead. I love you. Take me to the marshal and let him handle it."

"You underestimate me, dear Jessy."

Leaning down, he kissed her passionately, then slowly pulled her arms away. He chuckled softly. "Keep that until I return."

Overwhelmed with grief, Jessy leaned against the wall and listened to Cort go up the stairs two at a time.

When she heard him come down and head toward the door, she didn't even look. She knew his gun belt would be strapped on, and the pistols would be inside the holsters tied to his muscled legs.

"Good luck, and goodbye, my love," Jessy whispered. "I refuse to have your child born in a prison, and I couldn't stand being here if news came that you'd been killed. This way I'll always think of you as alive and handsome, and a most delightful bastard."

Cort brought the lathered, snorting animal to a walk and entered the compound, watching for any sign of trouble. There was no doubt he'd be remembered from his last visit.

The area around the saloon was deserted except for a few drunken men staggering around or sleeping it off. Even though it was broad daylight, horses of every description stood at the long hitching rail. Cort heard laughter, cussing and even the tinkle of a piano coming from inside as he dismounted and tied his horse on the end in case he had to leave in a hurry.

Cort entered the saloon, his hands down and ready as his eyes scanned the room. It didn't take long for him to spot Jonathan at a poker table in the back. The large room quieted as the men, one by one, turned to look at the tall gunman standing in the doorway.

As Cort moved forward, he heard several comments. "He's a mean son of a bitch, and I ain't seen no one that can draw as fast . . ."

"Hell, I ain't gonna tangle with him . . ."

"Who yah think he's lookin' for?"

"I seen him shoot two men down the other night, faster than you could blink a eye..."

"Hell, I gotta see this, might prove to be a damn good fight."

Cort was getting the impression that his last visit would work to his advantage. Jonathan turned, and Cort could see the startled look on his pale face. The four rough cowboys behind him started to spread out. Cort recognized one of them as the man who had entered the dry goods store in Topeka.

Knowing a gun fight could break out any minute, the saloon girls started screaming and ran behind the bar. Some of the customers ran out front, while others moved off to the side and ducked, leaving a clear path to Jonathan's table.

Cort made his stand, waiting for the first draw.

"You're a dead man, Lancaster," Jonathan called out. "I been hoping you'd come see me. I guess you know sweet little Jessy and me planned this whole thing. Ain't she something in bed?"

Cort knew Jonathan was trying to distract him, but it didn't work. The man with the sunken eyes reached for his gun first, but before he could even get it out of the holster, Cort shot him dead. Another on the far side tried next, but Cort fired one shot and he crumpled to the floor.

Seeing what was happening, Jonathan dived for the back door, a bullet missing his head by inches. The other two men raised their hands toward the ceiling.

"Hell," one of them said, "we ain't wantin' no part of this."

"Did Jonathan send someone on a train?" Cort asked.

"Train? What train?"

"We're the only ones Jonathan ever hired to do anything," the other man said, "and ain't none of us been on no train."

Cort backed out the doorway and ran for his horse. By the time he leaped onto the saddle, the stallion was already in motion. Knowing there was only one way in or out of the compound, Cort jerked the horse around and headed for the opening at a full gallop.

Cort pushed the stallion hard and soon saw Jonathan ahead. The gambler's buckskin was heavy and lacked speed, and Cort's stallion was quickly closing the distance between them.

Jonathan turned in the saddle, and seeing Cort in pursuit, pulled out his derringer and fired. Realizing the weapon was of no use at long range, he threw it away and leaned over the buckskin's neck, kicking the horse frantically in the ribs for more speed. The horse had none to give. Bounding up a small bank, the buckskin broke through the thick crust of snow. Frightened, the animal threw back his head, his hooves thrashing as he searched for a foothold. Jonathan, in his frenzy, pulled back hard on the reins at the wrong time. The buckskin started falling backward. Too late, Jonathan jumped from the saddle. The horse landed on top of him with a crushing blow.

By the time Cort reached the scene, the buckskin was standing quietly to the side, and Jonathan lay dead. Cort picked the slight man up and tossed him over the saddle. "Looks like you saved me the trouble of having to kill him, old fellow," Cort mumbled as he tied the gambler down. Gathering the buckskin's reins, Cort climbed on his own horse and headed for town.

By the time Cort reached home, he was in good spirits and anxious to see Jessy. It was about time he told Jessy some truth of his own, and way past time for them to settle down to a happy marriage.

"Honestly, Mr. Lancaster," Prudence sobbed, "I don't know where she went. She just packed a few things and left just a short time ago. I've been so worried sick, especially with her in her condition.''

"What are you talking about?" Cort stormed at the shaking girl.

"The baby. Didn't you know?"

The words took Cort by surprise. "Are you sure?" he asked, suddenly in awe.

"Yes, sir."

Cort broke out in a thunderous laughter of joy. He was actually going to be a father! He knew why Jessy had left, and he knew just where to find her.

When the ticket master told Cort the train for Kansas City had left five minutes ago, Cort was glad he'd taken the time to get a fresh horse.

By taking short cuts, Cort beat the train to the Hampshire Crossing by only a few minutes. Hearing the whistle, he pulled his horse up close to the track and waited. As the train came by, he gave the animal a good kick, and it leaped forward, maintaining the same speed. Pulling back slightly on the reins, Cort waited until the caboose was alongside. He reached out and swung aboard.

When Cort stepped inside the passenger car, he had no trouble spotting Jessy. Her back was turned and her head was bowed as though she was crying.

Jessy, he thought with a chuckle, you are in for one hell of a surprise. Kansas City is a damn good place for a honeymoon. King Lancaster headed for his bride.

*   *   *   *   *

COMING NEXT MONTH

#41 HIGHLAND BARBARIAN—Ruth Langan

Meredith MacAlpin would make any sacrifice to protect
her clan from the infamous Highland Barbarian. Then her
plans for a marriage alliance were thwarted when the
legendary laird himself abducted her from her own
wedding. She soon learned Brice Campbell was anything
but barbarous!

#42 PASSION'S EMBRACE—Cassie Edwards

Country girl Katie Lee Holden yearned to be a singer in the
boomtown of Seattle. But when Bruce Cabot saved her
from an Indian attack, he decided the security of marriage
was the only thing that could make her happy. Katie Lee
wasn't ready to give up her career to marry Bruce—though
his passion was another story....

Have You Ever Wondered If You Could Write A Harlequin Novel?

Here's great news—Harlequin is offering a series of cassette tapes to help you do just that. Written by Harlequin editors, these tapes give practical advice on how to make your characters—and your story—come alive. There's a tape for each contemporary romance series Harlequin publishes.

Mail order only

All sales final

TO: *Harlequin Reader Service*
Audiocassette Tape Offer
P.O. Box 1396
Buffalo, NY 14269-1396

I enclose a check/money order payable to HARLEQUIN READER SERVICE® for $9.70 ($8.95 plus 75¢ postage and handling) for EACH tape ordered for the total sum of $_____*
Please send:

☐ Romance and Presents   ☐ Intrigue
☐ American Romance   ☐ Temptation
☐ Superromance   ☐ All five tapes ($38.80 total)

Signature_____

Name:_____
(please print clearly)

Address:_____

State:_____ Zip:_____

*Iowa and New York residents add appropriate sales tax.

AUDIO-H

The Pirate
JAYNE ANN KRENTZ

At the heart of every powerful romance story lies a
legend. There are many romantic legends and
countless modern variations on them, but they all
have one thing in common: They are tales of brave,
resourceful women who must gentle and tame the
powerful, passionate men who are their true mates.

The enormous appeal of Jayne Ann Krentz lies in
her ability to create modern-day versions of these
classic romantic myths, and her LADIES AND
LEGENDS trilogy showcases this talent. Believing
that a storyteller who can bring legends to life
deserves special attention, Harlequin has chosen
the first book of the trilogy—THE PIRATE—to
receive our Award of Excellence. Look for it now.

AE-PIR-1A